STRENGTH
UNDER FIRE

PRAISE FOR LINDSAY MCKENNA'S WIND RIVER VALLEY SERIES!

"The believable and real romance between Tara and Harper is enhanced by the addition of highly dimensional supporting characters, and a minor mystery subplot increases the tension by a notch. This is a fine addition to a strong series."—*Publishers Weekly* on *Lone Rider*

"Captivating sensuality."—*Publishers Weekly* on *Wind River Wrangler*, a Publishers Marketplace Buzz Books 2016 selection

"Moving and real . . . impossible to put down."—*Publishers Weekly* on *Wind River Rancher* (starred review)

"Cowboy who is also a former Special Forces operator? Check. Woman on the run from her past? Check. This contemporary Western wraps together suspense and romance in a rugged Wyoming package."—Amazon.com's Omnivoracious, "9 Romances I Can't Wait to Read," on *Wind River Wrangler*

"Set against the stunning beauty of Wyoming's Grand Tetons, *Wind River Wrangler* is Lindsay McKenna at her finest! A *tour de force* of heart-stopping drama, gut-wrenching emotion, and the searing joy of two wounded souls learning to love again."—International bestselling author Merline Lovelace

"McKenna does a beautiful job of illustrating difficult topics through the development of well-formed, sympathetic characters."—*Publishers Weekly* on *Wolf Haven* (starred review)

STRENGTH UNDER FIRE

LINDSAY McKENNA

ZEBRA BOOKS
KENSINGTON PUBLISHING CORP.
www.kensingtonbooks.com

ZEBRA BOOKS are published by

Kensington Publishing Corp.
119 West 40th Street
New York, NY 10018

All Kensington titles, imprints, and distributed lines are available at special quantity discounts for bulk purchases for sales promotion, premiums, fund-raising, educational, or institutional use.

Special book excerpts or customized printings can also be created to fit specific needs. For details, write or phone the office of the Kensington Sales Manager: Attn.: Sales Department. Kensington Publishing Corp., 119 West 40th Street, New York, NY 10018. Phone: 1-800-221-2647.

Zebra and the Z logo Reg. U.S. Pat. & TM Off.

First Printing: October 2021
ISBN-13: 978-1-4201-5084-1
ISBN-13: 978-1-4201-5088-9 (eBook)

10 9 8 7 6 5 4 3 2 1

Printed in the United States of America

To my grandfather, John Cramer, master carpenter.
He left Ohio in 1929, during the Great Depression
and in his family Model T, headed for San Diego,
California, to start all over.
He built a kitchen cupboard business from nothing,
and worked hard all his life, creating beautiful wood
cabinets, cupboards, and so much more.
I grew up watching him choose wood,
his hands so knowing with grain and texture, and
seeing the wood come alive beneath them.
His work ethic, love of Nature, love of trees,
was imprinted upon me forever.
How fortunate I was to be his granddaughter.
I wrote Silver Creek Fire
in dedication to his magical craft.

Chapter 1

"This is my new home. A new chapter in my life," Dana Scott whispered to herself, sounding unsure about her decision. She had just bought a broken-down old log cabin and a hundred acres with the only money she had left in the world. This was her dream home.

She stood there in the cool morning at ten a.m., a range of Wyoming mountains behind and east of the cabin, rising out of the Silver Creek Valley. Fifty acres of land was composed of timber on the slopes covered with conifers. The rest of the land was on the flat Wyoming valley that was an agricultural paradise.

A slight breeze ruffled her loose red hair that lay against her shoulder blades. Pulling her denim jacket a little tighter around her, she felt panic rising and wrestled it down, as she always did. No stranger to fear, it had been a frequent friend the last few years of her life.

Drawing in a shaky breath, Dana had spent most of what her parents had left her, and the last of the money was in a bank in Silver Creek. She had no job—yet. She was farm raised, but there wasn't much of a call for a woman who had farming skills nowadays.

Looking up at the sky, it was a pale blue, the morning air clean. The cheerful call of birds getting ready to nest was music that lifted her battered spirit.

Had she done the right thing? Spending money that could never be replaced, on this land and the broken cabin? Like the coward she was, she had run away from her traumatic past. Looking to make a break and start over, she'd left the Willamette Valley, a rich winery and agricultural country in Oregon, and headed to Wyoming. Having taken a master gardener course earlier in her life, she'd used her educational knowledge and checked out the pH of the soil here in this valley and it was perfect to grow many types of crops. Of all the places she'd had the potential to choose in four different states, this valley had the richest soil with the right mix of pH, consisting of alluvial silt from old rivers now disappeared, and loamy clay.

The Silver Creek Valley had just the right formula for a fruit tree orchard, too. Her mother, Cathy, had a green thumb that she'd passed on to Dana. She had plans for a huge garden just like the one she'd once had at their farm. Once more, Dana reminded herself that this was her dream home, no matter how dilapidated-looking the cabin was and how barren the Wyoming land seemed. It was just starting to come alive mid-April.

A new start. A new life.

Despite all these world-altering changes, she felt a void and emptiness within her heart that nothing, not even buying the Wildflower Ranch, could fill. This ranch had been established in 1900 by a German husband and wife.

Gazing left to right, she could see the harsh winter had tamped down anything that had been growing wild here for several decades. There was a creek out back, perfect as an irrigation source for that garden and small orchard she'd envisioned in her mind.

She'd made an appointment with Mary Bishop, owner of Mama's Store, the most popular place in town to buy anything, and she'd filled out an employment form earlier in the week. Today, she'd find out if she had a job or not. Mary sold only organic, non-GMO fruits, vegetables, and meat. Although she had not met Mary personally, everyone spoke highly of her, and she had an appointment in less than an hour to speak with her. Her stomach clenched in anxiety. She had to have a job!

Dana needed a line of income or she wouldn't be able to make the payments on her ranch property and make her dream a reality. There was a lot of fear gnawing at her. Could she pull this off? Had she just wasted her parents' hard-earned money?

Feeling anything but happy, she walked slowly around the log cabin. Behind her, the main highway leading into Silver Creek was a quarter of a mile away. The dirt road into the place was deeply rutted and lacked grading and the care it needed.

What was odd to her was that there had been a lot of vehicle traffic on it and she could see where the flat land had a road of sorts plowed through it, heading to the slope of the mountain, disappearing into the thick, dark woods. Maybe the locals were hunting and used the road? She didn't know, but now that she had bought it, the first thing she was going to erect was a stout gate to stop unwanted visitors.

Her green Toyota pickup, more than ten years old, had handled the rutted dirt road easily. Turning on the heel of her work boot, she stared at the two twenty-foot-tall wooden posts standing upright at the entrance to the place. Over time and lack of yearly care, the carved wooden sign that had once rested across them to create a wonderful entrance, had toppled off those two stout timbers, thanks to the fierce winds that scoured the valley during the winter. It lay in two broken five-foot pieces, near the entrance. Etched into the battered, weathered oak sign were the words: WILDFLOWER RANCH. Whoever had been commissioned to create it had been a wonderful wood sculptor, because the words were carved into it, as well. It had lost its varnish a long time ago, the wood roughened by the weather. Still, she wanted to do something with it, get it fixed and lifted back into place where it had been for the family who had loved this place.

Dana wondered if Hilda, the German wife, had been responsible for that sign, or if one of her later descendants had it created? Dana would never know because the family had died out in 2000, with no one else to pass the ranch on to in their family. Since then, the land had lain dormant, unused, the cabin's upkeep gone, leaving it and the land to the ravages of time and weather. No one, the Realtor had told her a week ago, would buy the ranch because of the small family log cabin. It would have to be razed and a new home built on the property. From his point of view, the land was worth something, but the log cabin was a total loss. She almost said her life was a total loss, too, but she bit back the remark. She had to rebuild her life, just like this cabin needed loving care and attention to come back to life, as well.

Dana didn't want to destroy the cabin, built in 1900, because, in part, it symbolized how she'd felt for the last several years. Destroying the log cabin, to her, was like symbolically destroying herself. She wasn't anywhere near healed from her experience, but saw the cabin as a reflection of where she was presently. Determined to save the cabin, and in doing so, she'd bought the place to save herself. Her mother had often said, *Life is always unfair*, but the way her entire world got upended, it was more than unfair. It was a daily hell on earth for her.

Glancing at her wristwatch, she noted that the appointment with Mary Bishop was thirty minutes away. Time to get a move on. Mary was considered the maven, the queen of Silver Creek, Dana had discovered in the last week of being here. The older woman, everyone warned her, didn't act her age at all. She was spunky, driven, full of great ideas and easily excited over new projects. Dana thought, from talking to several people over at the Silver Creek food bank and kitchen where she volunteered on one day each weekend, that maybe the word *passion* best suited go-getter Mary Bishop, according to others. She was a woman on a mission and she took it seriously. Dana wanted this appointment with Queen Mary, and she meant that label in kind terms, not making fun of the elder at all. Queens could rule with grace, responsibility, and in her idealistic world, a queen would have a great love for her people. Mary sounded like such a person and that's all Dana could ask for.

Mama's Store was bustling with townspeople, lots of children and some people with service dogs, mixed among the crowded aisles. It was a huge place, far larger than she imagined from seeing it from the highway. A woman clerk led her back to Mary's office.

Everyone was happy here, she noted. There were smiles, lots of laughter and neighborly chatting amongst those who pushed the grocery carts around the store. Stomach tight with fear of rejection, Dana followed, trying to keep her expression calm, not fearful or anxious. Pulse bounding with stress, she pushed through it, following the clerk through the loading dock area to a small glass-enclosed office. Inside, she could see a petite woman with short silver hair working at a large, messy-looking desk.

"Go on in," the clerk invited, opening the door. "Mary, here's Dana Scott. She had an appointment with you?"

Taking a deep breath, Dana moved forward, spotting a chair in front of the desk.

"Yep, she did. Come in, Dana," Mary invited, lifting her head, waving her into the office.

Instantly, Dana could feel the elder's piercing scrutiny. Her stomach clenched, the door closing quietly behind her. Would Mary have a job for her? "Yes, ma'am," she said, standing, hands clasped in front of her.

"Sit, sit," Mary murmured, and gestured toward the chair. She put down her pen and moved some papers to one side, grabbing a blank piece of paper and placing it in front of her. "It's nice to meet you. Are you new to Silver Creek?"

Sitting, Dana murmured, "Yes, ma'am, I am. I've been here for two weeks."

Squinting her eyes, Mary said, "I hear from Judy, over

at the food bank, that you've signed up to work a day on weekends over there."

Dana tried to keep the surprise off her face, but didn't succeed. "Well . . . yes, yes, I did."

"Why?"

This was supposed to be an employment interview. Thrown off by Mary's question, Mary's gaze fixed on her, making her feel as if she were being checked out, Dana tried to relax. Opening her hands, she said, "Because I was raised to give back to others who didn't have as much as we did."

Giving a nod, Mary said, "That's commendable. We need folks like you in our valley. Here"—she looked around at the busy loading dock area where boxes of goods were being off-loaded from the semitruck—"we're all one big, messy family."

"The Realtor said the same thing," she said, nodding.

"How's that sit with you?"

"Fine. I grew up on a large farm in the Willamette Valley of Oregon and everyone knew everyone else. We were like a large family, too, of sorts."

"Good to know." She pulled an employment form from another stack of papers, looking down, frowning and studying it. "So? Why on earth would you leave your farm in Oregon to come here?" She looked up at Dana.

Uncomfortably, Dana moved in the chair. "Life changed," was all she would say. "I needed to find something close to what we had in the Willamette Valley and start over."

"Hmmm," Mary said, giving her another searching look. "We buy organic produce from that valley. I'm very well aware of how important it is to Oregon. The Willamette is a north-south one-hundred-and-fifty-mile valley. Very rich soil there, and a wonderful place to grow any crop. Winery owners love that area, too. Silver Creek Valley has very similar soil conditions."

"Yes, it was why I chose to come and put down roots here. I just bought the Wildflower Ranch."

"Ah," Mary said, sitting back in her chair. "Did you now?"

Dana wasn't sure it was a smart thing to admit to Mary, who reminded her of an eagle, missing nothing. Her face was wrinkled, but that didn't take away from the authority or power she had. "I know it's run-down . . ."

"We all have times in our lives when we're run-down, too. Even ranches here go through that up-and-down cycle. What do you think of the place?"

"It has possibilities. The soil is an excellent mix of alluvial and loamy clay; perfect for plants and fruit trees."

"So?" she said, rocking back in her chair. "Tell me what your plan is for it?"

Dana wanted a job, not to discuss the broken land. Still, Mary's interest was there and her voice was kinder once she found out she'd bought the ranch. She didn't know why, but said, "I want to repair the cabin, use the fifty acres on the flat of the valley to grow organic vegetable crops and put in a small orchard of about thirty trees."

"It has a nice, year round creek behind that cabin," Mary said, nodding thoughtfully. "So, you're going to farm it? Any animals you gonna raise on it?"

Shaking her head, she said, "I'm vegan. I don't eat meat. I can't stand to see animals slaughtered. I plan to raise vegetables, have a small herb garden and plant fruit trees."

"Of course," she said, sitting up. "So? We're at the beginning of our gardening and farming season in about a month. You got a tractor and plow? That soil needs to be turned, aerated, before you can plant anything."

Dana admired Mary's intelligence. "You're right about that. The soil doesn't look like it has been turned over for decades. I don't have a tractor."

"Want one?"

Taken aback, Dana stared at her. "What?"

"My son, Chase Bishop, has an old, antique farm tractor that's not all electronic with wazoo doodads and computers in it. He was looking to sell it to someone who might have a use for it."

"That sounds good, Mrs. Bishop—"

"Call me Mary."

"Yes, ma'am—"

"Cut the politeness, too. I admire your respect, but remember what I said earlier, we're all family. You don't refer to family in those terms. Right?"

A sliver of a grin pulled at the corners of her mouth. "Okay, Mary, I can do that."

A quick nod. "You want a job here because?"

"I need money to restore the cabin and rent or lease some farm equipment so I can realize my dream of bringing the Wildflower back to life."

"You're not afraid of hard work, are you? Or really tough challenges? But then, you're a farm girl and been working every day of your life on your parents' farm."

"That's true," Dana admitted.

Mary scribbled a note on another piece of paper. "I'm gonna call my son, Chase Bishop, owner of the Three Bars Ranch. I'm gonna ask him to loan you that old John Deere tractor and have it brought over there by flatbed truck, so you can start using it. What else do you need?"

Taken aback, Dana's head spun with confusion. "I . . . well . . . Mary, I'm looking for a job."

"And you're volunteering a full day at our food bank once a week, giving back to the community. Right?"

". . . er . . . yes . . ."

"Remember? We're family?" Mary poked an index finger toward her. "Family works together as a team. You don't have the money to rent a tractor, so Chase is gonna loan you his old antique so you can get going turning that soil and readying it for planting."

Stunned, Dana blinked, unable to speak.

"And," Mary went on, making another note, "I'll make sure he brings over the disc and other plowing equipment that you'll need, as well as tools that go with farming. That place of yours needs a barn, you know? You have to have one to store your equipment, work on it, and keep it protected from the elements."

"Yes," Dana whispered, stunned, "I know that. It's in my plans."

"Good, good," Mary praised. "You also need a wrangler. Can you afford one?"

"Yes, I think I can. Part of my plan was to hire someone to help me. I can't do it alone and I know that."

"I got just the gent for you. His name is Colin Gallagher. He's a real loner, ex-military, has a lot of bad PTSD symptoms. He's working for my son as a wrangler over at the Three Bars Ranch, but wants something smaller to work on. Colin is a hard worker, takes direction well, and won't disappoint you."

Dana didn't know what to do or say. "I—uh . . . Mary, this is . . . well . . . amazing . . . thank you."

"Here's my plan for you, young lady," she said, scribbling a third note. "I've been looking for a local valley farm to provide me with certain vegetables and fruits in season. I'm needing a good, responsible farmer to fill in because the person who was doing this, recently died. I need a new individual whom I can work with. If you're amenable to that plan? I will pay *you* to do this, twenty-five dollars an hour, five days a week, eight hours a day. Fair enough?" She lifted her chin, eyes crinkling as she gazed at Dana.

Stunned by the offer, Dana whispered off-key, "You'd do this?"

"Well, of course I would! I believe in synchronicity. Pete, my dear old friend who used to provide my store for the last thirty years, passed on this last winter. I was looking for a replacement and here you are!"

Her mind whirled with the implications, the help she was going to magically receive.

"And," Mary said, "Chase will continue to pay Colin Gallagher. He's going to be 'on loan' to you to help you do the work that needs to be done around there. Your first priority, of course, is tilling the soil and getting the crops planted." She pulled a paper from another stack, handing it to her. "Here's a list of what I need vegetable-wise. You look it over and let me know if you're interested in raising these particular crops. With fifty acres of flat valley at your disposal, I'm roughly calculating that you can supply my grocery store nicely. We'll work out the details after you read up on my needs, and we'll have several future meetings on your ideas for the land, planting, and so on."

"You're paying me to raise crops for you?"

"Yep."

"Do you expect me to give them to you for free, even though you're paying me to do it?"

Mary laughed and rocked in her chair. "I don't do sharecropping. You'll be paid market price for all your produce. I believe in treating everyone fairly and like family. There's a lot of hard work involved in this farming and because you grew up on a farm, you understand that better than most."

"I do." Dana was relieved that she would be paid for the produce; she would need the income.

"For me, you're a very valuable resource for our valley and my grocery store. But I want you to sign a contract with me, agreeing that no chemical fertilizers, herbicides, pesticides, or GMO seeds will ever be used."

"I'm right there with you," Dana said, trying to take all of this unexpected news in and digest it.

"I figured you were, but we'll put that in writing because the people who come to my grocery store trust me. I'm not gonna let them down. Also, I'm assuming you're aware of companion planting and utilizing certain flowers, like marigolds, among others, to plant along with the crops. They're natural pesticides from nature, and that's all you can use."

"Yes, my parents never used anything other than what you're talking about. They produced alfalfa for cube manufacturers and they wanted 'clean,' non-GMO alfalfa for the animals that would eat it. My mother always used alfalfa cubes in her garden as mulch, as well as the benefits from it because it's a wonderful source of natural nitrogen in the right mix, for garden plants."

"Good to know! I'm pleased." Mary stood up and offered her long, thin hand across the desk to Dana. "Let's shake on it. Around here, in most cases, a person's word is her or his bond."

Dana stood, smiled a little unsurely, still dizzied by what had just happened, and gently closed her hand around Mary's. "You've got a deal, Mary. Thank you for this opportunity. I won't let you down. I promise." She released the woman's hand. Mary's face beamed, her eyes sparkling as she sat back down.

"Take my business card there," she said, pointing toward it. "My personal cell phone number is on there. The people who work to make my grocery store what it is, can call me anytime they want. Welcome to our family."

Colin Gallagher felt a huge, dark burden lift off his shoulders as he double-checked his flatbed load. The antique John Deere tractor was on board, the disc and other plows, plus a metal box filled with farm tools that this woman, Dana Scott, would need.

Earlier, Chase had come and gotten him out of one of the barns and told him his wish had been granted: He was assigning him to a small valley farm that had just been bought by a woman, that would be low stress compared to being around Three Bars. Mary had hired her to become her produce resource for the grocery store, and she asked that he assign a wrangler to help her. Colin jumped at the chance. He hated waking up at night, screaming, and then startling the other wranglers awake, as well. His PTSD was severe, and he was desperate to stop what was happening, but he couldn't.

Fortunately, Chase had been in the military and understood. They were working on ten houses that would start to be built for the wranglers with families and after those were completed, for the single wranglers.. Until then, the single male wranglers all slept in the bunkhouse. The women wranglers had a separate bunkhouse.

He had been ready to quit because he was causing major sleep deprivation for the rest of the hands, until Chase had come by with this new assignment.

It felt as if life were being breathed back into him as he slowly walked around the flatbed, one more time checking the chains that held the tractor in place on it, as well as the wide, thick nylon straps across the other items.

"Colin," Chase said, coming out of his office to see him. "My mother says there is no livable place on that ranch."

Frowning, Colin said, "You mean I have to come back here every night and sleep in the bunkhouse?" It was the *last* thing he wanted to do. He saw Bishop grin a little. Their military background had bonded them closely, like brothers, to one another.

"No, I have a fix for it. Mary is buying a double-wide mobile home to be put on the place. I guess Dana, the owner, knows nothing about this yet, so you can break the news to her. You'll both have a bedroom, one at each end of it, so you'll have full privacy. It has two bathrooms, as well."

Relief poured through Colin. "That's mighty nice of Mary to do that for this woman, Dana."

"Dana Scott is her name. Mary likes her a lot. All I know about her is that she's a farm girl from the Willamette Valley in Oregon. She's agreed to raise produce that Mary needs for the store, but don't be shocked by how run-down the Wildflower Ranch is. There's a small log cabin on it that should probably be torn down and plans drawn up for a house to be built on the site, instead. Mary counseled one step at a time, here. You okay sharing a trailer with her? It's large enough to give you both space and you can meet in the center of it where the kitchen and dining room are located."

"I'll make it work."

Chase clapped him on the back as they walked toward the front of the truck. "I know you've been worried about waking everyone at night."

"Yeah," he muttered, pulling his black Stetson down a little to shade his eyes from the rising sun.

"Well, these modern-day mobile homes are pretty airtight and soundproof, so as long as you close your bedroom door at night, I'm sure Dana won't hear you."

"That's a big relief."

"This mobile home has four bedrooms. Mary's equipping the room next to your and Dana's bedrooms, converting them into offices for each of you with two computer terminals. That way the two spare bedrooms become offices, something you're going to need. And she's arranging for a wide-screen TV for the living room."

"I don't watch much TV," Colin admitted, halting and opening the door to the truck.

"You also have my permission to come back here for

any tools or other machinery you need. Mary wants to make this as easy as possible on Dana, so she can make the planting this season, on June 1. You just leave a list of items you need in my office, and I'll have someone drive it out to the Wildflower Ranch for you."

Nodding, he climbed into the cab after pulling on his elk-skin gloves. "Sounds good, boss. I'll let her know."

"And get me her cell phone number, will you? Mary's already called the utility companies, and she's going to put in electric, telephone, and another construction contractor is coming out to dig out a septic tank for the mobile home. She's got a plumber and an electrician set up to put in what's necessary before it arrives. Mary says about a week. It's going to be busy and hectic the first week or so, Colin."

"I guess so," he said, shutting the door and rolling down the window. "I'll be in touch. As soon as I unload all this gear and machinery, I'm going to assess what else she needs out there and I'll talk it over with you by cell."

Chase raised his hand. "Sounds good. Adios, compadre."

Relief flowed sweetly through Colin as he turned on the ignition, the massive truck engine coming to life. As a wrangler, there wasn't anything he couldn't do around a ranch, and he was well-known for his mechanical knowledge of engines, heavy equipment operation, and carpentry.

As the truck rolled out of the driveway, he headed toward the entrance, making a left turn, having to take this load through Silver Creek. He knew where the Wildflower Ranch was. Often, last summer, he headed to the desolate ranch and hiked into the mountains at the back of it. When his PTSD got bad, going into the woods calmed his anxiety and his stress levels lowered.

He recalled the small ranch's history, aware of a family claiming it in the 1900s. Now, this woman, Dana Scott, had bought it. Who was she? How old was she? Knowing nothing about her made him curious. He hoped she was someone who was easy to get along with. Chase hadn't said anything about her personality at all. Still, he knew Mary Bishop well enough that she had an eye for good, loyal people who worked hard, were honest and easy-going.

He mentally crossed his fingers, turning onto the main road with his load. The sun was bright and he pulled down the visor, not having his dark glasses with him. Pulling the brim of his Stetson a little lower, he headed out for his new job. What would it be like? Could he do it? Always concerned his PTSD symptoms might inter-fere, he had no idea if Dana Scott was aware of his unseen wounds.

There was plenty for Colin to worry about as he drove through downtown Silver Creek on a Monday morning at eight a.m. Mary had hired Dana Scott yesterday. Less than twenty-four hours later, he was bringing her all the farm equipment she could handle. The question he had was: How much did she really know about farming? Because of his PTSD, Colin was a loner. He didn't do well in groups of people and especially, not a crowd. He was fairly good on one-on-ones, but if this woman hadn't a clue about farming, he saw that as a hurdle he wasn't sure he could leap.

As he left the busy morning commute into Silver Creek by those who worked in the industrious little town,

18 *Lindsay McKenna*

Colin pressed down on the accelerator. The ranch was eight miles west of the town on a two-lane asphalt highway. Not that far.

He wiped his upper lip with the back of his elk-skin gloved hand. Feeling anxious, he recognized all the symptoms starting to accumulate in him, making his stomach seize up, his heart pounding a little harder in his chest. He was going to have a woman for a boss, not a man. That was going to take some adjustment, because most of his life he had been around and worked only with men. Trying to tell himself that Mary Bishop, a woman, literally ran everything on Three Bars, her son Chase taking care of the ranch while she took care of everything else, hadn't proved to be a hurdle at all to him. He'd met Mary many times and genuinely respected her type A personality. He always liked the deviltry he saw dancing in her eyes, that quick smile and the way she would pat a person's shoulder, as if they were a well-loved family member. And no one was more generous than Mary was. Colin had seen her fund a number of start-up businesses for small business owners right here in the valley. She wasn't afraid to invest in people, and believe in them heart and soul.

Was there any possibility that Dana Scott was like that?

Chapter 2

Dana got her first look at her wrangler-on-loan as he slowly pulled up in a long flatbed. The nine a.m. sun was bright and strong in a cloudless sky. It was around forty-five degrees outside and she wore her heavy denim jacket. He wore a black Stetson hat, the same color as his military-short hair and maybe two-day growth of beard on his lean, hard-looking face.

When he rolled down the window, lifting his gloved hand toward her in a silent hello, she drew in a breath. He had the most startling blue eyes! The thick fringe of lashes did nothing but accentuate the color. She'd seen that kind of blue eyes in a famous Hollywood star, Paul Newman. It took away some of her initial reaction that he was hard, because his mouth was well shaped and the corners moved upward, hinting that he laughed or perhaps had a good sense of humor. Forewarned that he had PTSD, he didn't appear anxious to her. The tan on his face, she was sure, had come from being outside a lot. She lifted her hand to him.

The flatbed truck braked and the engine turned off. Curious about the wrangler, she walked toward the cab, which was near the log cabin. The door opened and she saw he was tall and wiry, not thin, but there was tight muscling from continuous work, she would bet, underneath that blue-and-white plaid shirt he wore. The cuffs on the long sleeves had been unbuttoned and rolled up a couple of times, revealing the dark hair across his forearms. When he turned to her after closing the door on the truck, Dana relaxed more.

There was an intensity to him that was palpable; almost as if he were some big cat, like a jaguar or leopard, beneath his skin. He did not scare her. Just the opposite. It was a sense she had and it made her understand that he was all warrior. Not a peacemaker. Even the way he moved in her direction, taking off his gloves and stuffing them in a back pocket of his Levi's, he possessed a boneless grace that told her even more of his unspoken lethality. What was that saying? You scratch a man's skin and just beneath it one found a warrior? Or something like that. It fit this wrangler.

His Levi's were well-worn, his cowboy boots scuffed, scarred from many years in the trenches of demanding work around a ranch. The leather belt around his waist carried a Buck knife, which was common in his kind of work.

He removed his hat and halted about six feet from her.

"I'm Colin Gallagher. Mr. Bishop sent me up here to bring you some farm machinery." He turned slightly, pointing in the direction of the flatbed. Returning his gaze to her, he said, "And I'm here to help you any way that I can, ma'am."

"I'm Dana Scott, Mr. Gallagher." She thrust out her

hand toward him. He took it, but she noticed he didn't crush her bones, just a nice, firm handshake.

"Call me Colin, ma'am. I don't stand on a lot of ceremony."

She smiled slightly. "Mary Bishop got riled when I kept calling her 'ma'am,' but I'm not going to get upset. Just call me Dana. I'm not much on PC stuff, either." Her hand tingled after they ended their handshake. He reminded her of the dark knight in a story she'd read when in high school; a knight without family, pledging loyalty only to the serfs and peasants who needed protecting from their many enemies. She'd read that book and fallen in love with the anti-hero knight. Colin reminded her of that character in spades.

She sensed a tension in him that wasn't obvious in his body language or face. Maybe it was the PTSD he wrestled with every day of his life? Her heart grew sad over that realization.

"That's a nice name, Dana," he said, nodding. "Where would you like me to put the tractor and other equipment?"

She walked with him over to the truck. "How old is that John Deere tractor, Colin?" She stared up at it. He came and stood nearby, lifting his hat, running his fingers through his hair and then settling it back on his head. "I honestly don't know. What I can tell you is it belonged to Mr. Bishop, Chase's father. When he died, it was still used on certain areas of the ranch. When Chase came home from the military about three years ago, his mother, Mary, put him in charge of the ranch. He loved this old Deere," he said, gesturing toward it. "While it doesn't have electronics or work on computer programs or apps, it's a reliable, hardworking piece of machinery." He gave her a glance. "Chase said you came from a farm family. Am I assuming you did all kinds of this type of work, too?"

"You can," she answered drily. "I drove my father's tractor, which was computerized, and tilled the soil every spring and fall starting at age twelve. I've never been on an old tractor like this before."

A one-cornered grin appeared on his mouth. "No worries. I know how to use it."

"You can teach me?"

"Sure, if you want."

"I do."

He looked around. "This place needs a lot of work," he murmured, "but then, I know you realize that, too."

"I need a barn, or something similar, to put all this equipment inside to keep it protected from the weather. Plus, a place to do oil changes, and repairs."

Nodding, Colin gestured to the elephant in the room, the log cabin. "What are you going to do with this?"

"Fix it." She saw his straight black brows rise. "I know it's broken-down, but it's part of the history, an important part of it for the ranch family who first came here. I want to save it."

He nodded slowly, holding her gaze and then lifting his chin, assessing the cabin. "You know? I feel like that poor ole cabin most days. At least no one has told me I should be scrapped yet."

She felt an immediate kinship with Colin. His words had come out low, emotion veiled in them, and the look on his face broke her heart. He was in just as bad a place as she was. Maybe the reasons were different, but the outcome was the same. "Funny," she murmured, giving him an understanding look, "I stood here a while back after buying this place and saw myself in that old beat-up cabin, too."

Colin turned, studying her for a moment, and then returned his gaze to the cabin. "You sure don't look beat-up," he said in a rasp.

"Looks are deceiving," was all she'd say.

Taking the elk-skin gloves out of his back pocket, he pulled them on. "That's true, " he said. "Chase is working with the local feed-and-seed store. He's going to get a Quonset hut structure out here that's made of galvanized aluminum and steel, a barn of sorts, that will take care and protect all this equipment. He said it will be coming in about a week and the crew that's delivering it will set it up for us."

Shocked, she stared at him. "A Quonset hut?" Mary had said nothing about putting a hut on her land! She knew the prices of Quonset huts; her father had one for his tractor. "That's a *lot* of money!"

"This is one that Chase has had on his ranch and he's not using it. He's going to have the wranglers take it apart and I'll haul it up here on this flatbed." He hooked his thumb toward the truck. Looking up at the cloudless sky, he said, "It rains a lot in April, but we have about a six-day window of no rain, and he's planning on getting it set up here so we have a place to store and work on the equipment, before the bad weather arrives."

"Still, that's amazing," she murmured, shaking her head. "I've never seen such generosity. Ever."

"Welcome to Silver Creek Valley," he said, giving her an amused look. "The folks here stick together like glue. They help each other out where and when they can."

"I'll need to repay him someday," she said, worried about that.

"Naw, Chase said it was yours to keep. Like I said, he has no use for it any longer. Just consider this a repurposing of it, instead of being junked."

Uncomfortable, she looked around the area, trying to deal with a surge of emotion: disbelief and wanting to cry all at the same time because people she didn't even know were giving her more than a helping hand. Clearing her throat, she tried to hide her surging feelings. "Where would you put that Quonset hut, Colin?"

"Why don't you give me the layout as you see it, first, so I know more before answering you?"

That was fair, and for the next ten minutes they walked around where the log cabin stood and she gave him a verbal map of what she was going to do, and where it would be located.

Finally, when they were done with the walkabout, they stood next to the flatbed. "What is your idea of where things should go?" she asked, looking up at him. Colin was not pretty-boy handsome, his face lean, nose clean and sharp, high cheekbones with that growth of beard making her feel things toward a man she'd not felt in a long, long time. Seeing the look in his gaze change, become more thoughtful, he glanced one way and then the other, his gaze sweeping the area.

"You want your barn near the road so you don't have to build a large driveway in order to get to it." He pointed to where she wanted the vegetable crops, which would be located behind the log cabin area. "You've got a wide, strong-flowing creek. That's good news and bad news." He pointed to the rutted dirt road that was covered by the creek. "That is going to require some construction to put a small bridge across it. You can't keep driving through it all the time, especially with heavier equipment. And you don't want your Quonset hut too close to it because in the spring, like now, it's flooding from the snow melting off the mountain range and coming down into the valley, here. If this were my ranch, I'd place the Quonset hut closer to the entrance to this ranch, and very close to this old road that's seen better days."

She lifted her hand, shading her eyes, looking at where he was pointing. "Because it's drier and out of the flooding area?" she guessed. She saw him nod and give her a look of praise. It felt good. Feeling pummeled by so many things that were happening at once, she was grateful that Colin knew so much.

"Exactly. Plus, if you have to have a piece of equipment taken out for major repair or something? It will make it easier to be on ground that doesn't have any other buildings nearby."

"All good reasons," she said. Giving him a grateful look, she whispered, "I'm really glad Mr. Bishop is allowing you to be up here to help me. Do you have a degree in engineering?"

"No, just common horse sense. And I'm sure Chase will be coming here within the next week to assess your place and give you some good advice and ideas. You can bet he'll see things I don't, and be able to help you set up the structures you need in good places."

"I feel like the cavalry just rode in. I never expected so much help and gifts." She turned, gesturing to the tractor on the flatbed.

"People of this valley pitch in and help. We've all been

in places where we need a hand up," he said, rubbing his jaw, looking around. "Did you know that Mary Bishop has a double-wide mobile home coming to your ranch next week? It's going to be our sleeping quarters, our offices and HQ."

Gasping, her eyes widening, Dana pressed her hand to her heart. "She what?"

Grinning a little, Colin told her everything that Chase had told him about the mobile home. She looked like a lightning bolt had struck her: stunned and with no words. When she said nothing, her hand still pressed to her heart, he added, "It's got four bedrooms. One at each end of it. Mary is going to have the bedrooms next to where we sleep, turned into offices for each of us. In this coming week? We'll be having a plumbing company out here, a couple of wranglers from Chase's ranch bringing in a concrete mixer to pour a foundation for the mobile home, plus the electric and phone company coming out. You're going to be busy, so we need to decide right away where you want your living quarters."

"I was hoping to sleep in the cabin," she said, sounding unsure.

"Dana, you see that roof?" He pointed to it. "When it rains? There's going to be leaks all over inside the cabin. That roof is dangerous and I'll bet it could fall through; those cedar shingles look pretty weather-beaten. There's no windows or door on it either. You can't sleep out here because the nights get really cold, sometimes freezing this time of year. It doesn't start warming up until mid-May. You'll catch a cold or flu, or worse, if you stay out here."

Frowning, she muttered, "I really wanted to be with the land. I love the feel of it, the energy."

"You will," he said, trying to sound a little less clipped in his answers. She looked bereft. "Where are you staying right now until the mobile home is set up for use?"

"I was staying at the women's shelter in town."

"I don't think you need to stay there, Dana. We have two separate bunkhouses for our single wranglers, one for the women and one for the men. The boss told me there's an open bunk in the women's and he'd like you to stay there. It has showers, restrooms attached to it, and there's a cookhouse, which is really a nice building and like a restaurant, for everyone to eat three square meals a day. He'd like you come and stay there until things get situated here. He would never charge you for it, either."

Touching her brow, Dana took a deep, shaky breath. "This is so much . . ."

"I'm sure it is, but you need this kind of help under the circumstances, and you chose a good place to buy a ranch."

He saw tears in her eyes, and she gulped a couple of times, turning away from him, taking swipes at her eyes.

"I-I do need the help," she muttered, turning around. "I never thought about the creek and how I was going to get through it to the crop areas," she admitted hoarsely, meeting his gaze. Running her fingers through her red hair, she wanted to be alone to cry. This was all too much for her to take in.

"I know it's a lot to deal with," he said gruffly, walking back to the truck with her. "I've been down and out in my life and it was the people of this valley who have helped me get a handle on my problem."

She walked at his side, arms across her chest, head down, the grass beneath her feet blurring now and then.

Sniffing, she focused on him. "Silver Creek should be considered a hospital in some respects then. It sounds like you've had a rough time, too, and yet, you look whole."

He managed a strangled sound that was supposed to be a laugh. "I'm sure Mary told you I have PTSD?"

"Yes, she did. Some of our farmhands that worked for my parents were military men, and they had it, too. It's awful to be wounded like that."

Nodding, he said nothing.

"If your parents had a farm, why are you here?"

Wincing, Dana choked out, "I can't talk about that right now, Colin. I'm dealing with enough as it is."

"I'm sorry," he rasped, "it's none of my business . . ."

She looked over at him. "Don't feel badly about it. Okay?"

Mouth thinning, he nodded, walking to the truck. "If I pull around the log cabin and drive up the main road, I can off-load the equipment. Have you decided where you might want that double-wide mobile home?"

She took a deep breath and pointed to the south end of the cabin. "It seems the only place to put it would be there? What do you think?"

"You're too close to the creek. There's a company that will come in and create a huge hole so that your septic tank can fit down in it. You don't want it near the stream or you'll possibly pollute it."

She came to a halt. "Oh, no. I wouldn't ever want that. Where would you suggest is a good place to put it, Colin?"

"You could put it here," he said, pointing down at his feet. "It's a hundred feet or so from the creek. The septic tank could be put up there, giving another sixty feet away from it."

"How big is this mobile home?"

"It's thirty-two feet wide and sixty feet long. The interior would give you 1,920 square feet of living space. A pretty large one, with lots of room. I don't think we'll bump into one another," he teased, seeing the pallor of her face turn a bit pink. Was she blushing? The freckles across her nose and cheeks were endearing to him, making her look a lot younger than she probably was. He had a lot of questions for her.

"I've never lived in one. Our home was only fifteen hundred square feet—" She abruptly stopped talking.

"There's a lot of room in it," he said, seeing pain in her willow-green eyes. "Once I off-load the equipment? I'll do the measurements and put down some orange flagging so you can see what it's like. You can then tell me if you like it there, or you want some changes."

Nodding, Dana was beginning to feel so overwhelmed with her good fortune that she needed time alone to deal with it. She almost blurted out the murder of her parents by a group of white supremacists, and abruptly stopped the words from coming out of her mouth. Colin was way too easy to talk with. He had a gentle side, despite that warrior energy she felt around him. She could see he was doing his best to be amenable to what her needs might be. Her father had a mind like Colin's, and that helped her relax. She had always told her father that he should have been a civil engineer because he considered things she just never thought about.

Colin climbed into the truck, started it up, and slowly

made a wide turn around the log cabin, heading out to where the Quonset hut would be located.

In another week, this place would suddenly be populated with buildings! And in the midst of it all, was her beloved little log cabin. She decided to call Mary and find out if she needed to pay rent to her for living in the mobile home. Dana didn't want to take advantage of Mary's generosity in any way. She would call and ask. She pulled out her cell phone and punched in the number.

"Mary here."

"Hi, this is Dana Scott—"

"I was just gonna call you."

Brows moving up, Dana said, "Really?"

"I want you to follow Colin Gallagher back to my son's ranch once he gets everything off-loaded. We want you two to have dinner with us tonight. That okay with you, Dana?"

Gulping, she said, "Well . . . yes . . ."

"Then we can answer all your questions. Chase is having our head woman wrangler get a bunk cubical set up for you at our single-women wranglers' barracks. You'll stay there until we can get that mobile home out there and set up for you and Colin."

"That's . . . I mean, I really didn't expect all this, Mary, but thank you." She tried to take the quaver out of her voice as she turned, looking at where Colin had parked the flatbed.

"Good! We'll see you sometime this afternoon."

The phone clicked off and Dana shut off her smartphone, feeling as if she'd been swept up in a tornado, her whole life upended, but in a good way. She had to walk about a quarter of a mile to where Colin was taking off the chains from around the tractor. He had already pulled down a sturdy ramp so that it could be driven off the truck. As she approached, she saw the intense focus he had on his job. Knowing to never approach him from behind, she angled her walk to the middle of the road so he could see her coming.

"Talk to Mary?" he asked, dropping the chains near the rear wheels of the flatbed.

Nodding, she took a moment to share it with him. A lazy smile pulled at the corners of his mouth. "Mary's a force of nature," he drawled, pointing to the other side of the ramp.

"You could say that," Dana said.

"I'm going to have you stand over there, out of the way. I've got the keys to the tractor and it needs to come down."

"Right," she said. "Is there anything I can do to help you, Colin?"

Shaking his head, he said, "I've done this a few times." And then he suddenly gave her a boyish grin. "I'm not used to having a partner to help me out."

Her heart wrenched as she stepped away. For a moment, that intensity in his features disappeared. She saw, instead, a little boy, carefree, living in the moment, his eyes shining with humor. It was a breathtaking change. And it was gone in seconds.

Hurting for him, Dana stood well out of the way while he lithely moved up the ramp to the old tractor. Every movement continued to remind her of the lithe jaguar of South America. That, too, made her heart beat a little harder. Colin seemed unaware of how sexy he looked to her.

She'd grown up with working hands, all lean like wolves, graceful in their own male way. Whatever it was about this man, he touched her heart and curiosity. Dana wanted to know a lot more about him and she was glad he would be working here with her. She watched him back the Deere effortlessly down the ramp to the ground.

The breeze was slightly warmer now, the sun higher and warming the jacket she wore. In no time, he had the disc plow and other items off the truck, all neatly placed in a row near the road. A box of tools was next. And then rakes, spades, post-hole digger, and a lot of other tools were set next to the box, which had a padlock on it. It took nearly an hour, and Dana was able to help him with the tools, all of them in one pile.

"Why don't you bring your truck up here?" he suggested. "We can lift the box and tools into the back and drive it up to the log cabin. I don't really want to have those things in sight of others."

"Agreed," she said. "I'll be back in a bit." She began trotting down the road to where her truck was parked. The sun was higher, the air warming, and by the time she reached her truck, she shucked off her coat, her long-sleeved blouse keeping her comfy.

They moved equipment until noon. Colin was easy to work with. He'd pulled a notebook and pen from the flatbed, a measuring tape, and they measured the width of the creek, how deep it was, and the distances for a bridge to be built. He had knee-high rubber boots that he'd brought with him, but she didn't have any.

He didn't say much, but would answer her if she asked

a question. How badly she wanted to know more about *him*, the man who was stirring her heart and emotions. Patience was something Colin had a lot of.

On another page, he started a list of things she'd need, explaining that Chase had a forewoman who took care of any and all of the tools that a wrangler might need out on a job site. He promised that he'd take Dana over to her office today, once they got back to Three Bars.

Dana was glad to see Colin wading into that cold mountain-creek water. She stood on the other side, feet dry, holding that long, cloth measuring tape. The water wet his Levi's, his thighs hard and curved, making her watch him more than was advisable. Did Colin know how beautiful he was physically? Dana kept it to herself. He probably had a special person in his life, and that thought slowed her heart to a more realistic beat.

She wrapped up the cloth tape as he came across and then stood nearby, finishing out his notes on the bridge. "Do you have someone who can build a bridge?" she wondered.

"Yeah, me." He managed a wry, one-corner hook of his mouth while simultaneously giving her a glance from beneath his hat.

"You trained for this?"

"Well, kinda," he admitted hesitantly. He stopped writing and looked up, gauging the place where he saw the best site for said bridge.

"Are you an engineer?" she pressed. His mouth thinned a bit.

"I was in the Army Rangers," he admitted quietly, adding more notes, "Seventy-Fifth Regiment, Special Ops. We had to learn a lot of things that we might need out on a mission."

So, he was in the army. In her eyes, he was a hero. "Afghanistan?"

"Yes." He tucked the pencil into his left pocket and slid his clipboard between his left arm and the side of his body. "Sometimes, we were able to stay in an area long enough to work with other army specialties and we would sink a well or build a bridge for the people there. Part of our plan to show them we weren't there to kill them."

Hearing the sudden catch in his gruff tone, she said nothing.

Colin pulled a smartphone from his pocket and took several photos of the area where the bridge could be made.

"I don't know much about the military," she apologized. "Sometimes my curiosity gets me in trouble."

Tucking the phone back into his pocket, he cocked his head, slanted her a glance. "I don't mind your questions."

"Really?"

"There isn't a mean bone in your body."

She laughed a little. "Now, how do you know that?"

His mouth curved ruefully, and he put his clipboard into his right hand. "Just do."

Turning and following him, she hurried to catch up to his long, lanky stride as he headed toward the flatbed. "Where are we going now?"

"To eat," he said, stopping at the truck. He opened the door and placed the board on the seat, then picked up a small plastic carrier. Turning, he said, "Lunch. Hungry?"

Blinking, Dana looked at her watch. Indeed, it was

noon. And as if to seal the deal, her stomach growled. She felt heat fly into her face as she put her hand over her belly.

Chuckling, Colin gestured to the end of the flatbed. "Want to sit on the ramp with me and eat? This morning Chase's wife, Cari, made this up for us. She wanted to make sure you were well-fed."

Dana sat down on one of the metal ramps. He came and sat about three feet away, placing the plastic cooler between them and opening it up. "That was very kind of her."

"You'll meet her tonight at dinner," he said. "She made us three sandwiches with beef, lettuce, tomato, and mayonnaise." Looking over at her, he said, "By any chance are you vegetarian?"

"I am."

"Humph, must explain this third sandwich then. Cari said it was for you."

"How did she know that?" Dana wondered, taking the thick sourdough sandwich and opening it up.

"Probably through Mary." He chuckled and opened up one of his sandwiches. "Mary knows everyone in Silver Creek Valley. And I mean everyone."

"I'm glad I'll be able to thank her tonight," she said, appreciating the homemade sourdough bread. There were slices of cucumber, apple, red onion, carrot, and tomato topped with thick hummus. Her mouth watered and she sank her teeth into the giant sandwich. Making a sound of gratitude, she closed her eyes and simply allowed the spices, the garlicky hummus and different textures to blend. It was delicious!

"You really like that stuff?" he teased unmercifully, watching her green eyes shine with laughter.

"I can ask the same of you." She pointed to the sliced beef sandwich he had to hold with two hands.

"But I'm a growing boy," he protested, the corners of his mouth drawing upward.

"I could never eat an animal." She shook her head, concentrating on the banquet of tastes that Cari had divinely put together like a five-star chef might.

"Mmm," he grunted, relishing the sandwich. "I need the protein."

"We have vegetable proteins," Dana said archly.

He drew out a bag of blue corn chips and opened it up, setting it on top of the cooler. "These are vegan, too."

"I share. Would you like some?" She took a triangle, munching on it, pleased with the sea salt on it.

"Only if I'm starving."

"And you're not *that* hungry, huh?"

A throaty chuckle.

"Is Chase vegetarian?"

"No. None of his family is. Cari is the only one. She's five months' pregnant. Doc said it is a girl and Cari already told the boss man that their daughter was going to be raised vegetarian"

"Good for her," Dana said, wiping her fingers on the thigh of her jeans.

"You don't get much work done eating plants," he drawled, finishing off the first sandwich and reaching for the second one. This time, he drew out a bag of potato chips, opened it and set it next to her blue corn chips.

Laughing, she said, "Is this how it's going to be from now on?"

"What?"

"Us. Two very different people trying to find peace in the middle?" ·

He tipped the front of his Stetson up a bit, looking around. "Oh, I think you and me, as different as we might appear to be on the surface, have a lot more in common than we really know."

Her heart tumbled when he glanced over at her, completely serious. "Are you psychic or something?"

"Me? Nah." He bit voraciously into the second sandwich.

Staring at him, a warm ripple went through her. "I think," she began slowly, "that you are not who you seem to be."

"Is anyone?"

"Yes."

"Like you, for instance? What you see is what you get?"

"I hope so," she said, impertinent over the curious, appraising look he gave her. It was as if he really was able to read a person's mind. He certainly seemed able to penetrate her world and know who she was. Under other circumstances, Dana might have found that disconcerting, but with Colin? He seemed like a safe, quiet harbor to her pressured world right now. Just sitting with him brought her stress levels down. "Aren't you the same?" she demanded archly.

Shrugging, he said, "The work I did in the army? They called us chameleons." He gave her a steady look. "We

became what we had to be in order to survive, to manip-
ulate or manage a pretty deadly situation."

She lost her playfulness. ". . . Oh . . ."

"Now, don't give me that sad-eyed puppy dog look,"
he admonished. "I don't like people feeling sorry for me."

The silence fell between them, and they each ate their
sandwiches, watching a red-tailed hawk flying above
them, across the wide-open meadow where they liked to
hunt for rodents and snakes. Dana wasn't sure what to say
for a long time. She ate and then would pull a blue chip
from the bag. He'd do the same, only it was from his
potato chip bag. Finished, she pushed her hands against
her jeans.

"I think I need to wash off these paws in the creek,"
she said, standing.

Colin nodded. "I'll be doin' the same in a few minutes."

Walking toward the creek, Dana felt a mix of emotions
clashing within her. One moment, he was a delightful
little boy teasing her. The next, deadly serious and she
could see the agony in his blue eyes, as if he said anything,
some invisible dam within him was going to break open
and he'd have no way of controlling it or his emotions.
And yet, she felt comfortable and safe with Colin. And
drawn to him, man to her woman. Maybe he was many
things to many people. She simply didn't know. Her life
as a farmer limited her in some ways. The people she
worked with were literally the salt of the earth: honest,
commonsensible, what you saw was what you got.

Squatting down near the edge of the water, she put her
hands into it, the coldness snapping and jarring. Was
that what Colin was really like on the inside? She'd heard
that those who suffered from PTSD were often like two

different people. One nice, the other broken and hurting. His look had been haunting and her sensitive intuition told her he'd wanted to say so much more, but something was holding him back.

Pushing to her full height, she flung her hands a little and then dried them off on her jeans. Taking a deep, unsteady breath, Dana sensed that because she was so magnetically drawn to Colin, that one day, he might tell her. But from the look in his narrowed eyes, she wasn't sure when it might be.

Chapter 3

Colin felt sorry for Dana as they walked up to the main ranch house at Three Bars. They'd arrived at the ranch around three p.m., with Dana following his flatbed in her truck. He could see the fatigue in her eyes, understanding only too well that her world had been upended once again.

It was all good news, of course, but there was a lot going to come down next week, and she didn't have much of an anchor to hold on to during this chaotic period. He wanted to be that for her, and that surprised him. Since coming home from Afghanistan, he'd been a dark, quiet loner doing his job and doing it well on Three Bars. Because the owner, Chase Bishop, had been a behind-the-lines Marine recon and had also been a victim of PTSD, he understood Colin's need to work alone, and not in a noisy crowd. He always gave him assignments where he could do just that.

As he drove the flatbed into an equipment area down below the ranch, Dana pulled up. He climbed into her truck, giving her directions to where the main ranch was located. The sun was low in the western sky and he knew it would be dark around seven p.m. He told her how to

STRENGTH UNDER FIRE   41

get over to see Tracy Hartimer, their forewoman who ran the ranch. Once there, he introduced Dana to blond-haired Tracy, who was tall and lean. She took Dana over to the nearby women's bunking facility, which they called "the barracks." In no time, she had a very nice four-hundred-square-foot cubical with a bed, TV, desk, dinette table, and stuffed chair. Colin hadn't been in the women's bunkhouse, but it was, by far, superior to the men's bunkhouse. He saw Dana was surprised and pleased.

He brought her suitcases in from the truck and deposited them into her new, temporary home. The men's bunkhouse was nearby, so it was easy enough for him to walk over there where his truck was parked. He told Dana he'd pick her up near six p.m. Both of them needed a shower and a change of clothes, for sure.

There was a horizontal swath of pale lavender along the western horizon when Colin drove them up to the main ranch house. He parked in the gravel driveway.

"Looks like Logan Anderson and his wife, Leanna, are comin' for dinner, too," he said.

"Who are they?"

"They own the largest ranch in the valley. Nice folks. You'll like them." He walked around the truck, opening the door for her. Seeing her shock, he said drily, "Bear with me? I'm old-fashioned," and he held his hand out, which she took, and helped her step down to the ground.

"I can live with that." Dana smiled over at him. "Looks like a party going on," she said, gesturing to the huge cedar home, walking through the picket fence gate that he'd opened for her.

"The ranchers and farmers are really tight here in the valley and their families are very good friends with one another," he said, taking the lead. A few more steps up to the porch and he knocked on the door.

"Well, well," Mary crowed, opening the door moments later, "you finally made it, Colin! Come on in. Hi, Dana!"

Mary Bishop was wearing a dark purple jacket, a fuchsia blouse with ruffles, and trousers.

"Good to see you again, Mary," Dana said.

Mary grabbed Dana and gave her a fierce hug and released her. "You're looking better!"

The hug reminded Dana sharply of how her mother would bear-hug her as a child and she quickly forced tears away over that memory. Stepping away after returning the hug, albeit a much more gentle embrace, she said, "Why wouldn't I? So many good things have happened to me in the last day, that my head is spinning. I can't keep count of all that's going on at the ranch this week and next."

Cackling, Mary reached over and squeezed Colin's left hand. "I think this gent here filled you in on everything?"

"He sure did." She looked around the huge space, the kitchen to her left, the dining room in front of her, and beyond that, a huge living room with a floor-to-ceiling fireplace where a fire crackled and popped, the warmth welcoming her.

Sliding her hand around Dana's left arm, Mary said, "Come on, you need to meet your new neighbors. We're all sittin' around in the living room chawing and waiting on our two-dinner meal." She grinned elfishly and added, "Wait till you taste Louise's cooking. She's made a vegetarian meal for us women, and a meat meal for the guys."

"That's wonderful that we can have vegan food here tonight. I was dreading an all-beef meal."

Mary led her into the living room. "Not while I'm

alive! I've been vegetarian all my life and look at me! No one thinks I've lived so many decades." She chuckled.

Dana was introduced to Logan and Lea Anderson, the owners of the largest ranch in the valley. Then she shook hands with Chase, and his wife, Cari, who gave her a warm, welcoming hug. Cari looked very pregnant and Dana guessed she might be seven months along. Sitting down next to Colin on an antique pink velvet settee, she was served peppermint tea with honey, while Colin received coffee from Louise, who held a silver tray with sugar, plus cream for those who wanted it. She noted he took his coffee black.

Dana liked all of the families, the feeling in the room one of coziness, camaraderie, and she absorbed their moments of laughter. Pretty soon, just listening to the chatter back and forth between good friends, she discovered Logan had also been in the military. The idea of hundreds of beehives as a business was new to Dana, and she listened intently whenever Cari spoke about the enterprise, which had been surprisingly successful.

"Cari?" she asked, "I'm planning on eighty acres of fruits and vegetables. Could beehives help pollinate more of my crop if I had them there?"

Cari nodded. "Absolutely. Originally"—she gave her husband a warm look—"when Chase hired me to come and create a major beehive plan for his ranch, his hay, vegetable, and fruit orchard production was at a certain level. I had our team install two hundred hives around the ranch. This year"—she smiled over at Chase—"his production has nearly doubled."

"Wow," was all Dana could manage. "That much?"

Chase said, "It blew me away, too, Dana."

"But I thought bees were in decline," she said to Cari.

"Unfortunately, they are globally, and it's mostly due to pesticides, herbicides, and now, the GMO threat to them."

Wrinkling her nose, Dana muttered, "I told Mary when we got together, that everything I am going to raise will be organic."

Mary said, "It's the only way to go. Did you know that Cari and her team are now reaching out to people in the Silver Creek area, and if they grow a garden, she will supply to them one free beehive, with bees? They're teaching a whole lot of our neighbors not only how to care for the bees, but their garden crops will produce so much more food for them and their families, as well. It's a win-win."

"That's a wonderful idea," Dana said, excitement in her tone about the far-reaching program. "But I'd like to be able to buy a lot of beehives."

"You're looking at roughly one thousand dollars for each one," Chase said.

Deflated, she glanced over at Colin, who sat listening intently to the conversation. "Gosh, I don't have that kind of money, Chase. I mean, I wish I did."

"We could extend you a one-year promissory note on, say, fifty beehives for your land," Cari urged, equally excited over the prospect. "We could start a monthly payment plan after your crops come in this fall. There would be no interest on it, either. What do you think?"

Stunned by Cari's generosity, Dana said, suddenly emotional, "I'd love to do that! I can't believe you're offering me such a deal. People nowadays don't do this."

Laughing, Cari sipped her tea and said, "Welcome to

the Silver Creek Valley, then. I didn't believe it when I came here, either. Chase made it his mission to show me how everyone worked together. It takes a village, or in this case, all the farmers and ranchers, plus individual folks, all our neighbors, to work together to pull it off. It was so inspiring to me. Since getting married to this guy"—she gave Chase a warm look—"I've instituted a neighborhood beehive plan outreach to anyone who wants it." She pointed to Mary. "It was Mary's idea, years ago, to help people living in and around the town, to turn their lawns into gardens. She would bring out wranglers, who volunteered their time to prepare the soil to be planted. This was given to the family for free. All that Mary asked was that they would grow organic and never use GMO seeds, and no poisonous pesticides or herbicides on the plants. And Cari and Chase wrote off the beehives as a donation."

"That's right," Mary said. "When I was growing up, we had what we called victory gardens. Every family who owned ground around their home created a huge garden that would give back to them. Canning became the rage and everyone contributed, had big gardens, and they managed for a decade to have food to eat. Otherwise, so many would have starved."

"And do you teach these neighbors how to can?" Dana wondered.

"At my grocery store, we put on weekly workshops on gardening, growing, canning, dehydrating, and freezing their food for use during the winter."

"Mary," Dana said sincerely, "you are just so uplifting. You have so many good, commonsense ideas."

"Thank you, dear. No moss grows under my feet. I

learned a long time ago that when you are successful at something, you pass it on, you teach it, you show others how to do it so that they, too, are successful."

Everyone traded knowing nods and looks.

"I feel like I've gone to another planet," Dana said, admiring the group.

"Nah," Mary said, cackling, "just down the rabbit hole, Alice, is all."

Dana laughed along with everyone else. "Call me Alice."

"Colin will help you turn your ranch and farm into a success," Chase reassured her. "He's been with us several years, knows about crop rotation, soil mixture, and so much more."

"I didn't have a choice," Colin deadpanned, hearing laughter erupt among the close-knit group.

"Is *that* ever the truth!" Mary giggled, slapping her knee.

"Is there anything on your idea plate for the future for the valley?" Dana wondered, absolutely enamored with Mary's ideas.

"Oh"—she rolled her eyes—"of course there is. We pass out a Q and A sheet to those folks who take our workshops at the back of our grocery store. The one thing that so many of them ask for is herbal medicine."

Dana smiled. "That's something I know enough about to be dangerous. What are you planning?"

"Well, I'm actually going to try it out on your back fifty acres once we get you settled onto your Wildflower Ranch." Mary wagged a finger at her. "You know? Names and words mean something. They're symbolic on a greater playing level. Wildflowers to me translates into herbal-medicine wildflowers. The history on that ranch is long and prestigious, Dana. I've got an old book that was written by the son of the people who came here to make a better life for themselves. It was the son's wife, Hilda, who worked hard to create not only a garden around their log cabin, but also, she was an herbalist. People from around the valley came to her. She was the local doctor, so to speak, because at that time, real doctors were rare as hen's teeth. That back fifty acres you're going to turn into crops?"

"Yes?"

"You and I sat down and went over what you would plant. You remember?"

"Sure."

"Half your crop is devoted to medicinal herbs. My vision is to have you grow them this year and we'll see how it goes. People want medicinal herbs. We get calls for calendula, peppermint, chamomile, comfrey, dead nettle, echinacea, and so many more. When you told me that your family raised a lot of these plants, besides the other crops, I felt you were the right person to tag and we would see what happens."

Excited, Dana said, "Oh! I didn't know the history behind your decision. This is so exciting! My mother dabbled in herbs just like the ones you named. I grew up on a lot of them and very rarely saw a doctor."

Nodding sagely, Mary said, "I was completely raised on medicinal herbs. Our family was too poor and could not afford a doctor to come calling. I'm happy to hear your mother was truly an herbalist."

Dana pushed her sadness away and rallied. "And if I

can grow those crops successfully? What then? The next step in your vision?"

"Then I'll get serious about hunting up a certified herbalist to come and live here in the valley with us. I've already got some ideas on that because I take several herbalist magazine subscriptions. There's a number of young women, and a few men, who have the kind of medical background I need, because they'd have to be able to ascertain when to send their client to ER or to their primary care doctor instead of utilizing a medical herb."

Sobering, Dana said, "We agree on that. I once stepped on a rusty nail and I asked my mother what herb she had that would help it. Instead, she took me directly to our naturopathic doctor, who gave me a tetanus shot and wrote a prescription for antibiotics. A puncture, especially with a rusty nail, can kill you because you can get tetanus from it. My mother knew those things."

"That's truly good," Mary said. "Traditional medicine and surgery aren't off my list. I'd use 'em if I needed them, but they're always a second choice. But first, and always, I go to the medical herbs my mother raised and gave me."

"There's many times when you don't need a prescription," Dana agreed. "And with so many drugs having awful, even life-threatening adverse side effects? Why not try something natural that could do the work for you and it's a lot cheaper, moneywise, too?"

"I've got a list of three individuals sitting in my file on this idea," Mary told her. "I'm going to be out to your ranch, often, walking that acreage of yours, and if the herbs are coming along like I think they will? I'll be interviewing those candidates to see if they meet my expectations and the vision I have for the job."

"And then get that person to move out here to Silver Creek Valley?" Dana wondered.

"Exactly. I don't take no for an answer." Mary gave her an elfish grin.

Everyone nodded, giving one another knowing glances. Mary was a force of nature, and everyone knew it and gave her the respect she was due.

Colin sat on the arm of the settee, cup of coffee balanced on one knee. He hadn't said much at all, but appeared interested and absorbed in the conversation.

The tinkle of a bell sounded.

"Time to eat!" Mary told them, getting up from her rocking chair in the corner near the fireplace. "I'm starving!"

The long trestle table made of beautiful oak could easily hold twelve people. Mary sat at one end with Cari and Chase at her elbows. To Dana's delight, she got to sit next to Cari with Colin next to her. As always, he was pretty quiet, listening intently to the conversation around them. Opposite them were Lea and Logan. The fragrance of all the food made her mouth water and stomach growl. She looked over at Colin, who held her gaze.

"Hungry enough to eat a cow, are we?" he teased her.

She tittered and shook her head. "Never!"

"Everything sure smells good," he said, patting his own flat, hard belly.

Louise came rolling out a huge service cart and everyone stopped talking, eyeing the steaming food coming their way.

"Oh, hurry," Lea begged Louise, "I'm soooo hungry!"

"That's 'cause you're feeding two," Mary said, smiling tenderly over at her pregnant daughter-in-law.

"Well," Lea said, grinning, "that's true!" and she gently caressed her swelling belly.

Louise halted, set the parking brake on the large cart and said, "Vegans are served first!"

The women cheered. The men took it with good grace, thinking of the beefsteaks that would eventually come their way.

"Guests first," Louise pronounced. She placed an antique blue-and-white willow plate in front of Dana. "Tonight, vegetarian enchiladas and a crisp green salad!"

Dana thanked her, making happy sounds as she inhaled the spicy scents.

Mary threw up her hands. "Hallelujah, Louise! My favorite meal!"

"You're next, Miss Mary." She quickly brought a plate over to her. Mary took the plate, and held it close to her nose, inhaling deeply. "Ah, Louise, you are the best!" She set the plate down.

Cari was happy to get hers, as well. It had two large enchiladas on it, instead of one.

Louise brought over T-bone steaks, mashed potatoes drizzled with a rich, brown gravy, along with French beans sprinkled with almonds and tiny onions. There were growls of thanks going to Louise, who took the compliments with a wide smile.

Colin kept his intuitional sense on Dana, whose cheeks had pinked up as everyone dove into the delicious food after Mary gave a short, sincere prayer of thanks. Louise brought in two baskets of sourdough biscuits, which made the men even more appreciative. The vegan eaters bypassed them on the first pass. But he, Chase, and Logan didn't.

There wasn't much talking, just eating. Dana ate heartily, finishing everything that was on her plate. He offered her the basket, two biscuits left. She smiled and daintily took one. After slathering it with butter, Dana closed her eyes, savoring it.

The tendrils of her hair, mussed from the day's work, but also cleaned in a shower, made her look almost fragile to Colin. He didn't know why he thought of her in that way. Today, she'd hauled ass and worked as hard as he had. She was very athletic. But then she worked on a farm, and was in top shape. Her face was a tad red from being out in the sun all day, he noted, mostly her nose. She needed to have a hat and he mentally made a note to bring one of his with him tomorrow morning so she wouldn't get sunburned. Tomorrow was going to be a super-busy day outside on the Wildflower Ranch, that was for sure.

"Is Louise not the best cook around?" Mary prodded Dana, noting her plate was clean.

"She is a wonderful cook, Mary," she answered, patting her stomach.

"Nothin' like home cooking." She wiggled her fork at Dana's plate. "Louise uses food from the surrounding ranches and farms that we have contracts with. Any food that passes our lips here at the ranch, is non-GMO, organic, and tastes like the food I grew up on in the past!"

"I can tell it's homegrown," Dana said. "And I'm happy that I've signed a contract with you, too."

"Well, that will come in time." Mary smiled. "Is Colin being a good helper to you out at your ranch?"

Dana turned and looked at Colin. As usual, his expression was unreadable. "I couldn't have done it without him"—she looked over at Chase—"or you allowing him to come and help me out."

Chase nodded. "No one works harder than Colin."

"I do like a coffee break sometimes," Colin replied, giving them a partial grin.

Everyone at the table laughed and hooted.

Colin saw Dana's reaction and didn't want her targeted because this group, who knew each other so well, might appear to be like a pack of wolves to her. "Dana and I brought thermoses and we had a couple of breaks today."

"So?" Chase goaded. "You think you'll stay and help her out?"

"Sure," he murmured. "She's easier to work for than you, boss."

More good-natured chuckling and guffawing followed.

"Hey, Dana, you'll get used to this cosmic family of ours," Mary said consolingly. "They like to razz the daylight outta each other."

"Well," Cari said, "just the boys do that." She gave Dana a warm look. "We girls don't do that kind of rough-housing and horseplay."

"Good to hear," Dana said.

"Nah," Mary said, "we usually get together—Cari, Lea, and me—and we have farm-grown herbal tea, it's organic, and some delicious dessert that Louise makes for us here at the ranch. We expect you to come to our weekly gabfests, too, if you'd like?"

"I'd love to do that," Dana said.

Colin saw her green eyes widen with happiness and it tugged at his heart, a sensation of desire for her. *Again.*

There was no evading that some part of him was fully drawn to her. Why now? He had been okay with being alone. As Chase had accurately pinpointed, he worked best alone. A woman in his life? The way he was? Broken into pieces even he couldn't control? No woman in her right mind would want someone like him. He knew how stressed he was daily, fighting to keep the monsters at bay, trying to seem normal, trying not to project onto others or get triggered by a silly situation that didn't invite an explosive reaction on his part.

Gently, Colin tucked away his yearning because he saw so much possibility with Dana in his life. No. He couldn't hurt her like that and he knew he would. Somehow, he was going to have to move to being her support, her teacher, and helping her to bring her dream to reality. That gave him a good feeling. He wasn't totally worthless, after all.

April 18

The scudding gray clouds signaled an end to a swift-moving front that had hit the valley with rain yesterday. Dana looked forward to the concrete platform that would be created this afternoon for the double-wide mobile home.

The sun was peeking out here and there, warming her against the gusty breezes that came and went against her green winter nylon coat. She was glad to have the hood over her head to protect her neck from that late morning windchill.

Her gaze moved to Colin, who was dressed for the weather as well, a heavy denim jacket over his hoodie as he toiled to get everything into place for the cement mixers that would be coming in after lunch. He worked tirelessly and she didn't know how he did it, exhausted just looking at the energy he consistently gave to her ranch the last day and a half. He worked as if it were his own place.

Pulling on her heavy sheep's-wool-lined gloves, she went back into the dilapidated cabin. Yesterday, Colin had an outfit bring out a huge PODS metal container, where all their refuse could be put and later on hauled to the dump outside of town. There was a lot of debris inside the cabin and she looked around, wistful, because she'd wanted to save it because of its history. Reaching out, she ran her gloved fingers down the dark brown wood that had been roughened with age, across the white plaster, now yellowed, many parts of it having fallen out between the hand-hewn logs from so long ago. And where it had fallen out, cold air whistled in.

Getting down on her hands and knees, pulling a big bucket next to her, she took a whisk broom and dustpan, beginning to sweep up the debris. Her nostalgia continued as she wondered where the family had slept. Down at one end was a huge river boulder fireplace, handmade, rising up the wall, through the roof. How long had it taken them to build it? She imagined, looking at it, that perhaps it could be saved.

"How's it going?"

Snapping her head up, gasping, she hadn't heard Colin enter the cabin. "You scared me!"

"Sorry," he said, wiping his brow with the back of his arm. "Old habit from my military days." Giving her a close look, he asked, "Are you okay? You look pale."

Shrugging, she quickly swept up the debris and put it

in the can next to where she knelt. "Just an old reaction," she muttered, shaking her head, unhappy.

He didn't say anything, his brows dropping for a moment as he watched her move down the floor, sweeping up the chunks of fallen plaster. "I'll try not to do that again. I'll make some noise beforehand so you know I'm coming in," he offered quietly, seeing the darkness come to her eyes.

She sat back on her heels, pointing to the fireplace. "What do you think of it, Colin? It's really beautiful and it looks like the smooth, rounded stones are from the creek in back of this cabin."

He ambled down to it, leaning over, checking it here and there. "Yes, those must have come out of this creek. Did you know, the glacier from ten thousand years ago came through here and dropped tons of rocks around the valley?"

"No, I didn't."

"As it receded and melted, toward the end of the Ice Age"—he motioned out the back door toward the creek—"it would sometimes drop thousands of tons of rocks one place or another. I think that's what happened here on your ranch. There's patches that look like a gravel deposit here and there."

"Yes, I saw those." She sat on her heels. "So? Can the fireplace be saved?"

"I think it can. Needs lots of work, some support, and of course, getting a chimney sweep out here because I'll bet there's stuff in the flue of the chimney that needs to be removed."

"But it's fixable, right?"

Nodding, he turned toward the open entrance. The sun was returning, starting to warm up. "Right, it is."

"I really want to save this cabin, Colin."

Hearing the determination and sudden emotion in her low tone, he turned, watching her at work. "We'll figure out a way to do that."

"I was thinking that maybe, when things are pretty much finished and working around here, that I could get some expert craftspeople in here to put this cabin back together like it used to be." She frowned and pointed to the floorboards. "Look at these. They're so old and worn, especially in the center."

Colin looked closely at the floor, the morning sunlight making it easier to see. He pointed to one board. "That one looks awfully new, Dana. Someone replaced it." It was a board in the center of the floor and was much lighter than the grayed ones surrounding it.

"Who?" she wondered, staring at where he was pointing.

"Don't know. This place has been abandoned for decades." Shrugging, he picked up a broom and began sweeping from the other direction toward where she was working. "We have folks here in the valley. We call them barn builders. There's quite a few cabins just like this in the valley because it was settled around the 1870s by pioneers. They saw how fertile this valley was. We have some old-timers still around that know how to rebuild these things, so I think you'll get your wish." He saw the relief on her face. "What are you intending to do with it?"

"I thought it might make a wonderful meditation room.

I can't stand to see this cabin, which was built by hand, the logs chopped, cut and an ax smoothing them out enough, to be destroyed."

"Hmmm, a meditation room? I hadn't thought of that, but it sounds good."

She grinned. "What? Don't you meditate?"

"Nah, can't settle my mind down and turn it off."

"Mmmm, I used to be that way until someone got me into it. Little by little, over the past couple of years, it has helped me stop my mind from churning . . . from going over stuff from the past."

"Maybe I should give it another try," he agreed.

"You'd be more than welcome. Have you had any formal teaching in it?"

"None. Just heard about it. Cari is a big believer in meditation, though. She doesn't start her day, from what Chase told me once, without meditating first. She's even got Chase doing it." He chuckled.

"Meditation helps everyone. Maybe that explains why the bees love her so much," Dana said, finishing off the pile that Colin had swept for her. Getting up, she pushed her hands against her pantlegs, dusting them off. "I can hardly wait to go over and see her with the bees."

"I've helped her from time to time," he admitted, walking with her to the open entrance. "She really is one with those ladies. I didn't know that most of the bees in the hive are female. Did you?"

"No. I have so much to learn. I'm afraid of getting stung." She gave him a silly, shy grin. "I guess I'm afraid of a lot of things, even my shadow . . ."

Frowning, he watched as she leaped down to the ground. He made a note to build a set of steps for her soon, because a person could break their ankle, otherwise. He wanted to support her dream for this dilapidated place. If only someone could have that kind of care toward himself, broken as he was. That was a pipe dream.

He followed her as they walked up the muddy road to where the concrete would be poured. Colin had put in orange flagging where it needed to be. He'd dug the trench yesterday in the rain with the old John Deere. They'd both gotten soaked to the bone, but it had gotten done.

"The sun feels good," she whispered, standing nearby, her hands in the pockets of her jacket.

"Spring around here is up and down," he offered. "Some days warm with a blue sky, and then the rain hits and we have gray skies, which are depressing to me, but later on, it clears away."

Gazing up at the sky, Dana whispered, "I feel like those gray and white clouds, the darkness and rain, all the time." Realizing she'd confided too much, she managed a strained laugh. "Hey, look! There's the concrete trucks coming in!" She pointed to them slowing down on the highway to make the turn into her ranch's driveway.

She was glad for the distraction because she'd seen the sharp, penetrating look Colin had given her. Along with it came an unfamiliar but oh, so welcome feeling of warmth blanketing her, even though the sun was hidden by the clouds right now.

What subtle, quiet magic did Colin possess? Dana had made a promise to never reveal her past. But with him around? She was talking in metaphors. What was going on? She was afraid to confide in anyone about her past. Scared to death that it would overtake her, Dana was fearful she would drown and spin out of control. Colin was way too easy to confide in. Maybe it was his quietness, the way he studied her that made her feel safe . . . something she'd lost a long time ago.

Chapter 4

April 28

Brock Hauptman was happy to see the sun finally come out at nine a.m., the light rain having stopped. He watched through his binoculars from where he hid on the forested slope of the Wildflower Ranch, far below him. He wasn't pleased. At all.

He sat with his second-in-command, Richfield Jones, an ex-Marine and of late, an escapee from the Navy brig in San Diego. Hardened, thirty-five years old, he was as tough as they came. He, too, watched a few feet away, sitting on the dark brown ground, binoculars to his eyes. For the last week, Richfield had come over to the ranch under cover of night, watched and reported.

"This isn't good," Richfield muttered, drawing deeply on a cigarette. "At first, we thought that woman was just a vagrant, passing through, like so many others do."

Snorting, Brock watched the activity on the other side of the creek. "First, a double-wide trailer. Now, a Quonset

hut for the tractor and the other equipment. What next?"
He'd ground out the words in a low growl.

"The FOR SALE sign was taken down. Someone
bought it."

"Yeah. I'd like to waltz into Silver Creek and find out
who, but I'm a wanted escaped prisoner. My mug is in
every sheriff's department in the West." Hauptman
dropped the binoculars on his broad, deep chest, pushing
a large, scarred hand across his shiny bald head.

Grinning lopsidedly, Richfield lowered his glasses as
well, letting them hang around his neck. Taking two more
drags off the butt, he ground it into the wet ground, snuff-
ing it out. It had rained this morning, but now the sky was
clearing.

"No, you're a pretty big boy, boss. Hard not to notice."
And that was true. Hauptman, pure German, pure white-
supremacist, was more like a comic book character; huge,
broad shoulders, meaty as hell and no flab on him. The
years he'd spent in the pen in San Diego, California, had
bulked him up because he constantly worked out. For the
size of his face, he had what Richfield thought of as "pig
eyes," very small, dark, and intense-looking. A killer's
eyes, which is why he had been in prison until he broke
out and ran. But Hauptman missed little, and what he did
miss, Richfield was very good at catching and bringing
it quietly to his attention. He never put Hauptman into an
embarrassing position where he'd feel that he'd screwed
up. Richfield learned a long time ago to be politically
astute and always take the blame himself, leaving his
leader feeling good about himself—and him, as well. It
was easy to play the fall guy and the fool.

Hauptman's group of four other white males, all convicts with a record, had accepted Richfield as the leader's right-hand man. They'd met up shortly after Brock had broken out of prison. Hauptman regrouped his men and they had held up three banks in the city, and then successfully avoided law enforcement, getting out of the state for good.

Knowing that he was the exact opposite, body-wise, to Hauptman, Richfield figured his wiry leanness was an asset. Never mind his muscles were like steel cords. He'd killed a Marine officer with his hands. At five-foot-ten-inches tall and barely one hundred and sixty pounds, he posed no outward threat to anyone—until it was too late. He got his name in the brig, Chameleon, the hard way; proving that messing with the narrow-faced white dude in the brig, surrounded by bulked-up prisoners, was a mistake. Everyone left him alone.

He was good at mimicking another person, getting them to like and trust him. Gaslighting others was his way of taking the offense. By then, he was using his vast manipulative skills he'd learned in early childhood in order to survive, and literally lead from the rear. Hauptman didn't have a clue and Richfield wanted to keep it that way.

"Are they a married couple?" Hauptman groused.

Shrugging, Richfield said, "Dunno. Does it matter? You always see them coming outta the trailer together in the morning and going in at night."

"Probably bought the place, you think?"

Preening silently, Richfield put on an I-don't-know expression. "Could be."

"It screws us royal," Hauptman growled. "We used to be able to use our ATVs and cross that creek to get to fields high up on that other slope. We could steal from outlying ranches around here in the dead of night, escape across this highway, and hightail it onto the slope to our encampment."

"We won't be able to use this shortcut anymore," Richfield said, shaking his head. "They're living there full-time. And more and more other ranchers are visiting this place, bringing equipment and tools over to the Quonset hut. Looks like they're gonna make it a garage of sorts for their stuff. They're also building a large set of corrals, too. Not to mention pipe fencing on two pasture paddocks."

Grunting, Hauptman said, "They plowed the fields right up to the slope. They're planting that whole fifty acres."

"Poppies, maybe?" Richfield chuckled darkly. "It was a great crop over in Afghanistan, and this place looks pretty fertile. They could be raised here, too."

"Doubt it. Feds wouldn't let 'em." Hauptman made a gesture toward the dark rows of soil that had just been seeded with unknown crops. "I found out real early that the ranchers in this valley are tighter than fleas on a dog. They help each other out."

"I've been watching them this past week," Richfield agreed with a nod, "and I've counted at least ten other ranch pickups with different ranch names on their vehicles, coming and going. You're right about that. Way too much activity for us."

"Did you see that Mama's Store truck out here two days ago? I'll lay you odds this ranch is gonna start supplying fruit and vegetables to that store in town."

"I was in Mama's Store last week," Richfield said,

"and I was impressed. All organic. No GMO. Prices were decent, too, not ripping people off like other grocery chains do."

"You were in there getting us vegetables and other things we needed," Hauptman said.

Moving his slender but calloused fingers through his beard, which he'd grown after leaving California behind, Richfield said, "I like going into town. You can't go because law enforcement probably would recognize and arrest you. I'm a prisoner on the run, just like you, but because of my size, no one pays any attention to me."

"That's good, because we always need stuff," Hauptman said, nodding.

"Yeah, they don't call me the Chameleon for nothing." Richfield chuckled. "Besides, I get tired of living out in the wilds."

"You're a damn shadow," Hauptman grumbled, but there was respect in his tone.

"Right. You won't see me coming until it's too late." Richfield grinned wolfishly.

"Glad you're on our side."

"Me, too. I like that you're working with that Guatemalan drug lord, Gonzalez. Him dropping off ten of his men, plowing up that slope area for growin' marijuana, was a good plan. He trusts us."

"Yeah, well, he put his money where his mouth is by joining forces with us. Just hope that damned sheriff here"—Hauptman made a gesture toward the town in the distance—"doesn't get into using drones. He ever flies over that hidden meadow on that slope next to this ranch where they planted all that stuff, we're DOA."

"Well, your plan B is good if that happens, and now

we have a backup place we can go and hopefully escape any law enforcement if they do find it."

"Everything in life is risky, and I always have a plan B."

"Too bad the ranch was bought. We're gonna have to figure out a work-around. It takes us twice the time to get to that second slope meadow."

Nodding, Richfield had been here long enough to see the trails created by his group in the thick of the forest. They had an encampment far above the working ranches down along the highway on the valley floor. They tried to plan if a nosy drone from law enforcement or the US Forest Service were flying over, they wouldn't be able to locate the encampment.

Hauptman was an excellent strategist. But to get across the highway, up to the slope that was owned by the recently bought Wildflower Ranch, was another matter. Part of their need was to never be seen or recognized. There were white-nationalist groups all over the West who had gone into the mountains, gathering racist men and military weapons; and the leaders of each group talked regularly with one another via throwaway cell phones. They wanted to build an army and carve out fiefdoms, all the while doing it out of sight of the civilian populace. Several drug lords were working with groups in various other states. Hauptman had claimed the northwest corner of Wyoming into the Wind River mountain area and everyone agreed it was his turf.

"Did you see a dog around?" Hauptman wondered.

"No. That's strange. Most of these ranches have a number of them." Which made it hard for them to sneak into buildings and steal tools or other things they needed, carrying them out beneath the cover of darkness, often aided by bad weather to cover their tracks.

"That Quonset hut is very close to the trailer. It would be tough to get in there, with or without a dog."

"I'll worry about that when our date to meet the Gonzalez representative in June happens. Until then, we'll leave this place alone," Richfield said.

"For sure . . ." Hauptman muttered.

"They'd better not knock it down and get rid of it or we're all fried."

"I'm going back up the slope," Hauptman grunted, scowling darkly at Richfield's comment. "You stay another couple of hours and give me a report later today."

"Will do, boss."

April 29

"What's on your to-do list today, Colin?" Dana sipped her third cup of hot coffee at the dining room table. He was fixing them pancakes for breakfast. They had decided to swap out every other day to do the cooking, and it seemed to be working well for them.

"Plow the rest of the other field," he replied, scooping four light brown pancakes onto a nearby plate. "I've got to go out and check the dryness of the soil to make sure, first. I don't want to get the wheels stuck. That'd ruin my day."

"That rain was pretty light the other day," she said, hope in her tone. "I'm going to build corrals today with the wranglers coming from Three Bars to help us." She watched as he brought the pancakes over, sliding two onto her plate and two on his, then sat down at her elbow.

Colin didn't shave every day, but on him, a day or two

of beard accentuated his high cheekbones and made him even more desirable to her. They'd been living in the mobile home for the last week and there was a new ease that had just naturally seemed to grow between them. She didn't know why because they were basically strangers in one way, but in another, he had made the transition from the Three Bars bunk barracks to here, seamlessly.

The décor Mary had chosen pleased her and she wondered if the elder was psychic or something. There was homey country furniture throughout, reminding her of her parents' home. She had always liked light blue pastel colors; anything that would brighten or lighten up a space. The walls were a pale cream color, the drapes in the living room a cream with a bright wildflower design, with accents of tangerine, another one of her favorite colors. How did Mary know that?

Colin had already fried up the bacon, and they both dug into the vanilla-scented pancakes with eagerness. Today, as every other, they had worked from dawn to dusk. Her muscles were sore, and every night, after a hot shower, she would fall into bed at nine p.m. Only to be jarred awake at six a.m. the next morning by her alarm clock. But Dana liked it this way because it was how she'd grown up. *Dawn to dusk.*

"These are good," she said between bites.

"My mother insisted on me learning how to cook."

"She did a great job, Colin." Glancing over at him, she saw a faraway look in his eyes for a moment, and then it was gone. How badly she wanted to ask about how he was feeling at that moment. With all the other wranglers coming and going from various ranches, making this a working ranch, Dana usually didn't see him much during the day. She did most of the plowing and seeding. He was directing how to get the Quonset hut set up and stabilized. Or, he was on the other side of the log cabin where they planned several large, grassy paddocks. For horses? Cows? Gosh, she hadn't even had time to ask!

"Your waffles yesterday were heaven," he said, sliding three more slices of well-cooked bacon onto his plate.

"Belgian waffles. It's a treat. My mother taught—" She abruptly snapped her mouth shut. Tears rushed to her eyes and she turned away, a flood of grief filling her. She could feel Colin's intense gaze upon her, but also, his genuine concern.

"Are you okay?" he asked quietly.

"Umm . . . yes . . . fine . . . just . . . well . . ." She pushed the chair back, her plate empty, heading for the kitchen sink with it, an excuse to get away from his intense gaze. Blinking several times, she gulped and forced her tears back. She was still swamped with untimely and unexpected grief about her parents. Every time she mentioned their names, this reaction would happen.

Turning on the faucet, she washed the plate off and put it in the dish drainer. Turning, she saw Colin studying her, but the look wasn't one she could decipher. He was so closed up. Care, maybe? Unsure and not wanting to encourage any conversation, she hurried to the other side of the living room where her bedroom and bathroom were located.

Shutting the door quietly behind her, Dana pulled a tissue from the box in her bedroom, blotting her eyes. How badly she wanted to cry! Far too soon, the Three Bars wranglers would arrive and she needed to be out there to help them with the corral. Swallowing hard, she dropped the tissue in a wastebasket and went to brush her teeth. Her red hair had already been plaited into two braids, keeping it out of her eyes and face as she worked.

Her heart twisted in her chest, replaying the concerned look on Colin's face as she had abruptly left the table. Her heart told her that he cared deeply for her. That was silly; they barely knew one another. Yet, her heart persisted. She'd been so alone for those years, that she felt dehumanized in some respects due to her past. Dana tried to shrug off that caring look from Colin as she quickly brushed her teeth and rinsed her mouth out.

The temperature outside was forty degrees and she was going to bundle up for a day of corral building. Still . . . when she didn't focus on the work, she instantly thought about Colin. How she wished they had time just to talk and get acquainted. She knew so little about him. And she always felt that asking him a personal question was invading a privacy wall he kept up to keep everyone out. Even her.

Wiping her mouth, she glanced at herself in the mirror. She looked tired. And stressed. Well, why not? They were right on top of plowing and planting. Spring was always an intense time for a farmer. This was no different; only this time, it was *her* farm, not the family farm in Oregon.

Barely touching some tendrils on her right temple, she pushed them behind her ear. As she exited her bedroom, she heard a door close. Colin had just left, and she caught sight of him in his thick denim jacket, heading down the road toward the Quonset hut where the tractor and plows were now kept and protected from the weather.

She sighed inwardly. Yearning for some quiet time, Dana knew they wouldn't have any. At least, not in the next two or three weeks. Once the fields were plowed and planted, which would be this week, provided they weren't turned to mud by the rain, the focus then turned to building a barn, a tack room, and a few box stalls. She picked up her jacket, pulled on a baseball cap, and then settled a bright red knit cap over it to keep her ears warm. Next, a pair of gloves and a knit muffler around her neck. She was wearing a pair of knee-high rubber boots because where the corrals were being built, the rain had probably made things muddy.

Looking up at the sky as she left the mobile home, there were low hanging, ragged-looking gray and white clouds. The front had passed and with it, the rain. The day was chilly, the wind blowing off and on.

The warmth of the sun's rays on her back as she walked down the road toward the old log cabin, lifted her spirits. She had so much to be happy about. And yet, it reminded her sharply of her parents and the life she'd had with them. Wildflower Ranch was looking just like their farm in the Willamette Valley. That brought her grief, an ache in her heart and at the same time, a comforting reminder of her growing-up years. It was a trade-off.

She heard several trucks coming down the road and turned. They were Three Bars trucks and she saw a flatbed behind the two pickups bearing the wranglers who she'd work with today.

Lifting her hand in hello as they parked nearby, giving the flatbed the road, Dana walked over to the lead truck. It was Chase himself, and she was surprised.

"So?" she said, smiling. "You're going to build a corral with us today?"

Chase grinned. "Yes, and I brought our women wranglers

out to help you." He gestured toward the five women bailing out of the trucks. "And I'm not staying long, Dana. My forewoman, Tracy Hartimer, is going to lead the charge here."

Walking with him, she saw the five women wranglers gathering and waiting for them to arrive. Dana shook Tracy's gloved hand, and Chase introduced her to the other four women. They all had firm grips. All looked lean, like wolves. Easy smiles. Excitement in their eyes. This was a happy crew.

Chase waited until the intros were done and then said, pointing toward the flatbed slowly coming their way, "Dana, we figure that the wranglers will be done about noon with both corrals. You and I talked about a barn that needs to be raised nearby."

Nodding, Dana said, "Yes," and she pointed to the other end of where the corrals were going to be created, "and it was going over there? Right?"

"Yep," Chase said. "We got a surprise for you."

"Oh?" She looked from Chase to Tracy, who stood nearby.

"We thought," Tracy said, "that you might like a hen-house? Fresh eggs?"

"Ohhhh," Dana said, smiling, "that would be wonderful!"

"Me and the ladies can build you a sweet little hen-house after we get done with the corrals," Tracy said. "You just tell us where you'd like to have it. Plus, we need to lay out the barn foundation, too."

"Wonderful," Dana said, deeply touched by their generosity. She knew Chase was paying his wranglers for coming over here. Grateful, she added, "If we finish around noon? I'd like Colin to talk about the positioning of the barn."

"Of course," Chase said. He pointed to the flatbed that had stopped at the Quonset hut, and three wranglers were taking off a lot of lumber and storing it within the building. "If you'd like, I have blueprints for my barn in my truck. We can look over the dimensions and layout, From that, we can figure out how much lumber and concrete will be needed. Plus"—he hooked a thumb toward Tracy—"she's an ace at barn building. Her father is from West Virginia and he and his crew do nothing but go around the state reclaiming old log structures like your own. She knows barn building from the inside out."

"Indeed, I do," Tracy said. She pointed to the log cabin. "Dana? Maybe you and I, after we get the women assigned to jobs on building the corrals, could mosey over to your little cabin and talk about it in detail. I'd like to hear your ideas and what you'd like to do with it."

"Is it salvageable?" Dana asked the forewoman.

"From what I can see from here? Sure, no problem. There's a log cabin crew in Silver Creek and I know the owner, Charley Swanson, really well. Once you and I discuss the cabin, and with your permission, we'll get Charley out here. He's the owner of Swanson Log Builders."

"I'll need to know what he charges."

"He's fair in his pricing," Tracy said. "I can give him a thumbnail of what you want, then he'll come out and give you an estimate of how much it might cost to repair it."

"That sounds great," Dana said, feeling excitement run through her. "I was thinking of a nice place to meditate."

"For that size?" Tracy said, nodding, "that would be a perfect place."

"I really want to save it. There's so much history with it."

Tracy patted her heart with her gloved hand. "Music to my ears." She turned to Chase. "Okay, boss, you're outta here. The girls and I have work to do."

Chuckling, Chase gave her a humored look. "Yes, ma'am. I'll get a lift back to Three Bars with the flatbed crew. You know my cell number if you need me, Tracy."

"Sure do, boss." Tracy turned, waving to the women wranglers to follow her. Dana smiled, feeling right at home, following the boss lady past the log cabin and where all the postholes had been dug two days ago. It was a thrill to see women doing it all because she'd helped build corrals with her father, as well as other small buildings a farmer always needed. In some ways, it felt so good . . . as if she were home once again . . .

Colin saw how flushed Dana's cheeks were when he came in for lunch from the field he'd just plowed. The tilled soil would have to lay fallow for a couple of days, to oxygenate, before planting. These were cool-weather crops he'd be putting in: Kale, broccoli, cabbage, spinach, chard, arugula, collards, and peas. He had sketches that showed where to plant each of them.

He'd come home first, washed up, and was fixing them some tuna sandwiches with a slice of sharp cheddar cheese on each. The door opened behind him and he glanced over his shoulder.

"Looks like you got those corrals up," he said as Dana shut the door.

"Put six hardworking women on a task, and it gets

done," she said, giving him a grin while she took off her baseball cap, dropping it on a peg near the door.

"Looks fine. Hungry?"

"Starving," she admitted, heading for her side of the mobile home and her bathroom.

"One sandwich or two?" he called.

"One, please."

Colin was used to their daily routine. Every time he got to see Dana, it was like a breath of air fanned through his dark soul. With her red braids, she looked like a much younger woman, cheeks a bright pink, those freckles across her cheeks and nose a darker brown. He was glad to see her forest-green eyes was sparkling with life. Maybe happiness? He'd find out, washing his hands after placing the three sandwiches on two plates.

By the time Dana arrived at the kitchen table, he'd added a bag of chips and hot coffee in mugs, along with the sandwiches.

"Looks good," she said, thanking him as she pulled up a chair and sat down.

"There's more tuna if you want another sandwich," he offered, sitting at her elbow. He'd rolled up the long sleeves of his blue denim work shirt just below his elbows.

"I think this will do it," she murmured, giving him a warm look of thanks.

"Got everything plowed. Wasn't as muddy as I thought it would be."

"Whew, that's great. Is everything done, then?"

He picked up the sandwich and took a bite, nodding his head. Pulling the bag over, he poured some chips on his plate. "I figure two days of letting the soil sit and oxygenate, I can go back with the planting."

"Great. We're right on time.""

"I have to take a closer look at the corrals. You ladies kick butt and take names. Over at Three Bars, Chase would pit men against women on similar jobs that needed to be done." He grinned. "The women always won."

"Of course they did," she said. "We're sticklers for details and we think it out and organize everything before we start the project. Doesn't matter if it's sewing a dress, quilting a quilt, or making supper for a bunch of family members."

Giving her a thoughtful look, he murmured, "You're right. A lot of men don't give women the credit they're due, but Chase always has. I think it's because his mother, who was probably a feminist long before the word was ever coined, influenced him profoundly."

"Mary hasn't let her gender detour her at all. She's built, quite literally, an empire in this valley."

"And, like a woman," he added, "the place has bloomed under her leadership. There's no one in town who is jobless. She pays a fair hourly wage, too. Far more than what most grocery stores ever offered their hardworking employees."

"I hope that someday, when I have this ranch and farm under control and working, that I can do the same for my employees," she said wistfully, munching on a salty chip.

"In some ways, you remind me of Mary."

Brows raising, she said, "Oh?"

"You're a visionary like she is. You can look at this land of yours and see gardens, vegetables, fruit trees, and how it will all work together. Mary does the same thing. And she has people around her that can show her how to accomplish what she wants. Last year when Cari was hired to start up a beekeeping company, it was Mary who found her and brought her here. None of us knew what it would take to make this valley a known commercial honey producer, but Cari did because she'd done start-ups in many countries around the world. Mary and Chase laid out their plans, their vision, to Cari and she brought it all together."

"Experts are worth their weight in gold," Dana agreed.

"Has Cari come to you about having hives on your ranch yet? I know you discussed it with her at the dinner."

"Yes, we did. And I want to give her some land on the eastern side of the ranch, well away from the main area here, and the animals. With all our fields and the flowers, Cari felt about a hundred hives with the accompanying beekeepers, which she would hire, could be maintained here."

"Bees are good for everyone and everything. The fact that no one in this valley uses pesticides, GMOs, herbicides, or any other type of soil enrichment except natural ones, is why. Bee die-off is directly connected to those poisons."

"I detest them, myself," she muttered, scowling.

"What's up this afternoon for you?" he wondered.

"Tracy sprung a surprise on me. We're going to lay out a foundation for a henhouse. I love chickens. We can use the eggs."

"Is Mary wanting to buy the eggs?"

"No, I just want about a dozen hens, is all. Enough for us, here," and she gestured toward the kitchen.

"Nothing like fresh eggs," he agreed.

"We go through half a dozen nearly every morning,"

Dana said, finishing off her sandwich and wiping her fingers on a paper napkin.

"That's because we work hard for ten hours a day," he said. "Good thing we're young."

"Seriously," she agreed. "I hope you don't think this is too personal, but I have so many questions I'd like to ask you."

Colin felt his gut clench a little. "I'll try to answer them." He saw instant surprise in her expression, her eyes widening.

"Where were you born?"

"Outside of Billings, Montana," he said. "My family has had a pretty large spread and cattle ranch out on the plains west of the city about fifty miles."

"Do you have any brothers or sisters?"

Shaking his head, he said, "No . . . only child, but believe me, not spoiled."

Smiling a little, she said, "I was an only child, too. You grew up on a ranch and I grew up on a farm." Hesitantly, she whispered, "I feel a real kinship with you, Colin, and I was trying to figure out what experiences we might share between us."

"Curiosity was killing you, right?" He couldn't help but tease her and saw a flush across her cheeks, realizing that this meant more to Dana than he first realized. Taking the teasing out of his voice, trying to be serious, he said, "I feel the same about you. There's a nice, comfortable energy between us. And it's been there since I met you."

Sitting back, she whispered, "Really?"

"Do you feel it, too?"

"From the beginning. I mean, it was almost as if

meeting you was like meeting an old friend from my past," she admitted.

He shook his head. "That's kind of amazing. That's how I felt about you. Where were you born?" he asked.

Hesitating, she said, "Fairfield, Oregon, in the Willamette Valley."

Colin felt her tensing. He didn't see it, but he felt it. Why was she always so gun-shy about discussing her family? Of course, he wasn't much better, was he? But he'd gone through a war and the PTSD had blindsided him. Looking at her, she appeared, on the surface, to be a very attractive woman, used to hard work, responsible, and possessing a lot of kindness, which drew him powerfully. He decided to ask, "You wanted those two corrals put up. I know you're a vegetarian, so you're not going to raise cattle here, right?" He instantly saw her relax, her shoulders dropping, that darkness that came to her eyes, dissolving.

"No cattle. I grew up riding horses," she admitted, putting the plate aside and folding her hands on the table in front of her. "I've dreamed of having them again."

"How many?"

"Two. Horses aren't happy if they are alone. They're herd animals. I figure as I make some money, I can buy two of them here in the valley somewhere."

"What gender?" He smiled a little, watching her eyes become dreamy looking.

"I like mares. Oh, I know you guys don't, but I do."

"Now, wait a minute," he said, holding up his hands. "The horse I use from the Three Bars string is an older mare named Dolly, and she outclasses the boys every time."

Dana regarded him. "Seriously? You're not joshing me?"

"Not in the least. Yeah, I take razzing from the other guys, but Dolly is twelve years old, a barren mare, and she's good or better than any gelding those guys ride. Matter of fact, it was Mary who was in Casper about a decade ago on business and she saw a bunch of mustangs being sold to a chicken product plant."

"Oh, no!" Dana's eyes went huge at the same moment she pressed her hand to her mouth. Those horses were heading to be slaughtered and made into dog food. Her stomach turned over at the thought.

"Mary bought all of them at the auction, had them trucked back here, and she gave them to seven different ranches. Dolly was one of those mustangs. She's small, fourteen and a half hands high, wiry, tough, and so smart. All the ranchers got an influx of mustang blood and to this day, most of them are still working hard every day on the ranches around the valley."

"Are there any more mustangs available, then? Younger ones?"

"Logan Anderson has a small herd. He's always got some for sale, some already broken. After we get the barn built and get some hay bales and straw in there, how about driving over there and we can look at them?"

"I'd love to do that, but I have to be careful with my money, Colin."

"I'm sure he'll give you a fair deal, so don't worry too much about that."

"But . . . we'd need a horse trailer, too." She frowned. "There's just so much to buy."

"Let me inquire around. All the ranches have some older ones they'd let go really cheap. Let me see if anyone is willing to part with one."

"That would be wonderful!"

Colin felt as if he'd received an invisible hug from her, warmth sheeting through him, spiking his yearning for her, to be close to her, and more . . .

Chapter 5

Colin made his nightly tour of the central heart of the Wildflower Ranch. It was Saturday, and Dana always spent the day working as a volunteer in the kitchen line for the food bank in town. He liked that she wanted to give back to the community. She got paid nothing for it, but she didn't care.

He moved around the empty corrals that now had a good, thick bed of sand in them, which was easy on a horse's legs. He was hoping that since all the main structures were built and in place, horses coming in to be a part of Dana's life would be next. Going to the henhouse, which had a huge one-quarter-acre enclosure that wild animals couldn't dig under or climb over, was a masterpiece created by the wrangler women of Three Bars. The dozen happy, safe hens were all tucked into their henhouse for the night and he ensured the door was locked, another layer of protection against raccoons, skunks, foxes, owls, and other hunters who'd like a chicken dinner.

Beyond and to the south of the henhouse was the newly erected barn. It was roughly two thousand square feet and two stories high. They'd had a barn raising last week, over a hundred hardworking people from the other ranches coming together to put the barn up in a two-day period. There was already alfalfa, sweet grass, and timothy hay bales inside, plus straw bales with huge gunnysacks of cedar shavings. Those shavings were for the two box stalls for the horses. During the day, the horses would be out in one of the paddocks to eat grass and get fresh air and sunshine. At night, they would be put in their box stalls, fed grain and any other supplements they might need.

He inhaled the scents, fragrances that always made him feel good. Pulling the barn doors closed, he locked them. The barn had been painted green with a steep tin roof to force heavy snow to slide off during some of their worst winter months to prevent the weight from collapsing the roof.

Walking toward the house, he saw headlights and knew it was Dana returning from town and her duties at the food bank. His heart bloomed with need of her. The last month had been the best in his life. And he knew it was because of her quiet, gentle presence.

There was now a large, round, graveled area, a small parking lot created near the mobile home. Logan Anderson had contributed loads of gravel from one of his dump trucks. The rain coming through about every five to seven days had made the area little more than a rutted mud pit in front of their home before that had happened. Now, there was a clean gravel surface.

He came and stood between the new sundeck that had just been built around the front half of the mobile home, waiting for Dana to arrive. Several of the smaller ranches had gotten together, brought wood they had on hand, and loaned their wranglers, and in one day gave Dana a large, beautiful deck. Even nicer? Tracy, the forewoman from Three Bars, brought her women wranglers over and they created a two-person swing to put out on that deck. They had done this on a Sunday, and Dana and he made sure the crews were well fed.

Mary brought over a brand-new gas barbecue, a fancy one, with beefsteaks for some and plant-produced burgers for the vegans in the group. They had all sat around on the deck, trading stories, laughing and eating heartily. It didn't hurt, on the warm May afternoon, that Lea Anderson, Logan's wife, had brought over a huge cooler filled with ice and cold beers, either.

His heart warmed with the goodness and teamwork of the people of this valley. He'd never been anywhere like this, and he sometimes thought Silver Creek might be like the mysterious, never found, Shangri-La of Asia, come to life here in the US.

Dana drove in, where huge railroad ties denoted the parking spots, turned off the truck engine, and climbed out. "Hey," she called, closing the door. "Done with the nightly duties?"

He grinned and nodded. "Yep, just finished up. How'd it go today?" Even at dusk, he could see faint shadows beneath her eyes, and she looked more tired than usual.

"We had ten new people come in, and finding them a space, a bed, getting them used to the rhythm of three square meals a day, takes time. Two of the women were out sick with the flu, so everyone was multitasking like crazy."

"This time of year," he said, walking with her up the

stairs to the deck, "with it warming up, we get a lot of transients coming in for the summer. And yes, flu hangs around till June around here." She normally wore her hair in pigtails and today was no exception. About the only time he saw her hair down, a shining red cloak around her shoulders, was after she'd taken a shower.

"We have a very good network of tiny homes for them, plus food, dental, and medical services," he said, opening the door for her.

"Thanks," she whispered, giving him a weary smile, and brushed past him.

He closed the door, placing his straw Stetson on the wooden hook on the wall. "Are you hungry?"

She hesitated halfway to her bedroom. "I am. I'm going to take a shower, change clothes, and I'll be out in a bit."

Calculating, that would be about thirty minutes. "It'll be ready."

"You're spoiling me, Colin."

"I like doing that. Go get your shower."

"I wish I felt less tired," Dana complained after dinner, helping Colin take the plates over to rinse them off in the sink and then place them into the dishwasher.

"You were probably trying to fill in for those missing people," he said sympathetically.

She warmed to his closeness, hungry for his nearness, which didn't happen often. "Probably," she grumped. Drying her hands on a nearby towel near the sink, she said, "One of the women took my temperature there. I'm running a low-grade fever. I'm going to go to bed early,

Colin. I'm feeling really rugged. I hope I haven't caught that darned flu."

He leaned his hips against the counter, a few feet separating them. "You've been running hard ever since you got here. Maybe it's all catching up with you?"

She managed a quirk of her lips. "You're probably right."

"You look a little pale," he observed, meeting her darkening eyes. The shadows beneath her eyes had not gone away.

"The ladies on the food line said the flu hangs around here until June, just as you said."

"Yes, it does." He reached out, placing the back of his hand against her forehead. "You do feel warm." Forcing himself to remove his hand, he saw the look in her eyes change when he'd connected briefly with her overly warm skin. "Sorry," he rasped, "I should have asked if it was okay to touch you."

"It's okay, Colin. Your heart's in the right place. You care, and that means everything to me."

Her low, husky words were like honey drizzled across his tightly guarded heart. The sense of worthlessness started to dissolve beneath the softness he saw in her eyes, even though he knew she wasn't feeling well at all. "I do care, Dana." The words slipped from beneath his tightened lips before he could stop them. A new tenderness came to her expression and he ached to reach out once more, touch those crimson tendrils at her temple, a way to silently tell her just how much he was grateful she was in his miserable life. There were times when he swore he could feel her wanting to be held by him for just a moment. And how many times had he wanted to be the person who did that for her? Over the months, Colin was slowly beginning to realize that wounded part of his being, so withdrawn from the world, wasn't what he wanted to live with anymore. Being around Dana was bringing out needs that he thought had died and had been buried, like his friends. But they weren't; there was a new, bright, hopeful pulse flowing through him, whispering that he was worth something to someone, even as broken as he was.

"Want me to take your temperature?" he asked, his voice thick with tightly held emotions. "There's a thermometer in the medicine cabinet in my bathroom."

"No . . ." she answered. "I think I just need rest."

"I'll let you sleep in tomorrow and I'll take care of everything, so don't worry. Okay?"

Reaching out, she briefly touched his elbow. "Thanks. You seem to be handling all of this pressure and stress far better than I do."

"That's because you're around." Colin saw her tilt her head, her gaze on his. "I mean"—he stumbled—"you're the kind of person people like to be around, Dana. You make them feel good about themselves. I've seen your touch with a lot of the wranglers, and you are good with people."

"You're no less that way," she said, giving him a weak smile. "I'll see you in the morning. Good night . . ."

"Good night." He stood there, watching the gentle sway of her hips as she headed toward her end of the home. A sense of freedom fueled by hope ribboned through him like quiet creek water moving across a flat, grassy plain, beginning to wash away that constant heaviness in his chest, that yapping voice in his head that, daily, told him how worthless he was to the human race.

Dana had been pushing herself too hard, but his concern had remained unspoken. Maybe he should have said something? It wasn't his place, but he wanted it to be.

These weeks had melted the barriers each of them held in place and every day after their first meeting, he liked what he saw in Dana. There was a closeness being woven silently, yet strongly, between them. There was trust, and Colin knew that wasn't something anyone could ever buy. It had to be earned the hard way, over time and challenges. He wondered how Dana felt toward him. Was it mutual? Or just him and his wild, crazy imagination that wasn't based in reality at all? Colin didn't know and wished to hell he did.

Glancing at his watch, it was nearly eight p.m. He heard the door shut to her area of the home, feeling sad because he wanted—no, needed—Dana. He wanted to give her whatever she needed, unsure of what that might be. It wasn't about sex. It was about one human comforting another. How many times had he wished he'd had someone that he could turn to in his despair, cry until his gut hurt, and all the time, the arms around him giving him a sense of worthiness he'd lost so long ago.

Angling out of the kitchen after shutting off the lights, he headed in the opposite direction, to his office to finish off some paperwork for the day, as well as pay the bills. That was another area Dana had trusted him to do: take care of the finances. He was good with math and had taken a course in accounting, knowing just enough to keep the books straight. Always wanting to help Dana, he hoped, would show her that he was someone who could be counted on through thick and thin. Someone she could trust.

As he sat down in his office, pulling the accounting books out of a drawer and turning on the computer, he worried about her. Was she getting the flu? Instinctively, he felt she was, but he was no doctor. And in dire times, he did not trust his own gut reaction as much as he used to. It had gotten himself and fellow Army Rangers into a hellhole where most of them died in an agonizing, pro-longed firefight.

Shaking his head, Colin forced himself to look at the software that held Dana's ranch account, pressing a button and getting lost in the numbers and bills that needed to be input into the program and electronically paid. Why didn't she ever talk about her family? Hell, he didn't talk about his, either. Were they two of the same kind, just different genders? The times she had suddenly stopped talking or switched topics mid-sentence were few, but each one stood out because it concerned family, and he could see the look in her darkening eyes, the unexpected scratchiness in her voice, plus, she went pale. *What* had happened to her? Again, his instinct kicked in strongly, and he knew something tragic and life-changing had occurred to her. And no, he wasn't the kind to go to his boss, or his friends, to share this with any of them. Colin knew he was locked up tighter than Fort Knox. He was super private; allowing no one in, except, a little, for Dana, whom he trusted with his life.

Shaking his head, he tried to stop that wave of longing that was getting stronger, more demanding, within him every day, to have some kind of positive, personal con-nection with her. It gnawed at him. Since that night in

Afghanistan, at a supposedly "safe" village, working with the 75th Ranger Regiment, he'd felt numb inside. Dead, really. Nothing made him smile. Nothing made him cry. He was stuck in an emotionless hell, he supposed. Maybe that's what hell was like? Since that night when they were attacked by two hundred Taliban soldiers, who used grenade launchers and mortars to tear down the huge wooden gate and break through the mud-and-rock wall that surrounded the village, his whole life upended— forever.

Brow scrunching, he forced himself to focus on the numbers on the bills and punch them into the computer, not replay his grisly past.

May 16

Dana awoke feeling hot and then chilled. She raised her head, looking at the old-time alarm clock on her bed stand. It had been one of several items she had taken from her parents' empty house.

Frowning, sweat dribbling down her temples, she struggled to sit up. The radium dials read three a.m. Captive to the fever and then chills, she realized she'd most likely caught that same flu that had taken out her two food-bank worker friends on Saturday. With a soft groan, she pulled the covers off and her sweaty, bare feet touched the cool wood of the floor. It felt so good. Stabilizing.

Wearing pink long-sleeved pj's with purple trousers, she pushed off the bed. Her mind wasn't working right and she plopped down on the bed, gripping the mattress to steady herself.

Shutting her eyes, she kept seeing flashes from her

traumatic past. *No! Not now!* She didn't feel strong enough to fight off the horror washing through her. She remembered feeling light-headed and nearly fainting upon hearing the information about her parents. Tears, huge ones, rolled out of her eyes and no matter what she did, they continued like a river whose dam had broken, washing down her hot, flushed cheeks, gathering on her chin and then dripping off.

Still holding on to the sheet with her left hand, she pressed her right one against her tightly closed eyes, soft sobs punching up through her chest and jamming into her throat. She was a mess! How long had she held this at bay and all it had taken was a flu and fever to break down the walls she'd constructed? She hadn't cried at her parents' joint funeral, or when she'd laid two pink roses on each of their caskets. Oh! If only she could forget her past, but that was impossible.

Gulping and sobbing, she forced herself to her bare feet, dizzied and disoriented by the raw grief flooding through her, her flu symptoms smothered by the emotions churning up through her.

Gripping the doorknob, she yanked the door open, thinking it would help if she got to the bathroom and splashed cold water on her face. Stumbling down the hall, Dana tried to be quiet, her hand against her mouth, her sobs muffled.

Making it to the bathroom, her hands shaky, she left the door open and turned on the cold spigot of the wash basin. The cold water was shocking to her fevered state, but oh! It felt so good. Leaning down, pressing her hips against the wooden cabinet, she splashed several handfuls across her face. The water washed away her tears, soothing the heat she felt in her face from crying so hard, plus taming the fever.

How long she gripped the sink with her hands, head hanging, allowing the water to drip off her nose and chin, Dana didn't know. She'd used the cabinet to steady herself; otherwise, she wasn't sure she would remain standing, even with her legs apart.

Torn between going back to bed and making herself some hot tea, she gathered her internal grit and left the bathroom, padding out into the darkened living room. Everything was quiet. There was a small light above the kitchen stove and it gave her just enough light to reach the counter and open the cupboard. With a shaking hand, she brought down a ceramic mug. Tea was in a nearby drawer and she chose chamomile. There was already water in the copper teakettle sitting on the rear of the stove. Turning on the gas, the blue flame lit and she pulled the kettle over it.

As she turned, her elbow hit the mug, sending it flying off the counter.

Gasping, Dana saw it hit the floor, shattering into large pieces. The sound was like an electric shock through her system and she froze. Her hearing was acute and it sounded like a bomb had gone off. Instantly, she knew Colin would hear it.

The door to his bedroom and office flew open.

Eyes widening, Dana froze. In his hand was a weapon, the look on his tight, darkly shadowed face hardened and frightening. He wore a gray T-shirt and a pair of dark blue pajama trousers. Startled, she gasped again, her gaze riveted to the pistol in his hand.

"I-I'm sorry," she said, her voice trembling. "I hit the cup . . . I didn't mean to wake you."

Instantly, Colin allowed his hand to drop, the weapon's barrel pointed at the floor. "What's going on?" he asked, his voice thick as he moved toward her in his bare feet.

Leaning her hips against the counter, she whispered unsteadily, "I have the flu. Don't get too close, Colin. I-I was coming out to make myself some tea, hoping to bring down my temperature."

He halted and looked around where the mug had shattered shards. He set the gun on the counter, putting on the safety. "I thought it might be." He scrutinized her.

"Yeah," she muttered, pushing her fingers through her damp strands, moving them away from her eyes. "I picked it up at work."

"Are you okay?"

She heard the urgency, the low, gritty tone in his voice, and felt her raw emotions dissolve. "It's a middle kind of fever . . . nothing to worry about."

He moved closer, assessing her. "What's 'middle' to you?"

"Probably around a hundred and one, I would guess." She made a cursory point to the tea bag on the counter. "I was going to make some chamomile for myself. It's known to bring down fevers. I hate taking any medications. I was raised on medicinal herbs. I wish I had some feverfew . . . It's well known for dealing with fevers, but chamomile can do it."

He gently squeezed her shoulder. "Why don't you go sit down over there?" He led her away from the broken ceramic mug on the floor and toward the dining room table. Pulling out a chair, he said, "Take a seat. I'll make the tea for you and clean up the broken mug. Are you cold? Chilled? What about your feet? Can I get you a bathrobe and slippers?"

"No . . . I'm okay." Deeply touched by this thoughtfulness, she hungrily absorbed his care, the rawness of his expression startling her. Colin was genuinely concerned for her welfare. Now he was like a lover attending the woman he loved. That unexpected idea startled her. Dana wasn't sure where that thought had come from as she sat down and he left to pick up the broken mug.

Watching him, down on his hands and knees, swiftly getting every shard, she became emotional, probably thanks to her fever. As he stood, she could see the T-shirt stretch wonderfully across his broad shoulders, outlining his chest and flat stomach. He was beautiful to look at and Dana no longer tried to fight her yearning for him. Care radiated from him and she swore she could feel that unseen energy of his feelings, wrapping around her as she wearily sat at the dining room table.

"There," he said, dropping the mug pieces into the trash, "done. Now? Can I make you that cup of chamomile tea? Are you up for that, or do you want to go back to bed?"

Dana's heart ballooned with raw need of Colin as he stood there before her, his eyes tender as he held her gaze. The crazy thought that she really wanted him in bed with her, holding her, again shocked her muddled senses. Just holding her. This wasn't about making love with a man. This was about one human caring for another, and inwardly, Dana ached to say those words, but she was a coward. "I'd love that tea, thanks . . ."

"Coming right up." He grinned lopsidedly and turned, heading to the counter.

The copper teakettle was whistling in no time. She watched Colin, his movement economical as he took down another mug, deposited the tea bag into it, and then poured the boiling water over it.

"Did your mother teach you how to take care of people?" she asked, her voice scratchy.

He glanced over his shoulder. "My mother, Margaret, is a person who believes everyone should have some basic life skills."

"She taught you well." Dana knew these were personal questions, but the flu and fever seemed to have taken down her normal reserve. Right now, she hungered to know more than the surface of Colin.

"My mother made very sure I could cook, clean the house, and do everything she was doing." He set the kettle down and went to the silverware drawer and opened it up. "Do you like honey with your tea?"

"That sounds good," she said, her voice low. As miserable as she felt, Colin made her feel better with just his quiet presence. "I didn't expect you to come out of your room with a gun in your hand, but I guess I made enough of a noise to make you think someone had broken in?"

He dipped the tea bag. "Yes." He shrugged. "I'm sorry, I saw how much it scared you. I didn't mean to do that. I seriously thought someone had smashed a window out in the living room and was breaking in."

"I'm sure you did. I scared the hell out of myself, too," she managed wryly, watching as he brought the jar of honey over to the mug.

"One teaspoon of honey or two?"

"One, please."

Colin brought it over along with a paper napkin and

a saucer for the tea bag. "I think I'll make myself some coffee," he said.

"I'm sure this whole fiasco woke you up completely," she said, apology in her tone.

"I sleep lightly, anyway."

"Tell me about your growing-up years?"

He began making the coffee. "My father is a beef rancher and has a spread of fifteen-hundred acres just outside of Billings, Montana. My mother is an English professor at Montana State University."

"Is she an author?"

"No, but she says that when she retires, she has a book or two in her to write. She did read to me as a kid, every night. I really loved listening to all those fairy tales and myths she'd read to me."

"That's wonderful . . . My mother always read to me before I went to bed." The memory was warm and a deep ache settled in her chest. She saw him twist a look in her direction, surprise in his expression.

"We share something, then." He brought the coffee over and sat down at her elbow, the mug between his long, spare hands.

The chamomile tasted more than good. "This tastes wonderful," she managed softly, giving him a look of thanks. ". . . And, yes, it looks like your mother and mine both read to us."

He frowned, took a sip of coffee and rasped, "This is the first time you've talked to me about your parents."

She shrugged. "I keep avoiding it, Colin."

"Because of me? Was it something I said or did?"

A pain shot through her heart. "Oh . . . no! No, you've done nothing. You've been the most wonderful person to have stepped into my life since . . . well . . . I lost my parents." Her voice cracked and she stared down at her teacup.

"I'm sorry," he rasped, reaching out, briefly touching the back of her hand that felt damp and warm with fever.

"A-are your parents still alive?"

It was an odd question, but he made nothing of it, seeing the anguish in her eyes. She could barely hold his gaze. "Yes. They're in their sixties now, but in good health. They each like what they do. My mother is looking forward to retiring at sixty-five, but my dad said he's never giving up ranching until his last breath." He managed a one-cornered quirk of his mouth. "When I got out of the army, I had always planned on going back to the ranch and helping him, but"— he sighed, looking away for a moment—"things didn't work out that way."

"But you stay in touch with them?"

"Always. I love them. And I worry about them. Sometimes, I feel guilty for not going home to help them."

"Do you want to?"

Nodding, he said, "Yeah, but that's not going to happen."

She moved her fingers around the warm ceramic mug. "I'm sorry to hear that, but I'm glad you're here, with me, Colin. All of this"—she looked around the room—"wouldn't have happened without you being the lynchpin."

"Well," he admitted quietly, "I've really taken a shine to this place. But really? It's the person who bought it that has made it what it is. Your vision and love of it."

"I'm glad you're okay with being here, since you're on loan from your other ranch jobs."

"I'm glad I'm here, too," he admitted, opening his hands around the mug, giving her a look of apology. "I'm pretty stoved up from my years in the army, and I have problems working around other wranglers."

"Because of your military experiences?" she guessed.

"Yes."

"You never seemed stressed being here," she whispered, giving him a questioning look.

"I haven't been. Not once. That's kind of a miracle in itself, Dana, and I guess it's because of your quiet presence. You're sort of like that creek out back of the buildings, quiet and calm."

"Oh." She sighed, shaking her head. "There's times when I feel anything but. With you here, Colin? A lot of my stress just melts away because you're so reliable and steady. It's like nothing ever rocks you."

"It's all a mask," he murmured. "I feel plenty of stress at times, but in the military, you don't let it show or let others know you're feeling that way."

"You are hard to read," she said, giving him a weak smile as she sipped the tea.

"It's not on purpose. Just trained into me, is all."

"Did you get that steadiness from your dad or mom?"

"Both my parents. They are the type of people that don't get rocked by much at all, they've got an attitude in place that sort of defuses the event or situation. I guess, in most ways, I'm like that, too. I don't mean to be unavailable to you."

"It's nice that you're sharing all of this with me. I really appreciate it."

He held her gaze, her cheeks flushed, her eyes dulled with the fever. "I want to be there for you, Dana. I guess I don't really know a lot about your background, but I try to put myself in your place buying this broken-down place, trying to rebuild it and make it breathe and live once more. I imagine there's a lot of stress on you, worry, maybe."

"All of that," she agreed somberly. Tears filled her eyes and she wiped them away, seeing that Colin noted it. "Maybe it's my fever and I'm not feeling good," she groused softly, "but I'm tired of trying to avoid a major part of my life by never talking about it to anyone. It's so hard to swallow it, to pretend it didn't happen, when it did."

"I'm a good listener," he urged quietly, holding her watery gaze. "I keep what we say in complete privacy, Dana. I hope you can see me as a shoulder to cry on or lean on, if you need one."

Taking another swipe at her eyes, she managed, "Funny, I've already seen you like that. I've felt you were sympathetic to other people's plights even though you never said anything about it. I watched you working with the people of Silver Creek who helped us raise that barn, and the wranglers from other ranches who have come in to help us, as well." She studied him in the quiet. "I've seen how much they like you, Colin, that you're a hard worker, your word is your bond, and I feel so lucky to have you here with me to rescue this ranch."

"I like it, too. And, yes, I care about people, animals . . . our environment . . ."

"The dogs that the wranglers bring with them absolutely idolize you."

He grinned a little. "I like dogs. They're honest in their feelings for you."

She wiped her eyes again. "I like hearing about your parents, about how much you love them even if you can't go home right now. I want to tell you about mine . . . it's been so long since I said anything to anyone about them."

"I'd like that," he said, giving her a kind look.

"My whole life," she began, her voice thin and broken, "was upended when I was seventeen. It was a Saturday, and I was out with the school photography club for a nature day shoot. My mom and dad were at home . . ." She stopped, trying to fight the tears, her hands tight around the mug. "I—uh . . . it was three p.m. when we had just gotten back at the high school, wrapping up our shoot for the day, when a sheriff's deputy came into our lab and asked for me. I didn't know him, and I had no idea why he was there. He . . . he had a grim look on his face and it scared me. I went out with him and he took me to his cruiser. We sat in it and he . . . he told me someone had broken into my parents' home." She squeezed her eyes shut, leaned back in the chair and pressed her hands to her tightly shut eyes. "Oh . . . Colin . . . they told me they'd been murdered . . ." She broke down into deep sobs.

Stunned, Colin instantly shoved the chair back, raggedly whispering her name and going to her. He set his chair next to hers, sitting down close to where she was. Barely able to stand the way her mouth was contorted, the awful sounds of sobs filling the space between them, he slid his arms around her shaking shoulders, gently pulling her to him. She came, her arms opening, sliding around his torso, her face pressed hard into his chest, her cries tearing him apart.

He held her as if she were fragile, but allowed her whatever space she wanted, her hands opening and closing. The cries tearing out of her . . . my God, the sobs and animal-like sounds . . . He'd heard those same anguished cries before, back in that Afghan village where half of the populace had been arbitrarily slaughtered by the Taliban that night.

Jamming his eyes shut, he eased her head to his shoulder, her brow pressed to his jaw and held her. Just held her.

Chapter 6

Colin felt his heart melting. The sensation was like a deep, powerful earthquake moving through his chest, and it caught him completely off guard. Was it the cries from the terrified people in the Afghan village, the horror, the shock and trauma of losing family members, or was it Dana's sobs, which were slowly lessening, over the murder of her parents? The depth of loss was the same.

He held her close, giving her enough room if she wanted to be released. Her arms had wrapped around his waist, still snug around his torso, the material on the top he wore, damp with her warm tears, a flood of grief that he sensed she'd held for a long time. And what a helluva secret to carry, not speaking about it to many people she trusted. He savored the feeling of his cheek against her silky hair, tried to remain immune to the cinnamon scent tangled through the strands. This was no time to be aroused. This was only a time to be someone who cared enough to hold her while she shook with grief in his arms.

Closing his eyes, he couldn't imagine losing his parents like that. As soft and gentle as Dana appeared? She had a backbone of titanium as far as he was concerned. Carrying that loss, no one to turn to when she needed someone, dove deeply into his own heart and he grieved for her. How brave she had been to start her life all over again, coming out to Wyoming to buy a broken-down old ranch and try to start again. She had been seventeen when she'd lost her parents. She was still a minor. Did she have other relatives who could step in and support and help her? He didn't know, but hoped that it had happened. What other struggles did she have to surmount? It hurt to think she'd had no one to support or help her during that period.

Without thinking, he ran his palm slowly up and down her back. The tension he felt in her was real and, little by little, his soothing strokes were diminishing that tension.

Losing track of time, Colin could feel her giving in, surrendering to the terrifying losses in her life. He had so many questions for her, and yet he knew he couldn't pepper her with any of them right now. Another part of him was shocked that she'd come into his arms at all. He thought she would push him away when he set his chair next to her own. But she hadn't. She'd instantly fallen into his embrace, face buried in his upper chest, arms around him, as if she were clinging to her last hope: him, of all people. She was like clear, clean water to his thirsty soul.

He lifted his head, blinking away the tears he was crying for Dana, and, maybe, for himself. Over sixty-five families in that village had lost one or more loved ones during that nightmare night attack in Afghanistan. How badly he'd wanted to do something other than provide first aid relief to those who had survived the bloody assault. He remembered bitterly getting on a Night Stalkers helicopter transport after dawn arrived, his clothes stiff with blood, the stomach-churning scent in his nostrils and throat.

He wasn't the only one of the Rangers who had vomited out of sheer emotional trauma as they flew toward their US base. He'd sat in the shaking, shuddering helo, crammed in with fellow Rangers, head buried against his drawn-up knees, crying, but no one could see him or hear him. Helicopters were infamous for ear-slamming shaking and rattling sounds. Talk was impossible, so weeping would not have been heard at all, either.

Gradually, Dana's sobs stopped. She clung to him, and it reminded him of a frightened child clinging to a parent for protection against that harsh brutal world. How would he have reacted to the same thing happening to him? His parents gone? Forever? He simply couldn't conceive of it.

Gently, he laid his hand against her hair and whispered, "What can I do to help you?" His own voice was hoarse and choked sounding. Getting to stroke her back, hopefully soothing and supporting her emotionally with his touch, he felt her arms slowly begin to relax from around his waist. She'd held him as if letting him go meant she would be swept away with uncontrollable grief, lost forever. Hell, who didn't need holding and human compassion after experiencing something as earth-shattering as this? How many times over the years as a Ranger had he seen horrific, deeply shocking scenes, and felt the anguish soaring up through him, his emotions ripping him wide-open, too?

Dana cleared her throat. She sniffed several times.

Colin reached over and pulled several tissues from a box sitting on the table. As her arms slipped from around him and she slowly sat up, he pressed them into her hand. In the bare light she looked beyond pale, her eyes wounded holes of loss. Her fingers curved around his fingers. Unable to turn away from her hollowed-out gaze, it took everything inside him to hold it. In that moment, it felt as if she was shoring herself up as she sat up, tears running down her face, gathering on her jaw and chin. Her mouth, so tight, withholding more emotions, parted. She took the tissues in both hands and pressed them against her face.

It hurt just to sit there and say and do nothing. Hell, at one time, he'd been a hard-charging, ball-busting Ranger. Today, he was a thin, shadowy reminder of those younger years when he'd felt impervious to death or being wounded. In this precious moment with Dana, he focused on her, not himself. He watched her wipe her face several times, the tissues crumpled in her hands.

"Here," he murmured, reaching over for the box and placing it in her lap.

"Th-thanks . . . I feel," she whispered in a rasp, "like I've cried a million tears . . ." She saw his hand open, palm up, and she gave him the moist tissues.

"That's okay," he managed. "That's a million that aren't inside you anymore."

She lifted her head and she studied him in the growing silence. "How do you know this?" Her voice was thin and scratchy. She pulled more tissues from the box, continuing to blot her eyes.

"Long story," he admitted, suddenly feeling infinitely old and tired, far beyond his present years. His mouth drew into a weak one-sided upward movement. He couldn't call it a smile, that was for sure. Maybe more a grimace. "Someday? I'll share it with you. But not right now." He lifted his finger and moved several strands of red hair that were tangled in her lashes. Her eyes softened and he felt his heart burst open. It was a look of gratefulness.

"I-I never thought . . . well . . . anyone, except for my mom and dad, could be so caring as you've been. I never believed there was another person out there who could make me feel . . . well . . . safe . . ."

"You are safe with me, Dana. You always will be." His voice tightened and he felt a welling up of so many emotions, some needy, some hurting, some crying out to be held just as he'd held her. Battling all those powerful urges back down deep inside himself, as he'd always done since that awful night in the village, he allowed himself to feel the invisible, yet so palpable care that radiated like fragile, golden light between them. Maybe he shouldn't have been so intimate, pushing those soft, shining tendrils away from her eyes. Dana didn't look upset. In fact, his instincts, which were screaming at him, told him that she needed that kind of tender touch, that human thoughtfulness from him right now.

". . . Safe . . ."

"Yes, I'll always be here for you. You aren't alone anymore, Dana. We're kind of a mix-and-match family, but we're here, together, and from what I can see? We make a pretty good team. I'm glad I could hold you." Because no one held him after that terrifying, catastrophic night in that village and it was the one human response he needed more than any other. At least he'd been able to share it with Dana, and he hoped with all his heart that it had helped her through this. Human touch should never be discounted. So often, in times of crisis, it is the first gesture that is needed the most. As a person's world spins out of their control, touch grounds them, brings them back to reality, feeds them hope when all of it has been brutally taken from them.

Dana blotted her eyes again and wiped her nose, her hands clasped in her lap as she stared at him in the grayish light, the darkness surrounding them like a warm, invisible cloak. "That's so funny," she murmured, her voice still low and hesitant. "The first day I met you? I felt safe with you. I didn't even know you then, Colin, but for some crazy, unexplained reason, you made me feel like I haven't felt since before my folks were murdered." She winced, hardly able to raggedly whisper those words.

Reaching out, he placed his hand over hers. Skin chilled across her hand, he wanted to pull her into his arms, against his body, to warm her up, but he hesitated. From his point of view, there was enough intimacy already initiated, based upon what she'd just admitted, as his large, calloused hand covered her clasped ones. Dana didn't pull away. Instead, he saw her bow her head, a soft sob in her throat, but she didn't draw away. That told him he'd been right about his knowing that she *wanted* his touch.

"I hope this makes you feel better," he croaked, watching her as tears once more beaded on the red lashes of her closed eyes. "Just tell me what you need, Dana. I'll try to do it for you." Him, of all people, thinking he could help someone when he couldn't even help those sixty-five men, women, and children in that village, much less, himself. He had no business saying those words, and yet they almost tore out of his mouth, and he was unable to stop them.

"Just . . . be here . . . with me. I feel so broken, Colin . . . so broken . . . like I'll never mend, never heal. I feel a hole, a dark, huge hole in my heart." She lifted her chin, opening her eyes, staring into his gaze. "I feel . . . so . . . lost . . . I'm trying to put my life back together, but it's so hard . . . and I drag out the memory of that day the sheriff came and told me what happened . . ." She shook her head.

"I understand those feelings," he rasped, his hand tightening for a moment over hers, and then he relaxed, allowing the heat of his hand to warm her cold flesh.

"Do you?" she asked.

"More than you know."

"Oh . . . no . . ."

He saw the anguish in her shadowed eyes. "Someday we'll talk about it, but not right now. Tonight? We take care of you. Keep you feeling safe. That's all that matters right now, Dana. What else can I do for you?"

Nodding, she whispered, "I-I'm so tired all of a sudden, Colin . . . Gutted . . . feeling like I'm a top spinning out of control." She reluctantly pulled her hands from beneath his large, warm one.

"You need to sleep," he agreed quietly, seeing the anguish in her eyes recede and exhaustion in its place. "Can I walk you to your bedroom?"

Shaking her head, she said, "No . . . could you . . . would you, just sit in the corner of that couch in the living room and let me lie down against you? Just hold me?"

She sounded like a frightened child of seven years old, not the woman he knew. Totaled by her unexpected request, he managed, "Sure. Do you want a blanket? A pillow?"

"No, just let me lie against you. I'll use your shoulder as a pillow. Would that be all right with you?"

Suddenly he felt as if he had wings and were flying so high into the beauty of the sky above, that he went breathless for a split second. His heart was pounding, but it was the *feeling* in it that startled and took him by utter surprise. He was actually feeling again, like a normal human being would! Since the village massacre, he'd been numb, unable to feel his own emotional reactions at all, and that had frightened him. Now? He was *alive*! That realization shook him to his soul. His ability to feel was back! Shocked wordless, he dumbly nodded to Dana's request.

Pulling out the chair so she could walk to the couch, she moved slowly, not only sick with the flu, but sick with grief. "I'll be there in just a moment," he rasped, reaching out, touching her elbow. She barely nodded. To Colin, it looked as if she were carrying the invisible weight of the world on her shoulders. Without a word, he doused the light in the kitchen and walked to the couch. She sat there, hunched over, looking like a scared child. His heart was pounding wildly with so many feelings that he felt swamped by all of them, unable to really sort any of it out right now. Instead, he sat down in the corner and lifted his left arm in invitation so that she could come and lie against him in a way that suited her.

His heart thudded as she came to him, her arm sliding like a whisper around his waist, her head resting on his shoulder, strands of her red hair tickling his jaw.

"Okay?" he asked thickly as he slowly moved his arm around her shoulders, not wanting to startle her. He felt a fine shudder move through her, and then she collapsed fully against him. Breath warm and moist against his neck and upper chest, he felt her barely nod her head.

"Just close your eyes," he rasped against her hair. "You're tired. Just . . . rest . . . You're safe . . ."

A thrill went through him as he felt her sag fully against him, their thighs pressed trustingly against one another as well. He wondered how many men would take advantage of such a situation. *Too many*. But he wouldn't. Not *ever*.

At the Afghan village, the little girls and boys used to follow him around, laughing and smiling. He always had candy for them in his pockets, and sacks of canned food for their mothers because these people lived on the edge of starvation as farmers. One bad crop, and people did starve to death. That was how tenuous their hold on life really was.

Colin closed his eyes, convinced that he'd never be able to sleep with Dana in his arms. Just the softness of a woman against him after so many years of being alone, haunted by the PTSD, the nightmares, it felt like his life was suddenly being handed back to him. He would never put a woman into this situation with him, where she might feel taken advantage of. He couldn't begin to tell her how badly damaged he was. No one could understand.

Eyes shut, listening to her shallow breathing, Colin felt her body go lax, telling him she really was asleep. And in his arms. My God, he'd never dreamed of something like this happening to him, of all people. His heart was feeling deeply, and he had so many sensations; all good, all welcoming him home to himself. Finally, maybe, that numbness was gone? Forever? Dana, whether she knew it or not, had helped him reclaim some small, healthy part of himself; a missing piece returning to him.

Euphoria spiraled through him, and suddenly, without warning, happiness bubbled up through him—filled with light, happiness, and most of all, hope.

Tears filled Colin's tightly closed eyes. His mouth thinned and he tried to stop them, but it wasn't going to happen. He lay there in a semi-prone position, a beautiful, caring, resilient woman in his arms, someone he had been drawn to powerfully from the day he'd met her. How often had he hungered to just be with her? Talking and sharing with her? Listening to that soft, husky voice of hers, the joy dancing in her spring-colored green eyes and aching . . . yes . . . aching, to be touched by her.

He'd wake up at night, wondering what it would feel like to have her hand sliding across his chest, her breath mingling with his, what her lips would taste like against his, the scent of her firm, satiny skin. All his dreams had just come true. Her arm was curved around his torso, holding on to him even in sleep, afraid she might become lost. Her breath flowed across his lower neck and the opening of his shirt.

Her hair so soft, to Colin it felt like the strands were a quiet, cooling river against his flesh. Most of all, he allowed himself to enjoy the scent of her skin.

In one way, Colin felt guilty for all the pleasures thrumming through him, unbelievable gifts granted to him out of nowhere, feeling as if he were a hunter and finally discovering the otherworldly treasures that were being given him. *Of all people.* He deserved nothing and he knew it. Absolutely nothing. Innocent people died because the Rangers were there, taking up residence in their village with medicine and vaccinations. Nearly every family had a loved one taken from them by the Taliban that night. All the Army Rangers had done was bring death inside the walls of where they lived. *No gifts.* Just loved ones jerked away from them. *Gone forever. Forever . . .*

As he felt himself sinking more deeply toward sleep, he surrendered over to the luxurious and priceless gift of Dana in his arms. His feelings were alive, vibrant and glowing; his heart throbbed with such undeserved joy in his chest. She made him feel hope. *Hope.* He'd lost that, too. And faith, also. Colin had no faith in anything until Dana walked into his life, and suddenly the faith ignited within him and then it morphed into hope. He hadn't hoped for years. But with her in his life, even though he was just a wrangler, she fed his wounded soul and broken spirit with her breathy laughter, the way she saw life and adored living simply, in communion with the earth.

Spiraling downward, all sounds disappeared, with the exception of Dana's breath feathering across his skin, her subtle scent combining with his awakened feelings, allowed him to surrender fully, not afraid of having a nightmare. No, maybe this one time, with this incredible miracle in his arms, he could sleep deeply because he had the woman of his dreams in his arms.

May 20

"We need a cover crop," Dana said to Colin as they stood near the slope where tall pines covered the area. She waved toward the fifty acres of untilled land in front of them. They had driven out to the area after Colin and several ranchers from the surrounding area cut in a good road and added gravel to the surface of it.

"I heard my boss, Chase, talking one day to his mother about cover crops." He slanted a look in her direction. "I really didn't pay much attention to their conversation."

"Cover crops, when it comes to organic gardens or acreage like this, are vital. It's a natural way to put nutrients back into the earth so that the crop you want to grow, has 'food' to grow strong and healthy." Making a face of sorts, Dana said, "That isn't exactly a scientific description of a cover crop, but you get the idea?"

He smiled a little, resting is hands on his hips, surveying the plot. "What is used as a cover crop?"

The flu had taken her down for three days. Today was the first time she looked like her old self. He couldn't erase, nor did he want to, that night she'd slept in his arms until long after the sun rose.

"I talked to Mary about it and she said Chase uses cowpeas. They're a bean crop high in nutrients, food for the next crop we plant after they are plowed under. When you're talking fifty acres here? You need a tractor and plow to do it. In small, organic gardens there's several methods of doing it."

"I can plow it," he offered.

"I've ordered the cowpeas, and they're going to be trucked in and arrive in three days."

He pushed his straw hat up on his brow. The morning air was chilly, but the sky was clear and the sun's early morning rays shot across the land. "How long do you allow that cover crop to grow?" he wondered. Something had changed between them; he could feel it and it was almost palpable. She stood close to him and he swore he could feel the heat from her body beneath her clothing.

"Only until it gets to the bloom stage, then we plow it under, let it sit for about three weeks to begin breaking down, back into the soil, feeding it."

"Then? You plow again and plant the real crops over it?"

She nodded. "Yep. It's something my dad and I did every year. We have a long growing season here, a hundred and twenty days versus what most people have, ninety days, to grow a crop."

"Because we're in a special place thanks to the mountains?"

"Yes. We'll let the cover crop grow for a month, plow it under, and then get to work on planting different medicinal herbs in this first area." She gestured toward it.

"Okay, let's drive back to the barn. I'll get things going on plowing this up, starting now."

"Great," she said.

Not for the first time, she felt like she was drowning in his light blue eyes that glinted with something undefined, and yet, it made her heart swell with need of him.

Ever since that night he'd held her, their lives had changed. Colin was more open and talkative with her, not as withdrawn as before. Just knowing what he was thinking, what was on his mind, Dana realized he was allowing her private access to him as a human being. It was breathtaking for her to have such an entrance because before he'd been so closed up and unavailable. The tenderness he'd shown toward her had changed her, too. It was something she wanted to share with him. Maybe tonight, after dinner? Unsure, Dana didn't want to lose what had been gifted to them through the fires of her own personal experience.

Absorbing his tall, lean body so close to hers, maybe six inches away, made her feel happy as never before.

"I don't know about you, but I need more coffee," Colin said. "Good thing you brought a quart-size thermos with us on this early morning trip."

She smiled a little at his teasing. "Let's go," she urged, briefly touching his lower arm. The look in his eyes filled with warmth over her light touch. It made her feel good, too. Just getting to touch him sometimes, salved her soul and her heart. Just seeing how he felt, allowing her to read the expression in his face and eyes, was feeding her in so many wonderful ways. She felt like they were two wounded animals attracted to one another, and yet afraid to trust what lay between them, which was rich with promise and happiness.

Turning on her heel, she moved down the gentle slope toward the truck parked nearby on the newly created road.

Hearing the whistle of a hawk, Dana looked up as Colin matched her stride, at her shoulder, distance between them, but not that much. "Look," she said, pointing skyward. Above them were the resident red-tailed hawks, a husband and wife that Dana had seen often out here in their territory.

"Nice to see them," he agreed, slowing his pace and watching them circle above them. "They're searching this plot of land for gophers, mice, or anything else that might make a breakfast." He grinned a little, meeting her gaze.

"It all works together." She sighed, her lips drawing upward as she watched them continue to circle and gain more altitude. "Nature, if we let her, allows the great circle of life to endure."

"Despite man," he snorted, moving around the truck and opening the passenger door for her.

"Thanks," she murmured, climbing in. The console between them held the thermos. She strapped in and he shut the door. Sliding the thermos out of the console, she opened it and poured a fragrant, hot cup. Once Colin was in, she handed it to him. There was a second ceramic cup in another holder and she filled that for herself. They sat in the truck, the land spreading out before them. Sipping the strong coffee, she whispered, "I feel so lucky in being able to buy this land, Colin. Every day, I pinch myself to see if this is really real. You know?"

He leaned back and said, "Yes, I do understand what you mean. The land has its own magic. When Chase hired me as a wrangler, I didn't really have a sense of the land, but working with him, with Mary, I began to see it differently, like they did. Mary always said the land breathed; that it had its own set of lungs. I liked that idea."

"I love working with Mary. She just infuses all of us with her love of the earth."

"With your farm background," he murmured, sipping the coffee in hand, "you have to feel at home here in a certain kind of way?"

"Yes, very much so." She watched his brows draw down. "What?"

"Oh," he muttered, "I was just thinking about your parents' farm, how you let it go. I mean"—he gave her a searching look—"that had to be hard on you, Dana. You were born there, grew up there . . . I'm just trying to put myself in your shoes on what you shared with me the other night. The way you love the land is something I see every day, in so many different ways, with you. Out in the greenhouse, with all those seedlings in cups and containers, I see how happy you become, how relaxed as you dote over them like a mother with her babies."

Her heart twinged with old pain, but she welcomed knowing what was on his mind, what was important to him. This was all so new to her since he'd held her. They might be two scared people, broken, searching on hands and knees, trying to find a new niche in life, but she could feel the trust, however tentative, growing between them.

"A huge part of me didn't want to leave it after they were murdered," she admitted quietly, her hands around the cup, warming them. "I seesawed back and forth. So much of me was with that house, that land . . . all the memories . . . and yet"—she sighed, giving him a troubled glance—"I couldn't overcome what had happened to them there, in the house I grew up in. I just . . . couldn't do it."

He reached over, gently touching her shoulder. "I'm sorry, maybe I shouldn't have brought this up."

Her skin tingled where he'd lightly touched her for a brief moment. There was pain and understanding in his eyes and she could feel his care radiating toward her. "In the end," she admitted quietly, "I had to walk away from all of it. I couldn't be there, live with it, my imagination going wild . . . losing sleep, being sleep deprived. No . . . I had to sell it and walk away."

"I'm sure I'd have done the same thing," he admitted, his voice low with emotion. "One of these days, I'll share with you what happened to me. I think we're a lot more alike in our pasts than either of us realized before."

"I'd like that," she said, finishing off the coffee. "Anytime you want to share it with me, Colin? I'll be there for you like you were there for me."

He finished off his coffee and sat up a bit more. "I wanted to be there for you, Dana. I'd like to do that in the future if you ever need someone to hold you again."

She put the cap back on the thermos, setting it in the console. "I'd like that," she admitted. Her voice sounded choked, even to her. Colin had a way with a look, with the rasp in his low voice, that just seemed to her like a penetrating fog. She was going to continue to allow him entrance into her secret, inner world that was filled with such anguish and loss. "You don't know this," she whispered, giving him a searching look, "but whatever it is that is going on between us, is helping me in so many ways, Colin."

He turned over the engine, the truck going to idle.

"Maybe part of it is that you're finally giving that trauma a voice, Dana?"

She shrugged as he turned the truck around and they headed back toward the main ranch area. "I've thought about that," she hesitantly admitted. "But it's different with you. I don't think I could have talked to just anyone about this. There is something good and clean and hopeful between us, Colin. I feel it every day. And it heals me in an emotional way I can't explain. But I feel it. I really do, and it's helping me. You need to know that."

Colin wiped his jaw. He'd just shaved earlier, before coming out with Dana to this plot of land. "I didn't know that . . ."

She said firmly, "You're good for me in many ways, Colin. I can't explain it. I never thought something like this could happen, but you're helping me to heal and I can feel it in large and small ways every day. It's you. The sum of who you are reminds me of a salve my mom used to make for bruises and cuts I'd get. She'd gently smooth that salve on my hurt, and it would get better in minutes. In some ways, I think you're a salve for my broken soul. At least, that's how I see it. I know my dad, working with him, listening to his counsel and what he knew, always made me eager to be with and around him. In his own way, he was healing to me, too." She glanced over at him as he drove slowly down the road. "You are magic, Colin. And I can't explain it and I guess I don't want to, but it's like breathing life back into me after being in a desert of nothing but pain, grief, and memories."

Nodding, his mouth tightened for a moment and then relaxed, most of his attention on driving. "It makes me feel very humbled, Dana. I guess I never realized that I could have that kind of positive effect on anyone . . ."

"Ever since you held me that night? Let me sleep on your shoulder? I've changed. But it's a good change, Colin, not a bad one. I don't know what it is, or what's happening between us, but for me, at least, it's good and positive. The last couple of days, despite working my way through that flu, I've felt hope, real hope, for the first time in years, and I know it's because of what happened . . . what we shared with one another."

"Yes . . . I felt it was a special moment, too."

"Are you okay with me rattling on like this? On a personal level with you?"

"Of course I am."

She shook her head. "I know how one event can change a person's life," she whispered unsteadily. "I've lived through it. What I didn't expect was someone like you to walk into my life. You're like a dressing over my wounds. That's the only way I can understand and say it . . . I know it probably sounds weird."

"No," he said, giving her an understanding look, "I've sort of felt that way about you since I met you, Dana. When I'm around you, I feel lifted . . . maybe *lighter* is the word to use. And like you? I can't make sense of it all—at least, not yet. But I like it. I have always liked you and I like the friendship we're building. It feels strong, right, and good to me. Does that sound weird?" He gave her a quick grin, teasing her a bit.

"Not weird at all." She laughed softly. "But maybe we're weird, Colin. Just not normal people because of our earlier experiences?"

"I'm not a shrink," he said, following the curve of

the road that would lead them to the main road back to the ranch area. "Things happen to everyone in life. That's what I see over and over again. Some events are good and fortifying to us, and others rip us apart, destroy us, and we blindly go around trying to pick up the pieces left of ourselves, trying to figure out how to put it all together again so we can continue to muddle through life."

"But we aren't normal, Colin. Since my parents' murder, my life changed drastically and forever. I don't see things like I did before. I'm scared of men, if you want the truth. Deep down, I really am."

"It was men who took their lives," he rasped, braking and then making the turn. "That's understandable, Dana. I'd be distrustful of men, too. That's not weird, at all. What puzzles me is that you don't seem distrustful of me."

She thought over his words, seeing the barn come into view about a mile down the road. "Since coming here? Meeting Mary, and then Chase, and Cari, who I adore, a lot of my distrust toward men in general, has pretty much taken a back seat in my life."

"You must have distrusted me, though. Chase ordered me to come and help you. You didn't know me from anyone."

"You felt different to me, Colin. I can't explain it, but you did. I relaxed. And I trust you."

"Humph," he said, speeding up a bit on the wider dirt road, "I'm in so many pieces, I've lost hope of ever trying to put myself back together like I used to be. How can you trust someone who is so broken, Dana?"

She shrugged. "Broken doesn't mean bad."

"Both start with a B."

She laughed with him. "You know? In the Japanese

culture, pots that have been broken are not thrown away. Instead, they take them to a pot hospital and they gently put the cracks and breaks back together again with gold. It's called *kintsukuroi*, which means 'golden repair.' They see it as a metaphor of embracing our flaws and imperfections. I see it as scars healing my wounds."

"I like this idea," he said.

"It's really very beautiful and I love the symbology of it. Even though we're broken, doesn't mean we aren't of some use to ourselves and to others. That despite how we've been broken? The gold that cements our pieces back together again make us beautiful and more resilient. You should go online and check this out because the Japanese people, I feel, realized a long time ago that life is brutal and it breaks most people one way or another. What matters is how we pick ourselves up, mend, and go on living the best we know how."

"Hmmm, I will check that out. I like the concept. Broken beauty."

"Not bad. It would make a good book title." She grinned over at him. He gave her a thoughtful glance.

As they drove into the main ranch area, Dana gasped. "Look! The horses have arrived!"

"So they have," he murmured, braking near the barn where there was a four-horse trailer and a white truck with the Three Bars Ranch logo on it. He saw Chase and Cari Bishop, climbing out of the truck. "We've got company. And from the looks of it, several horses."

"Chase and Cari brought them," Dana said, excitement in her tone. She unbuckled and opened the door. "What a nice surprise! Come on, Colin! Let's see which horses they chose for us." Dana knew that these horses were on loan from Chase's ranch, which was very nice of them to be so caring and thoughtful. She raised her hand and Cari smiled hugely, waving back to her. Chase smiled a hello.

The day was turning into something magical for Dana as she hurried toward the couple. She loved horses! And it had been so long since she'd ridden one! Colin caught up with her and she saw the grin on his face. He looked just as excited as she was. What did the horses look like? Dana could hardly wait to find out!

Chapter 7

"We've been a little late in getting horses for you," Chase said in way of greeting Dana, shaking her hand and then Colin's as he approached.

Cari hugged Dana. "I kept bugging him," she whispered conspiratorially.

Dana released her and said, "Thank you! I've been so excited about having horses here."

"Well, we have four of them for you!" Cari joined her husband, sliding her arm around his waist, his arm coming across her shoulders.

"Thanks for bringing the horses, Chase. But *four* of them?" Dana asked, excitement in her tone.

"We wanted to pair you with the right horses," Chase said, getting more serious.

"Colin had mentioned you might need a packhorse," Cari added. "We have one in the trailer, if you still need him."

"Oh, we will," Colin said, nodding. "After we get that ten acres plowed and seeded for medicinal herbs that Mary asked Dana to grow, I wanted to do an overnight up on the slope of the mountain where Dana's other fifty acres sits. I'd like to spend a day or two looking around and assessing what she has and how the surrounding land is going to impact her ranch. And I was hoping"—he glanced toward Dana—"that she might want to make an overnight camping trip with me."

Brightening, Dana said, "I love the idea, Colin."

"Good," he murmured, meeting her enthusiastic smile.

Chase pulled his straw hat off, running his fingers through his dark hair, and then settled it back on. "Sooner or later, Dana, you'll have to decide what you want to do with those trees. It's a fine, mature grove. If you started a commonsense plan for cutting some of them, then planting young trees where the mature ones were cut down, you could have another source of income."

Frowning, Dana said, "I honestly haven't given much thought to it, Chase, because we've been so busy here."

"I know," he soothed. "But you need to assess your property as soon as you can. That way, you'll have a full understanding of its income capabilities, and what you might want to do about it."

"Nothing will grow up there on that slope," Colin said, "under shade and trees, that's for sure. The acidity of the needles they drop, really doesn't encourage growth because it makes the soil too acidic."

"I know," Dana said. "And the fifty acres we have available here on the flat will produce enough of what Mary wants for her grocery store, no problem. At least, for now."

"Well," Cari said, her eyes sparkling with excitement, "let's have Chase and Colin get the horses out of the trailer and into one of those beautiful new corrals you've just erected."

Dana was all for that. She tried to pretend she wasn't excited, but she was. Colin and Chase headed to the rear of the trailer and opened the doors, lowering the ramps so the horses could easily walk out. "Come on," she urged Cari. "Let's open the gate to the corral so they can bring them in."

"Good idea," Cari agreed, moving swiftly with her toward the corral.

In no time, as Cari stood by the open gate, the four horses were unloaded and placed into the large ring. Because the corral had inviting, deep sand they all rolled, using it as a way to get rid of bugs. There was a huge aluminum water trough and the animals, one at a time, after their dust bath, walked over and took a good, long drink. Because horses are naturally curious, they each came wandering back to where the humans were standing, just inside the closed gate.

"Now," Chase said, standing next to Dana, "you get first pick, since you're the owner."

Feeling heat move into her cheeks, she gave him a silly, excited grin. "They're all so beautiful!"

"Let me tell you about them," Chase said. The first horse to come over to the group was a blood-bay mare with a black mane, tail, and all four legs up to her knees, the same color. She went directly to Dana.

The horse had a soft, whiskery muzzle as she halted and then gently sniffed Dana's hair and neck.

"This is Gypsy," Chase said. "She's a ten-year-old mare and has worked hard herding cows and carrying our women wranglers where they needed to go. She's a real quiet horse, curious, likes to be around women more than men. Very trail broken, super trail-smart and savvy. She's a patient horse and does what the rider asks of her."

Reaching out, Dana slid her hand along the mare's long, graceful neck, moving her thick black mane aside. "She's beautiful, Chase."

"Sometimes," Colin told her, "a horse will pick you, like Gypsy just did. That's a good sign that she's probably the right horse for you, unless you feel differently."

Nodding, Dana gently pressed her fingers into Gypsy's withers, or shoulder, and the horse half closed her eyes as Dana gently scratched that area. All horses she had ever known, loved massages in that area because it's where the saddle rested. "I love her. My horse, Pattycake, when I was growing up, was a bay color, just like Gypsy is."

Cari came over. "Gypsy, when she was bought by Chase as a two-year-old, was going to be a broodmare. Unfortunately, she had medical problems with her first foal, and her days as a broodmare were over. Chase had one of the women wranglers train her to become a ranch horse after that, and she's excelled at it. Everyone loves Gypsy."

"Gosh," Dana whispered, worried, "how can you part with her, then?"

"Wrangling is hard work on a horse," Chase said. "By the time a horse is ten years old, their knees and legs are pretty much used up. We wanted to take Gypsy off the wrangling line and give her an easier next ten years or so, of her life. Cari thought she might be ideal for you."

Sighing, Dana said, "She's perfect for me! She reminds

me of so many good times growing up on my parents' farm."

"You can use her for riding, or trailing, or anything else you have to do here at your ranch," Chase murmured. "She's trained for ground tie, too, which is really important to wranglers when they're out repairing a fence line."

Rubbing her palm down Gypsy's strong, short back, Dana said, "She's really well conformed, too. Great, straight legs, and that's really important."

"She's half Arabian and half Morgan bloodlines," Chase said. "She's only fourteen-and-a-half hands high, which is why we always used her with women, who weigh less. But she's tough, excels at long-haul demands, and can out-pull any horse on our ranch."

"That's the Morgan in her," Dana guessed.

"Yes," Colin added, "but she is also one of the most intelligent horses they have, so you're lucky to have Gypsy. That's the Arabian blood in her coming out."

"Now," Chase said, "if you don't like her—"

Laughing, Dana said, "Oh! That will *never* happen! Gypsy is so perfect for me in every way. Pattycake was part Arabian, too, and I swear, she could read my mind or intent before I was even conscious of it."

They all chuckled and nodded.

"What about you, Colin? Which horse do you want?" Dana asked.

He pointed to a black horse in the corral. "That's Blackjack. He was my favorite horse over at the ranch. Hardworking, smart, patient, and I could always count on him in tight moments."

"He's a big, beautiful horse," Dana murmured, admiring

the gelding whose coat had a blue sheen to it when the sun's rays were just right.

"Sixteen-and-a-half hands tall," Chase said, "and weighs about thirteen hundred pounds. He's a mix of mostly thoroughbred with a bit of quarter horse blood in him."

"Mostly thoroughbred, though," Colin said wryly. "He can run a mile and not even be breathing hard."

"I suspect," Chase said, "he's probably three-quarters race horse, because I've seen him do some serious hauling speed-wise, when needed."

"Yep," Colin said, grinning. "Thanks for bringing him over for me. I appreciate it."

"We figure you'll be doing a lot of fence mending," Chase said, chuckling.

Dana admired the other two horses. One was a black-and-white paint, a gelding, and the other a beautifully colored palomino with a deep gold coat and cream-colored mane and tail. "Which one is the packhorse, Chase?" she asked.

"Domino, the paint gelding," he said, making a motion toward the heavy-looking animal. "He's part Belgian draft horse and his mama was a pretty paint quarter horse mare. He's fifteen now, and we use him in parts of our ranch where we need heavy wooden posts and other heavy items hauled in to do some work where vehicles can't reach."

Colin looked at Dana. "I used him a lot, along with other wranglers. He's patient, quiet, and just as smart as Gypsy and Blackjack."

"That's wonderful, but do you think we need a packhorse?"

"Well, if we're going to ride up into that fifty acres of timber on that slope of your property, he'll carry our tent, food, and all the other things we need. You'll be glad to have him along."

"Oh . . ." She turned to the palomino, who had come to stand and be with the group. "And what about him? What's his name? He's incredibly beautiful; his coat reminds me of shiny, old gold coins dappled across his barrel."

"We call him Trigger, after Roy Rogers's horse, who was also a palomino. He's a looker. We kinda talked it over," Chase said, glancing warmly at his wife, "that I'll be sending a second wrangler up here to help Colin from time to time. And he would need a horse. Are you okay with that?"

Clapping her hands, Dana said, "Yes! I mean, look how he goes over to be with Gypsy. They must be friends. I wouldn't want them separated."

"Trigger is in love with Gypsy," Cari agreed, smiling warmly. "He kind of looks out for her, but she really doesn't need that kind of protecting."

"He thinks so," Chase said, grinning.

"Typical male," Cari said, giving Dana a humored look.

"I think we all need help, regardless of our gender, from time to time," Dana said. She moved over to where Trigger stood next to the mare. "I think it's nice that they're friends. Gypsy would be lonely without him, don't you think, Cari?"

"I do. Certain horses just like one another, and ever since I came to the ranch, Trigger has always been in the same paddock with Gypsy before they're let out to eat grass in the pasture at night. He's never far from her side, which"—she gave her husband a one-eyebrow-raised look—"is why I insisted we bring Trigger along. Chase felt Gypsy was a good match for you, Dana, but I wasn't going to break up a bond between them, either."

"No," Chase admitted, rubbing his jaw, hiding his grin, "we decided that Trigger could come along if you two were okay with it."

Dana gave Colin a questioning look. "You all right with it?"

Shrugging, he said, "Sure am. There might be a time when Blackjack needs a rest and I can ride Trigger instead. He's fully trained for daily hard work around the ranch."

Satisfied, Dana said, "We'll take all four, Chase. Thanks for doing this for us. You and Cari have been our fairy godmother and godfather since I arrived. I honestly don't know how to ever pay you back for everything you've done for us."

"My mother would skin me alive if I didn't," Chase teased, laughing deeply.

They nodded. Yes, Mary was a force of nature. And Chase bowed to her just as quickly as everyone else did.

Dana sighed, placing her hands against her chest. "This is so wonderful. I'm so happy. This is a dream come true! When I bought the Wildflower, I was wondering how on earth I could afford to keep a horse here. I've been riding since I was three years old, with my mom and dad." Sadness moved through her, but she gently put it aside, no longer trying to hide it from everyone. "I had my own horse, a pretty pinto Shetland named Pattycake, when I was seven years old."

"So," Cari said, impressed, "you really are born to the horse. I'm so glad we could do this for you and Colin."

"Me, too," Dana said. "It's going to be tough to return them to you—"

Cari held up her hand. "These are a gift to you and Colin. We don't want them back."

Mouth falling open and then snapping it shut, Dana stared at the couple. Finally, she found her voice. "Are you *sure*? I was already thinking of how to ask you the price for each of them so that I could set up a budget to pay you back, if you'd let us keep them."

Cari's face softened. "Oh, dear, I wish Chase had made that clear." She gave her partner a significant, slightly chastising look. "I thought you already knew they were a gift from us to you."

"No . . . I didn't know that."

Colin cleared his throat. "That's my bad, Dana. Chase *did* tell me in an earlier phone call that they were a gift from them to you." His voice lowered. "I'm sorry, I forgot to tell you."

Dana nodded and reached out, squeezing his hand and then releasing it. She looked at the couple. "Things have been pretty rugged around here the last few days, so it's okay, Colin. I understand." Her hand tingled when she'd squeezed his large, work-worn one, the calluses across his palm sending tiny tingles through her hand.

"Hey," Chase murmured, "it's all okay. We're on the same page now, so let's just move forward? I'm having one of my wranglers bring up enough hay to fill your barn. He and Colin can move it from the truck into the barn, later today."

Tears came to Dana's eyes and she rushed forward, throwing her arms around Chase's broad shoulders and Cari's thin ones, hugging them fiercely. "Th-thank you . . . I feel I'm in some kind of wonderful fairy tale, where only good things happen to people!" She released them, stepping back.

Cari pulled a tissue from the pocket of her jeans, holding it out to her. Dana thanked her and wiped her eyes.

Chase said, "Colin? Help me get the ramps and trailer shut up so we can leave?"

Dana watched as the two men returned to the rear of the four-horse trailer. She looked over at Cari. "I've been meaning to call you or have lunch, and talk to you about how many beehives you'd like to have up here."

Reaching out, Cari patted her shoulder. "As soon as you have a diagram of what you're planting, and how large the area is, I'll drive up and we'll throw our leg over the horses and go out and see where the hives could be delivered and set up."

"That's the least we can do for you," Dana said, sniffing, wiping her eyes one last time, tucking the damp tissue into her jeans pocket.

"You'll get a lot more blossoms and produce this way," Cari said. "That will make you and Mary very happy." She smiled gently over at her.

Rubbing her face, Dana heard the ramp being pushed back beneath the trailer frame. "Wow . . . so many good things . . ."

"Hey, do you realize you're using the words *we* and *us*, instead of *I* or *me*?" Cari held Dana's gaze.

"Oh . . . no, I didn't." She saw a smile come to Cari's lips.

"Are you falling for Colin?" she asked in a low tone.

Blinking, Dana tried to think clearly. "Well . . . yes . . .

I mean, we live together in the same home and we're working together all day."

Cari slid her hand across Dana's shoulder. "I know that. But I feel or sense something good between you and Colin. Am I wrong?"

When Dana first met Cari, she had automatically trusted her and loved being in her company, which wasn't as often as she wished it could be. "I guess we just rub off on one another," she admitted softly, making sure the two men were not coming from around the trailer. This wasn't something she wanted to be overheard. "Lately, we seem to have gone to another level with one another. I mean . . . it happened naturally. I'm not thinking about a relationship and he isn't either, Cari."

"Hmmm, okay. Well, it would be kind of natural since you live and work in close confines with one another. And he's a very likeable guy. Chase misses him."

"He's got so many loads he's carrying," Dana admitted, pain coming into her heart over it. "We're both broken. Terribly broken, Cari. But somehow, we seem to help and support one another, despite those things. I see it as both of us having the glue to help put the broken shards in each of us together again."

"We're all broken," Cari whispered sympathetically, her hand on Dana's upper arm. "You aren't alone. And we're here for both of you. You know that, don't you?"

"You've very clearly shown us that."

"I mean . . . more on a personal level. I'm here to listen if you need someone to talk with in the future, Dana."

"Thanks," she said, seeing Chase and Colin emerging

from around the trailer. "I think Chase is ready to go. I will be in touch with you. Okay?"

"Good," Cari said, giving her a hug and then stepping away. "Enjoy your horses."

May 21

"Are you ready?" Colin asked Dana as they mounted their horses. He had used their four-horse trailer, loaded up Gypsy and Blackjack, and drove them to the end of the first fifty acres and where the slope of woods began.

The day was cool and the sky was brooding. There had been a brief, pink color on the eastern horizon announcing dawn earlier. Dana had checked the weather and by early afternoon, they were supposed to get rain through the area. Glancing at his watch, Colin saw it was seven a.m. They had plenty of time to scour the woods and get a feel for the area.

"Ready," Dana said, pulling on her warm, lined gloves. Colin had saddled and bridled the horses earlier, before loading them. She took the reins of Gypsy, who looked eager to be released from a box stall and out on the open land once more. Blackjack was antsy and she smiled, watching Colin easily step into the stirrup and mount his horse. She mounted up, and swung Gypsy around toward the slope.

The wind was coming and going, some gusts with it, but the horses didn't react to it, moving out at a good, long striding walk, side by side. Colin liked that sometimes, due to the narrowness of the trail leading up into the grove, his boot would brush against Dana's boot. She looked beautiful to him, her black baseball cap over her hair, and over that a bright red knit cap that came down over her ears to protect them from the chill. This morning, she wore a sheepskin vest beneath her nylon coat that protected her hips as well. He was used to this kind of cold and it was clear she was not. Oregon was a lot different than Wyoming, that was for sure.

All he had was a dark green goose-down vest with a thick Levi's jacket over it. His elk-skin gloves felt good, however, because he knew as this front continued toward them, the temperature was going to drop even more. He wouldn't be surprised if there was sleet at the altitude that they'd be climbing up to: six thousand feet. Dana's land was a long, rectangular-shaped area and it went from the floor of the valley and up to the top that they could see from a distance.

"What kind of trees are these?" she wondered as they began up the slope, up a narrow trail that looked as if wild animals routinely utilized it.

Lifting his butt off the cantle of the saddle, to take weight off Blackjack's hindquarters as they moved upward, Colin said, "All Douglas fir from what I can see." He pointed to the left. "Fifty acres is roughly four-fifths of a square mile," he told her. "Your land is very long and rectangular and narrow on the sides."

"I was studying a map of the area," Dana said. She looked up. The boughs of the mighty Douglas firs pro- vided shade but also protection against the gusty wind, the tops singing around them. "It's a narrow strip, for sure."

"Right," he said, resting his right hand on his thigh, looking around. "Someone planted these so that the trees could grow up straight and have enough room to spread

out. These trees look to be about seventy-five years old."
He pointed around at the many stumps in the area. "I think
the family who owned this before had started logging the
area and then replanted it, which is good land manage-
ment."

"I found out from Mary that the people who used to
own this ranch had cut the trees down once they reached
maturity and sold the lumber locally. For them, it was a
cash egg in their basket."

"Back at the turn of the twentieth century, there was a
silver rush in the nearby mountains," Colin said. "Wood
for tunnels was in short supply. That's how Chase's family
made a lot of money over time. They planted many different kinds of hardwood trees and later sold the lumber
to the mining companies." He saw her looking around,
assessing the area. Up ahead, he heard a blue jay squawk-
ing. Probably spotted them or heard them talking and
sounded the alarm.

"I was thinking a lot about this, Colin." She pulled
Gypsy to a stop, halfway up the slope. He pulled Blackjack to a halt and joined her.

"What ideas do you have for this?" he wondered, the
saddle creaking as he moved his weight a bit.

"Well," she murmured, "I'm not really interested in
growing trees for lumber."

"Then, cut it and sell it off?"

"I was thinking along those lines. But I want to use the
land. I don't want this slope to lose its stability because
that's what tree roots do: They hold the soil in place."

"Good thinking," he praised. "If this was cleared?
What would you do with it, Dana?"

"Mary said she's looking for a woman who's an herbalist to become part of the valley. Remember she talked about it that evening we had dinner with Chase and his family? She said Logan and Chase both raise some herbs, but she wants to make Silver Creek Valley a mecca for herbs and herbalists. She's even got ideas for putting up a building that would have classrooms, and a dormitory so that people could come here and study medicinal herbs and start bringing this way of living back into the present day."

"She has you planting a lot of herbs on your lower fifty," Colin noted.

"Yes, but not all herbs grow at lower levels. Others need different elevations in order to thrive. She showed me a list of bushes and other perennial as well as annual herbs that do well at these different altitudes. The bushes would sink deep roots, along with perennial herbs, and keep the soil from washing down this slope. We could stabilize it if wc remove the trees."

"Hmmm," he murmured, looking around. "Something like that could work here."

"She's given me a list," Dana said, "and I'll show it to you when we get back to the main ranch area."

"I'd like to see it." He gave her a grin. "I know next to nothing about herbs and herbalism."

"My mom," she said, "always raised culinary herbs. She knew how to use them in cooking, but I had them used on me, medicinally, growing up, too. For instance, she always had a big patch of yellow and orange calendula flowers growing in one part of our huge garden. When I got scrapes, burns, or bruises, she would make an ointment out of the flowers and put it on my injury. It always helped."

"Nice," he said. "It sounds like Mary has another prong of her business plan she's ready to initiate."

When Dana ran her hand down Gypsy's sleek neck, the horse's ears moved back and forth appreciatively. She added, "Mary called me a few days ago and I forgot to share it with you, Colin. She asked what I thought of having the herb school located in the main area of the ranch, along with a dormitory, which she would pay for to be built on my property."

"How many people would come to one of these courses?"

"She said up to twenty-five."

Whistling, he shook his head. "That means twenty-five cars. Where will they park? That would entail the use of a chunk of your land to make it happen."

"I know." She frowned. "I'm not keen on it, Colin. I told her I'd think about it and I was going to pull you into the loop to see what you thought."

"Wildflower is a dream come true for you," he said. "Does Mary share your dream, too?"

She appreciated his insight. Shaking her head, she said, "Not really. I don't mind raising vegetable and fruit tree crops for her store. But I needed a place like this, that is out of the way, lodged in nature, a place where I can try to retreat and heal from the past."

He reached out, squeezing her hand that rested on her thigh. "Good. I think it's a good dream for you. Maybe not for Mary. There's plenty of land for sale around here. She could easily buy it and put her school into reality on another plot. I don't think she'd be upset if you said no."

"So? You agree with me? That how I'm working with her right now is a good plan?"

"Yes, because it's in alignment with what you need in order to be happy, Dana. I don't think a school facility and dorm is going to make you feel calm and peaceful. People would be coming and going, there would be a lot of noise, and the pollution of the vehicles adding to it."

"It's not for you, either," she noted. An ache was building inside her. Every time Colin met her gaze, her heart melted a little more. She felt safe allowing him into her personal life.

"No," he said, shrugging, "I do better without a lot of people around due to my PTSD."

"I agree with you."

"So," he said, turning and looking up the slope, "would you want to take Mary up on planting medicinal herbs if this area was cleared?"

"I'm not sure yet, Colin. I need to do a lot more research on the land itself, the type of soil it is, and what would or would not grow in it, or deal with the four seasons we have here. I need to talk to the county extension agent about the possibilities for this slope. Right now, I'm just gathering info."

"Good plan. You know? You could still have a few of these firs left in place, maybe groups strategically located here and there, to be the anchor for this slope and soil."

She studied the area, loving the sighing sound of wind through the trees surrounding them. "That's a great idea. I hadn't thought of it."

"Aren't there some plants that are partial shade or shade types that would do well in that kind of condition?"

"I think so. But again, I'm not a botanist or an herbalist, and I need to study her list. I need to get ahold of the county people, to find out the type of soil we have around here."

"I've heard Chase and Logan extoll the soil in the valley, but I don't know if it's the same up here on this slope." He gestured upward.

"Let's keep going. I want to see the top of this hill," she said, urging Gypsy forward. The horses were fresh and trotted upward, side by side. The scent of the fir mixed with the scent of the horses made Dana smile broadly. It felt so good to be riding a horse once again! As they crested the area, coming out of the woods, the top of the hill was lush with ankle-deep green grass.

"Ohhh," Dana whispered, pulling Gypsy to a stop, allowing the reins to drop so she could eat the grass, "this is gorgeous!" Below them was a small, round lake, dark blue, half of it ruffled by the wind, the other half glass smooth. On either side of the slope where they were, it was nothing but grass, some bushes and colorful wild-flowers just beginning to bloom here and there.

Colin frowned and moved his horse over to where she was. "What's all these tire tracks?" he asked, pointing down at them. The tracks were along the top of the huge mountain that extended a mile toward the main highway in the valley.

"I don't know," she said, looking at them for the first time. There were ruts that the plants had grown over, but one could still see them.

Dismounting, Colin dropped the reins and Blackjack remained where he was, happily eating the thick, juicy grass. Moving past Dana and her horse, he walked a bit farther, following the two sets of tracks.

In one spot, the area was somewhat bare of grass and

he knelt down, pushing the grass aside, studying the tire treads in the soil. "Looks like ATVs," he muttered. "Two or three of them." He stood, glancing back toward Dana. "Those tracks stop and then make a left, going down through your land," he said, pointing.

Frowning, Dana looked, and sure enough, what Colin saw was correct. "This is US Forest Service land up here and for as far as we can see. Do they allow ATV trail riding around here?"

"Not that I know of." He took out his cell phone and took a number of pictures where the tire tracks came from and where they went to the left onto Dana's property. "We can call the ranger station and find out. In some places, in other state parks, sometimes ATV riding trails are allowed, but your land is private and they shouldn't be on it at all."

"Can you tell how long ago?" she asked hopefully, watching him walk to where the tracks came up the slope.

"No. They're not real fresh, but I'd guess it was maybe April when this happened." He leaned down, touching the grass that was not standing up straight, but growing at angles where the treads had run over the plants.

"April? This year?"

"Yes," he said, straightening. He held up his cell phone. "I'm going to download these photos, plus I got some really good tire tread tracks in the mud back there. Try and see if I can match the ATV type that's doing this."

"Maybe hunters?"

"It's not hunting season. And if they're caught, the game warden for the county will come down on them hard. They won't do it again, with a big fine being slapped on them. Even jail time, possibly." He picked up

Blackjack's reins and brought them over the horse's head and neck, mounting up.

"That's curious," Dana said. "Because when I first went out to the Wildflower Ranch, there were tracks somewhat like these, leading across the fifty acres, into where we have the mobile home and barn, and leading toward the only road in and out of our place that connects with the main highway."

"Those are long gone by now," he said. "I really didn't notice them, but then, I was bringing in a big rig, and those tires probably destroyed any chance of ever seeing them again."

"Probably so," Dana agreed. She sighed and smiled. "It's so beautiful up here. "

Glancing up at the sky, which was now a gunmetal gray and the clouds were lowering more, Colin said, "I think this front is moving in a lot faster than we thought. It looks like it's going to rain soon, and we'll get wet if we don't make our way down the slope to the trailer."

Dana agreed. They rode back into the grove of firs, swallowed up by the shadows, much darker riding through them than before. "I don't really want to get rained on," she muttered, giving him a grin.

"Me either. Maybe we should make some hot chocolate with melted marshmallows once we reach the ranch?"

"That sounds good," she agreed. "I like making the hot chocolate when it's chilly, damp, and windy like this."

"Let's just hope we can get our horses loaded up and out of here. We still need to lay a lot more gravel on that new dirt road to make it mud-proof for heavier trucks and a tractor."

As if the horses sensed a bit of urgency, they walked

quickly down through the grove and out onto the flat of the land, heading right for the trailer. The wind gusts were thirty or forty miles an hour now and Dana pulled her knit cap tightly down to cover her ears. When they dismounted and Colin took the horses into the trailer, she felt the first drops of rain. Going to the cab, she sat in the passenger seat. She was still learning the muddy conditions of this new road and didn't trust herself with a four-horse trailer on it. She trusted Colin.

"Okay," he said, moving into the cab. "Let's go! I want to beat this rain before we sink to our axles in mud."

"Hot chocolate, here we come." She laughed. It was an excuse to spend a bit of personal time with him. With the rain coming for half a day or so as it crossed the valley, they would both be stuck inside. It was a warming thought to her.

Colin laughed with her, putting the truck in gear and slowly moving forward, not wanting to jerk or jostle their horses around in the trailer. "It's sounding mighty good," he agreed, giving her a quick glance. "Lots of marshmallows . . ."

Chapter 8

May 22

It was a chilly rain with gusting winds the next morning as Dana made her way out to the old cabin. Colin had just finished feeding the horses, each having a box stall in the barn to keep them warm and dry. She wore her knit cap over her baseball cap, keeping to the gravel pathway that another wrangler, with Colin's help, had created to the cabin.

It was only eight a.m. and the sky was low, gray, and it reminded her of home, in Oregon, where there were many days in a row like this one. Pulling her rainproof jacket a little tighter around herself, she hurried along the gravel, the crunching mingling with the fairly heavy drops of rain. This was not a day to do any plowing or other field work. It would take three days for the field that needed to be plowed, to dry out enough so that the tractor wouldn't get trapped in muddy furrows made by the plow. They were still ahead of schedule on the planting of that field, so she didn't worry about it too much.

She loved that cabin, no matter how beat-up-looking

or how old it was. For Dana, it reminded her of a simpler time when humans moved with the seasons, not a clock on a computer telling her the next appointment she had to make. In many ways, she wished she could live back in that era, wanting not to get entrapped in the hurry, hurry, hurry, and the high-stress world that people lived in nowadays.

Opening the cabin's creaking front door, she was glad that Colin had, early on, put up plastic on the outside of the windows, to stop rain or snow from coming into the interior.

Stepping inside, she moved toward an electric cord that he had wrapped, strung, and brought inside the building so they could have some light, when needed. Right now, they were working on the plaster between the logs. Dana had wanted to start sizing up the work it would take to make the cabin livable. She had begun the process of taking notes and photos. Barn-builder Charley Swanson had already contacted them and made an appointment in mid-June to discuss what she wanted and what would or would not be possible to do to make the cabin livable once more. He had two other log cabin projects ahead of hers, but that wasn't going to stop her from nosing around.

This morning, she wanted to closely check out the flooring and look for wood rot along the windowsills. These were all things she wanted to take notes on to make a list for when Charley could come out and size up the job of saving this old cabin. She was sure he would find other things, as well.

The wood creaked badly beneath her boots as she

aimed herself at the light switch situated at the other end of the cabin. Suddenly, there was a loud *CRAAACK!*

Dana felt her right foot crash through the floorboard and it gave way without warning. In seconds, she found herself slamming into the floor, the air woofing out of her lungs. Her right boot had broken the board in half and was now lodged beneath it. Grunting, unhappy, the light grayish and hard to see by, she sat up, scowling. Her boot lay on something she couldn't see because it was jammed down below the break. Righting herself, she sat up and scooted forward. What was beneath her boot? It gave way when she wriggled it, whatever it was. Brows dipping down, she yanked and pulled away some of the jagged, broken pieces around her foot, trying to see what on earth the heel of her boot was resting on. It sure wasn't dirt! What then? A dead animal? Ugh! She hoped not! All the more reason to get her foot released!

Wrapping her hands around her ankle, she used her weight and strength to dislodge the boot. More wood cracked and broke as she pulled it out of there. Her ankle ached, but it wasn't major. Rolling onto her hands and knees, she wanted to see what was under the broken board. Unwilling to shove her gloved hand into the dark space, she got up and walked over to the light switch. Colin had strung five light bulbs across one end of the cabin. Wincing at the sudden light, she was careful not to walk on that same plank that had just broken. Circling it, she got down on her knees and peered into the darkness. It was gray. *What* was it?

She tentatively reached in with her gloves on, glad it wasn't the fur of some dead animal that had been trapped beneath the floorboards while hunting mice. Her fingertips lightly brushed a tough-feeling fabric.

Scowling, she inched closer, realizing that whatever it was, it wasn't an animal, nor was it alive. She placed her hand over it. It appeared to be a huge canvas bag of some sort. Pushing on it, she felt lumps of something contained within it. Glad it wasn't an animal, she positioned herself and pulled at it. Grudgingly, the long canvas bag eventually came out of the hole she'd made in the floor.

What was this? She rolled it away from the break in the floor. It looked a little like a modern-day gym bag, no writing on it, but it reminded her of one. There was a padlock on one end, a brown leather strip that could be closed and opened. Poking at the fabric, it felt fairly new, not something ancient. There was no sign the fabric was rotted or torn. Sitting up, she pulled out the Buck knife from the sheath around her leather belt. Pointing the tip beneath the leather, Dana used the knife to rip the bag open.

Gasping, her eyes widening, the knife froze in her hand as she stared down at what she saw. It was hundred-dollar bills all wrapped up neatly. So many, she couldn't count them all. The four-foot canvas bag was swollen with batches of bills ranging from five, ten, twenty, fifty dollars, plus one-hundred packaged bills. The more she pulled out from the bag, the more shocked she felt. *Who* had put this money down below the board of this cabin? *Why? When?*

Her mind reeled as she put all the cash on another floorboard. The bag looked almost new. The family that had lived here for generations before her had not put this here, that was for sure. So? Who?

She stood up and pulled the cell phone out of her

jacket pocket, calling Colin. He was over at Chase's ranch picking up some bags of grain for the horses after he'd fed them earlier in the morning. Going to the door, she pushed it open into the gray, rainy morning, hoping for better cell connection.

"Dana?"

"Yes. Hey, are you coming back here soon?"

"I just loaded up five hundred pounds of grain and oats to be stored out in the barn for the horses. Why? You sound worried."

Grimacing, she said, "I've discovered something in the log cabin. Can you come home now?"

"What's wrong?"

"Nothing . . . I don't think. I'm fine, Colin. Everything's okay around here. I just discovered something and I need your eyes on it."

"Well . . . okay . . . I'll be there in about fifteen minutes. Are you in the cabin?"

"Yes, but I'm going back into the house where it's warmer. I need you out here to look at something I just discovered."

Dana could hear real concern in his voice and she wasn't sure she wanted to tell him what she'd discovered over the phone. She trusted him completely and wanted to discuss what she'd found once he'd gotten here, first.

"I won't be long," he promised, hanging up.

Turning, Dana went back over to where she'd placed all the stacks of bills. How much was there? She had no idea. Had the canvas bag been there before she bought the place? Afterward? Someone was hiding something. Her skin crawled and she looked toward the open door, realizing it was the only entrance/exit point of the cabin.

Feeling dread and not knowing why, she left the cabin and shut the door, heading to the mobile home.

The rain had let up and now her mind whirled with so many questions. Why did she feel a threat around this bag of money? There was no reason for that feeling. Or was there? Glancing at the wall clock once she got inside the mudroom, she removed her damp coat, hanging it up.

She felt suddenly vulnerable, and Dana hated that feeling. She paced the living room, glancing out the window to see if Colin was turning into the ranch yet. Another part of her, the one that was on silent guard, glanced toward the cabin. Her mind was taking imaginative flight, and that wasn't good. Trying to shut it down, she poured herself a cup of coffee. Why this reaction? Right now, she felt like she was a target of some kind and no explanation for it. How she wished Colin were here!

Finally, she saw Colin making the turn at the large, open gate. Hurrying to the mudroom, she threw on her coat, hat, and knit cap, meeting him as he came out of the truck, a worried look in his expression.

"Hey," he called. "What's up?"

She met him at the door to the truck. "I found something, Colin. I can't explain it." She gripped his gloved hand. "Come with me." She saw confusion in his eyes, his mouth set, and that told her he was uneasy. Was he feeling it, too?

At the door to the cabin, she dropped Colin's hand and opened the door. "Go in . . ."

As he stepped in, he anchored to a halt. Dana almost ran into him.

"What's this?" he demanded, moving aside to allow her past him.

Breathless, she closed the door and told him. When she finished, she added, "I'm scared, Colin, and I don't know why."

He took her hand and squeezed it. "We're okay. Let me look at all this . . ."

She followed him and he took care not to step on that floorboard, either. Kneeling down next to the broken area, he perused the stacks of bills she'd laid out. The gray bag was opposite of where he knelt.

"Did you touch that padlock or opening?" he asked her as she came and knelt at his side.

"No. Why?"

"Don't touch it. There might be fingerprints or DNA on it."

"Oh . . ." she whispered, giving him a worried look. "Who owns this money, Colin?"

He sat up, hands on his thighs. "I don't know, but that bag looks pretty modern to me. It's a money bag, the kind the bank has, would be my guess."

"Oh . . ." she said again, more dread in her tone.

Looking around, he said, "I'd like to know when this happened."

Pointing to where the board broke, she said, "It appears someone sawed it." She pointed about a foot away from where the board had broken. "I noticed it after I fell through the floor. The wood just gave way."

"Did you hurt yourself?" he asked.

"My ankle's a little tender, but it's no big deal."

"Did you touch that money with your hands?"

"No, I had my gloves on."

"Good," he breathed. "We're not touching it again." He leaned down after taking a small flashlight from the pocket of his Levi's. Flashing it down beneath the broken opening, he peered both ways.

"Whoa," he muttered.

"What?" Her voice went high and scratchy.

"There's another bag to my left, Dana. Maybe more. I don't know . . ." He got up and handed her the penlight. "Take a look."

She got down and peered beneath the floorboard. Sure enough, there was another bag stuffed in there. "Oh, my God, Colin," she managed, sitting up, handing him the penlight. "What does this mean? Who put this here? Was it done while we were here? Or before I bought the place?"

He stood and offered his hand to her. "All good questions," he said, gripping her hand and helping her stand.

"What should we do?"

"I'm calling Sheriff Dan Seabert. He's got to see this, and I'm sure he'll bring along the forensics team to take over the investigation. What we need to do is get out of here and not make a mess of possible DNA or fingerprints. Come on, I'll call him once we get to the house."

Dana was glad to get out of the cabin. There was an air of tension, but also that feeling of threat that scared her. They shucked out of their coats and hats and went to the kitchen, where Colin made the call from the nearby wall phone, their only landline. She poured him a cup of coffee and another for herself, sitting down at the table, cupping the mug, a deep frown on her brow.

"Dan's coming out right away. He's bringing his forensics team," Colin said, hanging up.

"Did he say anything? What it might be? Or who?"

Shaking his head, he sipped the coffee. "No. They aren't

going to know anything for a while, Dana. I do want us out there when they lift that broken board completely out of the floor. There could be more than two bags stashed down in there. We just don't know, yet." He studied her. "You look pretty pale. What's going on?"

"I feel threatened and I don't know why."

"Finding something like that would be unsettling to anyone."

"I guess," she said, wrapping her hands around the mug, warming her hands. "I've got so many questions and no answers. It appears to me that someone hid them there for a purpose."

"And judging from the fabric on that bag, this wasn't done too long ago."

"I guess that's what has me scared. Whoever put it there? They're bound to come back to get it."

Shaking his head, he muttered, "This isn't good. A criminal would do this. Not some upstanding person. They'd put that money into the bank, not hide it under floorboards."

"I was thinking that, too. Has there been a bank robbery here in Silver Creek?"

"None that I'm aware of."

"I remember the first day I came out here to look at the property. As I told you, I noticed a lot of tread tracks that led up to and away from the cabin. And they either came or left by the main road because I followed them out to the gate that leads to the highway."

He rubbed his chin, his dark brows dipping. "Remember those tread marks up on the top of the hill that we rode up yesterday?"

"Yes?" Her throat tightened. "Could those be the same person or people?"

"I don't know. I have photos of those tracks. We need to give all this intel to Dan when he arrives. They're puzzle pieces and they may or may not fit into a larger pattern of what has happened in that cabin."

She sat back in the chair, sliding her arms around herself. "I just have a really bad feeling about this, Colin." She glanced at him to see if he believed her or not.

"My reaction isn't any better than yours. This smacks of criminal behavior."

"What bothers me, if this is true? That person, or people, are bound to come back here to get it. And I don't feel safe at all about that . . ."

Colin remembered starkly that her parents had been murdered out of the blue, wrong place, wrong time, the police had told Dana. He reached over and placed his hand over hers. "Listen, I'm here. Nothing's going to happen to you." The fear shadowing in her large, beautiful eyes, bothered him greatly. "What would make you feel safe again?"

"For Sheriff Seabert to tell me that those bags out there weren't placed there because of criminal intent."

"Well, we should know something fairly soon," he murmured, feeling how cool her fingers were. "They can run the numbers on those bills and tell which bank, and in which state, they came from."

"That would be wonderful," she murmured.

"It's a trail, and I'm sure Dan will follow it."

"Will he take all that money with him?"

"I'm sure he will."

Dana rolled her eyes. "I never even thought to look for

another one, Colin." She managed a half, strained laugh. "Some detective I'd make!"

"Dan will be here any minute, now." That seemed to soothe her a little bit. Colin didn't really understand the depth of the terror he'd seen in her eyes earlier when she'd realized this was a criminal activity that she'd literally fallen into. More than anything? He wanted to hold her. To make her feel safe. But when Dan arrived, this place was going to be, he would bet, a crime scene. And then, how would Dana react to it?

Dana led Sheriff Dan Seabert and Sergeant Pepper Warner, plus a two-woman forensics team, into the log cabin. The rain had stopped, thankfully, and the wind had died down as she reached to open the door for them. Dan stopped her.

"We need to see if there's fingerprints on this door," he cautioned, releasing her gloved hand.

"Oh . . ." Dana felt the flush of embarrassment sliding up into her cheeks. Colin came and stood at her side.

"We'll stay out here until you look around or need us," he told Dan.

"We will, for sure." Dan gave his forensics team the lead. Both he and his sergeant stepped back.

"I wish I knew more about things like this," Dana apologized.

"Don't worry about it," the sheriff told her. "You were just being kind enough to open the door for us."

Grimacing, Dana muttered, "Oh, sure. Wipe out the fingerprints of whoever did this."

Dan grinned. He was in his sheriff's uniform, a warm

black nylon jacket over it, wearing his black baseball cap with SHERIFF on the front of it. "You can help," he told her, gesturing around the outside of the cabin. "First, I want my team to check for anyone's footprints."

"I'm sure you'll find mine," Dana said.

"Mine, too," Colin added.

"We'll take photos and show them to you. If they match," Pepper said, "we know it's you and not someone else. Has there been anyone else out here since the last rain?"

Dana shook her head. "No. Colin and a Three Bars wrangler laid the gravel pathway about a month ago, but it only leads to the front door."

Dan nodded, peering at the mud and weeds around the outside perimeter of the cabin. "We need to try and establish a time when this occurred, if we can."

"Would you like some coffee? Anything to eat?" Dana wanted to help them in small ways if she could.

"Tell you what," Dan said. "You go on into your home and wait for us there. This will take about an hour. Pepper and I packed some sandwiches before we left."

"Would you join us for lunch, then?" Dana asked.

"That would be nice," Dan said.

"We both like black coffee," Pepper added with a knowing grin toward her boss.

"Done deal," Dana said, happy she could be of some assistance.

"Dana just made a cherry pie," Colin added, a sparkle in his eye.

"Ohhhhh," Dan murmured, giving Dana a pleased look. "Maybe we could beg a piece of it after lunch?"

"You sure could." Dana laughed.

"Great," Dan said. "We're lookin' forward to some home-cooked dessert."

Colin walked her back to the house. "It will be at least an hour," he told her.

He moved ahead, taking the stairs and opening the door for her. Dana thanked him and she shrugged out of her coat and hung it up in the mud porch, as did Colin. Inside, it was warm, the chill of the rainy May morning dissolving.

"My mind is going in all kinds of directions," she told Colin, getting dessert plates from the cupboard for the pie.

He poured them coffee and took it over to the kitchen table. "Mine, too. If this is recent? That's really disturbing."

"My gut is in knots," she admitted, sitting down at his elbow, taking the cup of coffee he slid in her direction.

"Until Dan finds something, it's anyone's guess, Dana." He reached out and squeezed her hand gently. "Is this bringing up your past?"

Sighing, she whispered, "Yes . . . yes, it is."

He lifted his hand away. "Do you feel like sharing it with me?"

Giving him a dark look, she managed, "Let's wait and see what Dan finds out. I've always had an overactive imagination, and many times, it's just that."

Dan and Pepper came in to share lunch with them an hour later. Colin had made Dana and himself grilled cheese sandwiches, along with butter pickles and potato chips. They all sat down and Dana delivered the hot, steaming coffee to all of them.

Dan unwrapped his beef sandwich and said, "We opened up that floorboard, Dana, and we found three other large canvas pouches under it. But they weren't from a bank that we could tell. Just the first one you found."

Gasping, Dana whispered, "Oh . . ."

"Four in total?" Colin said. He glanced across the table at Dana. She looked uneasy.

"Yes. And my forensics team has found some fingerprints on them, so that's a good sign," Dan assured them.

"And someone had worked to erase the name of the bank that had been stenciled on the one you discovered first," Pepper added.

"We think," Dan said between bites, "that we can lift the erased name."

"So? These are from a bank?" Dana guessed.

"Or banks," Pepper added. "We won't know until the team gets back to our lab and performs the testing needed to see if the name or names start to come up."

"Sounds like someone hit a cash transport van?" Colin asked them.

Nodding, Dan said, "That's possible, too."

"Did you have any bank robberies in the valley?" Dana asked them.

"None," Pepper said.

"What a mess," Dana muttered, shaking her head. "I'm glad you'll take all of them with you. I'm really upset that it's on my property."

"I would be, too," Pepper said sympathetically. She reached into the large bowl of chips and took a few of them to go with her sandwich.

"What I'm most concerned with," Colin said to the

sheriff, "is that whoever put them there will come back, sooner or later, to retrieve them. That leaves us vulnerable."

Dan traded a glance with Dana. "On the top of our list is to find out the who, what, where, when, and why, and get that information back to you."

"How long?"

Shrugging, he said, "Depends a lot on what our team finds."

"With fingerprints?" Dana pressed. "What will you do with them?"

"We'll run them through our databases," Pepper assured her. "It will be national, not just here in Wyoming. My job, once we get back to HQ, is to find the numbers on those bills and locate the bank or banks they came from. If there was a bank robbery, they'll let us know. We don't really have the kind of far-ranging facility that is needed to dig deep into these bills, but we'll get enough information in order to know what to do next."

"Dana and I rode up to the fifty acres on that hill at the end of her property," Colin told them. He gave the details and pulled out his cell phone, showing them the treads and track photos he'd taken. Instantly, Dan's eyes narrowed and he studied them, his mouth thinning.

Pepper handed Colin her card. "Can you send me copies here, to my email at the HQ?"

"You bet," Colin said.

"I'm more interested in those tracks you said that seemed to stop where Dana's property was located. Even though that is USFS property up beyond her land, they have certain ATV trails where these vehicles can go."

"And," Pepper said, "there's no trails on this side of the

highway. All the ATV trails are assigned between two ranches, and they go up into the mountains along certain routes they must stay on."

Frowning, Dana asked, "How much ATV tourist traffic do you get here in the valley?"

"Quite a bit," Dan said, "June through October."

"And even though it snows in the higher elevations," Pepper added, "the USFS does not allow any vehicles or snowmobiles into the area where your property adjoins it."

"The county has made this valley pristine, and the people don't want that kind of activity in the mountains, tearing things up, the noise and pollution, as well as scaring the wildlife," Dan said.

"That's good," Dana said. "But what do you think about those tracks up there on the hill next to my property?"

"Could be something as simple as avid ATV people seeing this ranch was sitting empty, came in here next to that cabin, off-loaded their ATVs, and used the land as well as that slope and running them back toward the highway."

"We need to check that out," Colin said. "That one photo I took shows the tracks heading toward the highway, but we didn't follow it down to verify that."

"I'm going to ask Pepper to come out tomorrow and maybe she can borrow one of your mounts. Either of you could take her up there to check it out more closely."

"I think Colin and I would both like to go with you. We have Trigger, the palomino, that you could use, Pepper. We have all the tack, so just bring yourself."

"Sounds good," she said, nodding.

"When I first came here, there were lots of tire tracks in and out of the road leading up to this area, Dan. All of it has been destroyed by now, but I saw a lot of signs of vehicle activity."

"That puts more weight on ATV riders stopping and using the ranch," he agreed, typing in a text to his office. "If this money is tied to a bank heist or several of them, and we get more info, there's a good chance I'll call in the US Forest Service people on this issue and widen the investigation."

"They would know more about ATV activity," Colin guessed.

"Yes, and they keep tabs on ATV users who break the law, a list of names, license plates, and addresses. That might be of help to us if the investigation curves in that direction. Right now, we have lots of theories and few facts."

Dana frowned. "Do you think we should stay here, Dan? I'll admit, I'm spooked." She had not told them why and wasn't about to bring it up. It had nothing to do with what was going on at her ranch right now.

Looking around, Dan said, "I haven't seen a dog around. Do you have one?"

"No," she said, giving Colin a look, "but do you think we should get one?"

"Dogs are the best alarms in the world," Dan added.

"I think we'll get one," Dana said grimly. "I won't sleep at night without one. I'll jerk awake, wondering if someone is skulking around outside our home."

"It's a good idea," Colin said. "I have a few leads on people who might have a dog they could sell to you, or give to you."

"Heck," Pepper said, "we're retiring our drug-sniffing yellow Lab, Bandit, today. That's rather serendipitous. We were going to start looking for a nice home for him. He's ten years old, smart as a whip, and loves people. Might you be interested in coming down to see him, Dana? He's totally trained and so loving."

"Would he bark if he heard someone around our house?"

"Sure would," Pepper said.

"I think that's a great idea," Dan seconded. "Why not come down tomorrow morning, around ten a.m.? He's out at our kennel at HQ. If you like him? You get along with him? Take him home with you."

"Don't you want some money for him if I like him?"

"Naw," he said, wiping his hands on a paper napkin. "We just want Bandit to have a loving home, is all. Money can't buy that."

"Sounds good," Dana whispered, suddenly feeling a little less threatened. "We always had dogs growing up. And I'd been thinking of getting one for the ranch, anyways."

"Well," Dan said, grinning, "here's your opportunity, Dana." He rose and so did Pepper. "We need to go back to work. If I find out anything before we leave, I'll let you know. Pepper is going to put yellow tape around the cabin and it's designed to keep everyone out."

"That's a good idea," Dana agreed. She glanced over at Colin, who also seemed to be relieved that they might be getting a dog. Fear gnawed away at her gut. Why?

Chapter 9

May 23

The morning was sunny and bright, the cold front having passed silently across Silver Creek Valley during the night. Colin could feel the tension in Dana as they drove to the sheriff's office to visit the kennel and meet Bandit, their retiring drug-sniffing dog. Would he be a good fit for Dana? He wasn't sure. There were shadows beneath Dana's eyes and he knew she hadn't slept well last night. He hadn't either, but for different reasons. How badly he wanted to become more intimate with her. It wasn't about sex, per se, but something more human and fundamental; the ability to hold her and make her feel safe in the unraveling world that suddenly whirled around her.

The sunlight made the green colors of the valley look like peridot and emeralds after the washing of the rain in the hours of darkness. Everything in downtown Silver Creek seemed normal. But there was nothing normal in their lives right now. It was unsettling to him, as well. His PTSD was kicking up and he wanted to will it away, but that was useless. His focus, his heart, was centered on

Dana and he could see her silently wrestling with the bombshell that had exploded into her life yesterday.

As he drove into the sheriff's HQ, he saw deputies climbing into cars or arriving back to the station. There wasn't a lot of crime in the valley, but in part, that was thanks to Dan Seabert, an ex–Navy SEAL who had come to the valley after retiring.

Sensing Dana's tension ratcheting up, he said, "Let's talk to the sergeant on the desk and find out if they know anything conclusive about that money found in your log cabin." Instantly, he saw relief come to her eyes.

"Yes, I'd like to do that."

"And then, afterward? We can have Pepper take us out to the kennel and you can meet Bandit." More tension dissolved in her features.

"I can hardly wait to see him, Colin."

Parking, he turned off the truck and unstrapped. "Let's see what's going on," he told her, climbing out.

The coolness of the morning was refreshing. With the cold front passing, it meant the temperature would rise and the soil would start drying out. He was anxious to get that back field plowed and planted. Moving around the truck, he met Dana and they walked up the concrete sidewalk to the one-story redbrick building that buzzed with quiet activity.

Colin opened the door for her and she gave him a nod of thanks, heading straight for the sergeant's desk offset to the left of the entrance. Dana smiled a little as she saw Pepper Warner come out of the hall, lifting her hand and motioning them to come with her. Changing direction, Colin at her shoulder, they met her out in the visitors' lobby area.

"Good morning," Pepper greeted. "We're still processing everything and chasing information down," she told Dana. "Nothing conclusive yet."

"I know this takes time," Dana said, keeping the disappointment out of her voice.

"It does." Pepper nodded to Colin. "Come on, we'll take a back way to get to the kennel. Bandit just wants to get out and get some exercise."

They fell in behind the sergeant, making their way down a highly waxed hall and exiting out a rear door.

Dana saw a nice canine kennel to her left as they emerged from the main single-story building. There was a grassy oval enclosed right in front of where the large, airy pens were placed. There were three dogs and all of them at their gates. She spotted two German shepherds, and in the nearest pen was a short-haired yellow dog. That had to be Bandit!

Colin felt Dana's tension ease as they came to the paddock where Bandit stood, waving his long, thick yellow tail in a friendly fashion at them. Another officer came up to Pepper. He introduced himself as Hank Evans, the keeper.

"Bandit's already been fed," he told the sergeant.

"Great." Pepper turned to them. "Hank is our dog trainer and deputy. He's going to bring Bandit out and we'll go to the oval where they do training and playing with them. It's fully enclosed and he's going to let Bandit off the leash so he can run and snoop around. All the dogs get an hour of what we call 'playtime,' out here in the oval every morning and afternoon. It's good mental health for them."

"I wouldn't want to be in a pen all day, either," Dana said.

"I agree," Pepper said, watching Hank go into the pen and place the leash on Bandit's collar. "If you decide you like Bandit, he'll be rid of his pen forever."

"The pens are large, clean, and airy," Colin noted with satisfaction. Each had a long concrete run, as well.

Dana watched Bandit's large, expressive brown-gold eyes sparkle as he dutifully remained at Hank's side on the leash.

"Let's go," Hank said with a smile, pointing at the oval. "This is one of Bandit's favorite things to do."

Dana itched to pet Bandit. The dog was at least eighty pounds, well proportioned, very athletic looking. She liked that he listened to Hank's voice and commands. Once inside the oval and Pepper had shut the cyclone fence gate behind them, Hank brought the dog to where Dana and Colin stood.

Dana smiled as Bandit sat down, looking up at her, tongue lolling out the side of his mouth, his tail thumping. "He's so well-mannered," she told Hank and Pepper.

Hank grinned. "Bandit is used to certain commands. Once you say the word, he'll automatically do what is asked of him."

In the next few minutes, he gave Dana the commands and then handed her the leash. "Okay, take him for a walk. He'll always go to your left side."

Patting Bandit's broad head, Dana smiled excitedly. "Okay."

"Bandit, walk," she said.

Instantly, Bandit moved out of his sitting position and took up a spot on her left side, about six inches away from her leg. Dana walked him near the fence line and the Labrador altered his stride to match hers, so he wasn't either behind or ahead of her. It felt so good to have a dog around again! Why had she waited so long to get one? Dana didn't have an answer, but as she walked around the clipped green grass oval, all the weight and worry lifted from her shoulders.

She would stop, and he would instantly sit, giving her a look, watching her.

Dana smiled, leaned over and petted Bandit profusely. "You are wonderful! Such a gentleman, and so well-behaved." She laughed. Bandit looked up at her with an adoring gaze. "Do you know what's going on, big guy?" she asked, kneeling on one knee, her hands moving gently across his head, neck, and thick, strong shoulders.

All she got was Bandit thumping his tail, but she took that as a yes.

After petting him, she walked him back to where Hank, Pepper, and Colin were standing, watching them.

"He's wonderful," she exclaimed.

Grinning, Hank pulled a red rubber ball out of his pocket. "Here's his reward. He loves to chase the ball. You throw it and he'll retrieve it and bring it back to you."

Instantly, Bandit sat, focused fully on that ball.

"Seriously? He'll bring it back to me?" Dana asked, impressed.

"Yup, he sure will. Go ahead and unsnap the leash. He won't go anywhere until you give him the command. As you can tell, all his attention is on that ball."

Laughing, she unsnapped the leash and stuffed it into her pocket. Bandit sat, tail thumping rhythmically, watching the ball in Hank's hand. "Wow, he stays right where he is! That's amazing, Hank."

"He's fully trained," Hank assured her, passing the ball to her. "Now, give him the command *walk*, and he'll take his place at your left side. If you want him to chase the ball, just tell him *fetch*, and he'll take off running at ninety miles an hour, nail it, and then bring it back and drop it at your feet."

Dana gave them a wide grin. "This, I have to see!" She walked out to the center of the oval, Bandit dutifully at her side, his tail like a metronome, excitement in every inch of his body. She threw the ball and gave the command. Instantly, Bandit leaped, racing full tilt toward it. In seconds, the Lab snapped it up as it rolled, galloped around in a large circle, and came right back to Dana. He sat down, dropped the ball at her feet, panting heavily, tail thumping with joy.

Dana felt that joy transfer to her. Bandit loved to run! She stood there for about fifteen minutes, tossing the ball and having him retrieve it and bring it back to her. It was freedom for her and the happy dog. Picking up the ball, she told Bandit, "Come," and the dog took his position at her left leg, prancing in place, elation in his face as she walked toward the group.

"Well?" Colin teased. "Are we taking Bandit home with us?"

A thrill ran through Dana as she met and held his smiling eyes. "Would you like to work with Bandit, Colin? He'd be in our home and with either of us when we're out on the land."

"Sure," he said, taking the ball from her. He leaned down and petted him.

Bandit became super alert, watching Colin.

"All you have to do is let Bandit know he's to go with you," Hank said. "Just use the word *come*, and he'll put it together and realize he's going to walk with you now, Colin."

Dana couldn't help but smile, warmth encircling her heart as she saw life leap into Colin's eyes. "Have you had dogs in your past?" she asked him.

"Always," he said, grinning and patting Bandit's broad skull. "Come," he told the excited dog.

Dana stood with Pepper and Hank, watching man and dog have a wonderful time with one another.

"They look so happy." Pepper laughed.

"With his PTSD, I wasn't sure about bringing a dog into our lives," Dana confided, "but now? I can see there's nothing to worry about."

Hank chuckled. "Bandit's used to having a man, me, working with him. You can see how happy Bandit is, chasing the ball for Colin. His favorite time of day, after eating in the morning, is coming into the oval to play."

"Hank? Will he adjust to farm life? To living indoors with us? Going out on the land?"

"Bandit's smart. And he's very flexible. We have a doggy bed here for him, a very nice one donated by the K9 Ballistics company. Bandit's a serious chewer and they provided us with a material that won't wilt under his chewing."

"That's very nice of that company to donate beds for your working dogs," Dana agreed. "It's nice to see generosity from a business to the people who are out in the field working with dogs like Bandit."

"They're a great company and they provided three of their elevated dog beds for their crates."

Pepper laughed, watching Colin play with Bandit. "Man and dog. They're just a duo, that's all there is to it. I've never seen Bandit so engaged and happy. Colin's really giving him a workout."

Hank nodded. "He likes Colin. And Bandit is a super athlete, Dana. He'll like being out on a ranch. He's a working dog, no question."

"I think Colin likes him, too," Dana said, smiling broadly. "Any worries I had about him and bringing Bandit into our lives is gone."

"So?" Pepper asked. "Are you going to take Bandit home with you?"

"I'd love to have him, but I'll ask Colin once he comes back here, if he'd like Bandit to be with us."

Man and dog were both panting and smiling as they returned to the group. Colin took off his straw Stetson and wiped his sweaty brow with his forearm.

"Bandit gives as good as he gets!" He laughed, handing Hank the red ball.

"Both of you were working out hard," Pepper said, smiling.

Dana met Colin's gaze that told her how happy he was. "I haven't seen you ever be a kid, but you sure were out there with Bandit." She leaned down, petting Bandit because Colin had come and stood so that the dog was between them.

"Brings up a lot of good memories," he told her, petting the dog's head.

"So?" Dana said. "Should we take him home with us?"

"I'd like that," he said, becoming more solemn. "But how about you, Dana?"

"We always had dogs when I was growing up. They stayed inside with us and I'd like Bandit to do the same. Do you have any issue with that, Colin?"

He wiped his forehead. "No, not at all."

"I have a crate for him," Hank said. "Since he was a puppy, he goes to his crate and sleeps in it at night."

"But," Dana said, "couldn't Bandit just sleep in one of our rooms with us? Without a crate?"

"Sure, he could. It's a pretty big crate and if you wanted it, we'd let you have it."

Making a face, Dana said, "I'd just like Bandit to be a dog, if that makes sense?"

Hank nodded. "He's worked hard for ten years, so in his other ten, I don't see why he can't become a family dog, instead. He's very flexible and easygoing. I don't think he'll miss the crate, but I would like you to take the bed he was given by K9. Otherwise, he might wander around at night and start chewing up something you don't want destroyed."

Laughing, Dana said, "We'd love to have Bandit's bed."

"Labs are well-known to be massive chewers," Pepper warned. "So watch that he doesn't take a fancy to the legs of your dining room table or a chair."

"I think once Bandit falls into our routine," Colin said, "he'll be too busy and active all day to do that at night."

"He's a super athlete," Hank agreed. "Let's take him over to the pails of water by the gate. I'm sure he's thirsty."

As they walked toward the oval gate, Dana looked up at Colin. "You really okay with this?"

"I haven't felt this good in a long time," he told her.

"When I was watching you and him out there playing with the ball? I saw all your worry lift. You were like a young girl with her dog, having nothing but fun."

"You're right," she murmured. "I'm so glad we're going to get Bandit."

"He'll be a good guard dog, too," Colin said, slowing. Ahead, Bandit had plunged his muzzle into the pail of water, slurping noisily.

Nodding, Dana moved to where Hank was standing. "What will Bandit do if he's in our home and he hears a car, truck, or a human outside?"

"Oh," Hank said, "he'll bark his head off. Labs, like golden retrievers, are super family-oriented dogs. They look at you and Colin as if you are a part of their wolf pack, so to speak. I was telling Colin how to introduce him to other people who come to your ranch, an official kind of handshake between Bandit and your friends or family. Once he's introduced, he won't bark if he hears or sees them come into the ranch. He'll simply consider them part of his expanded wolf pack, of which he's the chief wolf."

"I like that," Dana said.

"He will bark at anyone walking or driving onto your property, though," Hank warned.

"Dogs memorize faces, body stance, voice tone and gestures, too. If Bandit doesn't recognize that human? He'll alert you that someone is coming onto your property. In his mind, he's responsible for the safety and welfare of you and Colin."

"But he's not an attack dog?" Colin asked.

"No, but don't be put off by Bandit's friendly manner. He loves the people who love him. Or who he's been introduced to and they are made part of his expanding pack. But a stranger? He'll instantly go on guard and bark to warn you that someone he doesn't know is nearby."

"That's good news," Dana said, relieved. "Has he ever bitten anyone?"

"Nah. Labs aren't like a German shepherd or Belgian Malinois, who are both known to be aggressive."

"Great, because I don't want him biting someone by accident," Dana said, relieved.

"Let's go get his water bowl and a pail that has his brush, comb, and other items in it, so you can take Bandit to his new family home. Colin can help me get his bed and put it in the back of your pickup."

Dana watched with affection as Bandit was allowed loose in their mobile home. At first, he was confused because no one said "come" when he moved into the home. And when Colin opened up the bedroom doors at either end and then came and sat down on the couch near Dana, he stood there looking perplexed.

"He's used to being told what to do," Dana said.

"Yeah, for sure." He patted his knee and Bandit perked up his ears.

"Over here," he called to the Lab.

Dana felt for the dog because he was like a fish out of water. "His life has been so regimented . . ."

"I kind of see myself in his shoes . . . maybe his paws," Colin said wryly. "With my PTSD my life has been altered to what I can and can't do. I'm no longer who I used to be, and now Bandit's in the same predicament."

"I think all three of us have had our lives cut short and

we've had to make a lot of adjustments, no longer like we used to be," she murmured, giving him a sympathetic look.

Nodding, Colin held her sad gaze. "But that doesn't mean we can't carve out a good quality of life because of it." He patted his knee again. This time, Bandit walked over and sat down in front of him.

"Good boy," he praised, gently petting the dog's head. "You'll get used to being really free, Bandit, over time."

"Yes," Dana whispered, "you will." She reached out, smoothing his fur down his shoulders and back. "Think he's waiting for us to give him a command?"

"Probably. I need to go out to the hay barn for a while. We've got a lot of grain I've got to put away."

"Why don't you call him to you and let him go along without the leash? He has to get used to being around us without one."

Colin stood up. "Good idea." He called Bandit, and this time the dog walked over to him, at his left leg, attentive. "We'll be outside if you need us."

Smiling a little, Dana whispered, "Okay. Go have some fun and freedom, Bandit."

May 25

Colin was coming in for lunch when he saw the sheriff's cruiser turn onto the ranch road. The spring sun beat down upon his shoulders, the warmth feeling good. Halting at the bottom of the porch, he saw Dan Seabert easing out of the driver's seat.

"Hi, Dan," he greeted. "Are you joining Dana and me for lunch?"

The law enforcement officer grimaced. He kept his black baseball hat on, pulled out a beat-up-looking brown briefcase from the SUV and shut the door, locking it. "No, this is an official call," he said, walking up to Colin.

"You find something about that money?" he guessed, climbing the stairs and opening the front door.

"Yes."

"Come on in," Colin said, stepping aside. He saw Dana in the kitchen, putting final touches on their lunch: tuna sandwiches.

Bandit came trotting toward them. His tail was like a metronome, and once Dan was inside the door, he petted the dog fondly because he knew him well. It was a joyous meeting.

Colin hung his Stetson on a peg near the door.

"Hi, Dana," Dan greeted, taking off his baseball cap and hanging it on another peg.

"Dan!"

"I probably should have called first," he said apologetically, heading toward the kitchen.

"Don't worry about it," she said. "Have you had lunch?"

"Yeah, I grabbed something earlier."

"We're eating at the kitchen bar," she said, gesturing to the three seats. "Would you like some coffee?"

"Never say no to a cup of coffee," he told her, setting the briefcase at one end and taking the stool closest to the wall. "Thank you."

Dana poured three cups. Colin spied the plates on the kitchen counter and brought them over. "Are you here to tell us who that money belongs to?"

"Well," he hedged, ". . . sort of . . ."

Colin put a stool on the opposite side so she could sit down and face Dan. She smiled and nodded thanks to him. He worried about what Dan had found. How would it affect Dana? She hadn't slept well last night, a nightmare about her parents' murder—once again. In her own way, she had acquired PTSD from the shock of the event, too. He saw wariness in Dana's gaze as she sat tensely, not picking up her sandwich to eat.

Taking a sip of the black coffee, Dan set it aside and opened the briefcase, drawing out a sheaf of papers. "This money is a hodgepodge," he told them. "Pepper is working with our forensics team on what they found, and we're trying to put this together, but it's like a thousand-piece jigsaw puzzle."

"Nothing's ever easy, is it?" she said, looking at the papers in his hands.

"No." He frowned. "Okay, here's what we know so far. In three of the four bags, we ran some of the numbers on the cash. We aren't set up to put a lot of bills into a machine and have it hooked up nationwide to get info. Only the FBI and Treasury agents have that capacity. The cash that we did check, comes from all over the United States. I thought this might be a bank robbery, but in those three bags, it doesn't appear, so far, to have anything to do with robbery." He handed her some papers. "These are serial numbers, columns of them, on the first three bags. Forensics has found traces of cocaine, heroin, fentanyl, and meth on some of them, so at this point, we're assuming this is drug money."

"Drugs?" she said, her brows raising in surprise. "Here? In the log cabin?"

"I know. Like I said, we're at the front end of this investigation and right now we have disparate, illogical pieces we're looking at and haven't gotten a pattern yet to see the whole picture."

"We don't have much drug traffic in the valley," Colin protested.

"We have a Guatemalan drug lord, Pablo Gonzalez, who hit the western side of Wyoming, below Jackson Hole, a couple of years ago. He tried to infest Wind River Valley, but didn't succeed. Now"—he sighed—"I've called ATF, DEA, and the FBI for help on this investigation. We are in way over our heads on this one and I need federal assistance to sort it all out. This is absolutely turning into a federal investigation, not a county or even state one."

"Do you think this drug lord is trying an incursion into our area?" Colin asked, scowling.

"Don't know yet. Pepper went through the last year's arrest records, and except for some minor recreational drug infractions, there's nothing going on that would be a red flag that something bigger is taking root in our county."

"But who put those money bags under the floorboards of an old, dilapidated turn-of-the-century log cabin?" she wondered.

"Another question that hasn't been answered yet," Dan said. "Because of the enormity of this find? I didn't want to leave you worrying and hanging out there on this, Dana. It's going to take a month, maybe more, to get intel back from these federal law enforcement agencies, and by then, I hope they've put it together. We're sending those three drug bags to the FBI; they'll run all the serial numbers, and they have huge databases that will identify where each bill came from."

"You mean, like a state or a city?" she asked.

"Exactly. Plus, their forensics laboratory is one of the finest in the world. They will be able to take the traces of drugs off the bills and identify them, and, possibly, once they know the regions where the bills came from, will identify who the bad actor drug lord—or lords—are behind this. It's always a drug lord, and I'm hoping they'll find out which one, and that, in turn, will give us direction on where to investigate next."

"Wow," Dana murmured, giving Colin a look. "This is really crazy stuff. Who knew?"

Dan shared a photo of one of the money bags. "Remember? I said three out of the four bags were in that class?"

"Oh, that's right," Dana said. "What have you discovered about the fourth one?"

"The bills we've checked in the fourth bag so far show that the money came from three banks in the county of San Diego, California. This was a series of bank holdups that occurred about six months ago. We're working with different law enforcement agencies there to piece it all together. We have the names of the banks. And the bills match that string of robberies." He gave her another paper. "Here's the banks involved. Do you recognize any of them?"

Dana studied them. "Not at all."

He gave her a sympathetic look. "We stumbled upon something else in our investigation that we didn't see coming, Dana." He hesitated. Reaching out, he put his hand over hers, as if to stabilize her. Voice lowering, he rasped, "First of all, I'm so damned sorry your parents are gone . . ."

She gasped, her eyes widening. "H-how did you know . . . I mean . . . I haven't told anyone but Colin about my past . . ."

"The man who hit a string of those banks in San Diego was the man who murdered your parents. Brock Hauptman."

Eyes widening, she reared back. "But . . . how . . . he's in prison!" Her voice cracked.

Shaking his head, giving her a pained look, he said, "The prison system screwed up, Dana. Hauptman was put in prison, but he broke out and they still haven't found him."

Gasping, she felt the life drain out of her. Colin got up and stood behind her, hands on her shoulders. "He's . . . loose? Why wasn't I told?" Dana gasped.

Colin's fingers tightened against her shoulders as she slumped against him, her whole life, that whole, murderous time in her life, brought up again like a damned lightning bolt. He saw Dan's face grow apologetic.

"I asked them why in the hell they didn't contact you. They were supposed to, by law. They said there were a series of mistakes. They apologized, but that doesn't do anyone any good."

She made a choked sound. "He's loose . . ."

"Yes. He and his gang robbed those three banks and then they left town. There's APBs out on him, but he's disappeared, quite literally, and gone underground. I talked to the FBI this morning and they said he's disappeared. No one knows where he's at."

She wiped her brow with a shaky hand. "B-but, that

bag? The fourth one? It was under the floor with the rest of them."

"We're trying to figure out how long they've been under the floorboards, Dana. That bank heist probably gave Hauptman the money he wanted to get out of the state and disappear."

Placing her hands against her face, she fought back the urge to scream, to cry.

Colin moved his hand slowly up and down her shoulder and upper arm, wanting to assuage the anxiety and grief in her expression. "Try to take some slow, deep breaths, Dana. You're safe here. I'm here, and so is Bandit."

"And us," Dan reminded her gently. "The entire police force is going to keep you safe, Dana. We've had no indication that Hauptman is around here."

Her hands dropped, tears dribbling out of her eyes. "Yet. There's a bag full of his money that he stole from so many people in my log cabin. It's logical to assume he is here, somewhere in the valley or wherever . . ." Wiping her eyes, she sniffed and found Colin handing her his clean white handkerchief. She whispered thanks, blotting her eyes.

"I've come to the same conclusion, Dana, but we don't know where he is," Dan admitted. "It's possible Hauptman has hooked up with the drug lord who owns those other three bags. That would explain why they were using that log cabin to hide the bags of money. Maybe he's in with the drug lord, and until we figure out his whereabouts, there's a lot we don't know, yet."

Giving her a worried look, Colin saw how pale Dana had become. She clutched his handkerchief in her hands, content to lean against him, and he understood he was a port in her storm of shock. "Don't you think that Gonzalez must really trust Hauptman, since their bags of money were found together?"

"Yes," Dan said, putting all the papers back into his briefcase. "We think so. Drug lords tend not to trust their minions. But for whatever reason, Hauptman has wormed his way into Gonzalez's gang and, from my perspective, Gonzalez trusted him with probably around a million dollars found in each of those three bags. That's a lot of trust. This particular drug lord doesn't often hire anyone from the outside, particularly a white Anglo male. Most of his drug runners are from his own family, or families he's familiar with. I'd really like to know how Hauptman managed that trick."

"That means at least two people, maybe more," Dana said, her voice thick with tears, "know the money is *here*, on our ranch."

"That's why we need to make this investigation our number-one priority," Dan said gently. "I've already put out a statewide APB on Hauptman. There isn't a law enforcement officer who doesn't have his picture right now. We're in touch with the California attorney general and San Diego County law enforcement. They're very interested in a hunt for Hauptman and Gonzalez if they are here in Wyoming." He grimaced and muttered unhappily, "Probably in our county, from the looks of it."

Dana looked up into Colin's darkened gaze. "How do you feel about this?"

His hands closed on Dana's shoulders and he caressed them. "It doesn't matter how I feel. What matters is how you feel."

"I felt safe here," she managed hoarsely, looking around. "For the first time in years, I felt safe. This place is out of the way. I was going to start all over . . . the past . . . finally, in the past . . ."

Colin's mouth tightened. And now, Dana's whole, fragile, beautiful world had just exploded. The man who murdered her parents was on the loose and no one . . . no one knew where he was . . . and the likelihood was he was here, in this country. Maybe even a lot closer than Colin wanted to think about.

His sense of protection rose strongly within him. This whole, shocking event had torn away the fact that he knew he was falling in love with Dana. Colin didn't know if she loved him, but he felt something good, warm, and solid growing between them every day, something important, life-changing and good—for both of them. He swallowed hard. There was no way he could speak about his growing love for her right now. Dana was devastated, her face white, eyes mirroring anxiety laced with well-deserved fear. Hauptman was a murderer. What to do?

Chapter 10

May 25

"Dan, I don't think we can stay here on the ranch under the circumstances, do you?" Colin asked, giving Dana a questioning look. She gave a bare nod of her head, grief passing across her face.

"How do you feel about that, Dana?" Dan asked.

"How could we stay here?" She gave Bandit, who sat at her side, his big, long body resting against her leg, his gold-brown eyes always on her, a pat on his head. "We can't expect him to keep us safe."

"He'd bark," Dan agreed, "but if those criminals come in, they'll be armed and you wouldn't stand a chance. Drug runners don't care who they kill to reach their objective." Shaking his head, he muttered, "Here's my thoughts on your situation, Dana. We can discuss them, and since you're the owner, you can decide what you want to do after you hear me out."

"Okay," she whispered. "What do you think we should do?"

"We're taking the yellow tape down around the log

cabin as soon as I'm done here. It will be a sure sign to the bad guys that we're on to them. I'd like to have my team set up cameras inside and outside the log cabin. They'll be practically invisible. And, I'd like to put cameras on the four corners of your mobile home. One will be aimed at the entrance road and we'd have cameras on each of the other three corners to cover the other directions. I would expect them to come in the main gate, but Colin and you mentioned tire treads, probably ATVs, on the rear of your property, coming and going into this main area. We don't know if these other tracks were made by hunters, ATV folks, or the bad guys. I think it's okay if you leave the animals here. You can be here in the daylight hours, but no later than dusk, then you need to leave. I've talked to Chase about taking you in for a while. They have an empty three-bedroom home near where Mary lives on their ranch. It's ready for you, if you want it. He's not charging you any rent to be there."

"I like that plan," Dana said, clearing her throat. "That's kind of Chase to offer it to us." She twisted a look up at Colin. "What do you think?"

He squeezed her shoulders. "I think it's a sound plan." Lifting his chin, he pinned Dan with a dark look. "But I'll be packing a pistol, Dan. We aren't going to work out here during daylight hours without some kind of backup protection."

"That's fine. I'll get Pepper to work with you on getting an open-carry permit, so everything's legal."

"I don't want a gun," Dana said, shuddering, wrapping her arms around herself.

Bandit sidled closer, watching her, as if trying to absorb some of her terror and pain.

"It's up to you," Dan said, nodding. "I also want each of you to have a small radio on you that has the power to reach us no matter where you are in the county."

Relief in her tone, Dana said, "Oh, that's a *great* idea, Dan! That makes me feel safer already."

He managed a tight smile and pulled out two radios from the side pocket of his briefcase. "Here you are. I'll go over how to use them before I leave."

Dana managed a slight smile, taking hers and handing the other one to Colin. "You came prepared."

"Part of my job," Dan said. "I want to go over some other operational things with you. We don't want a sheriff's cruiser coming onto your ranch again, unless it's an emergency."

"For all you know," Colin muttered, "these dudes could be in the woods, set up in a camp, watching us right now."

"That could be happening," Dan agreed. "I want you to *assume* they are watching you, Dana. You have to remain alert and on guard." Dan pointed to Bandit. "He'll be your first line of defense. Dogs have a photographic memory. They know you are part of their pack, so to speak. If an unknown vehicle comes into your ranch? He'll bark. If he sees a person he doesn't know? He'll bark because he's alerting you. So, let's say you two are out in the barn working during the day. Bandit will bark. You'll drop what you're doing and come out and see what he's alerting you to. Then, look around and see who or what is on your property, and then take appropriate action from there."

"What about the FBI?" Colin demanded. "Are they involved in this?"

"Yes, but undercover. We were told yesterday that

they'll be sending this individual to us in about three weeks. It will be our job to keep tabs on him."

"What's his objective?" Colin asked.

Dan sat up and moved his shoulders around, as if to ease the tension in them. "I've talked to the FBI. They think that if Hauptman is around, he's hidden in the nearby forest. What we have to do is find him."

"A drone?" Colin suggested.

"Well, first, the FBI is going to position a satellite over this area and make several passes. It's infrared, so if it's alive, it will show up a bright red on their feed. Then, that undercover agent will go into the area and snoop around and find out who or what is there."

"But infrared will show red blobs and you can't tell whether it's animal or human," Colin warned.

"True, but the shape of the blob is in the hands of an FBI forensic person, who will probably be able to sort this out to a high degree."

"Can we know who this agent is?" Dana asked.

Shaking his head, Dan said, "No. He can't have people knowing who he is. Besides? Just as an example, let's say Hauptman kidnapped you, Dana. If you know nothing, you also couldn't recognize him and ask for help. Plus, if they tortured you and you gave up that information? He'd become a target."

"Oh . . ." she said, frowning. "I see . . . I'd be putting him in jeopardy."

"Yes. But this is just a scenario. I'm not anticipating any of that happening. The agent could be there to get you out of that situation. Not knowing who he is will protect him and you."

Rubbing her upper arms, she muttered, "This is real. It's awful . . ."

"I'm sorry it's happening to you," Dan rasped. "You've been through enough."

"Well," she said, scowling, "I'm *not* going to let Hauptman or his gang, or Gonzalez, chase me away from my home. Not a chance."

May 28

"How are you doing?" Colin asked Dana as they ate breakfast in their new home on Three Bars Ranch. It was a two-story, three-bedroom house filled with antiques from many generations of Chase's family.

She shrugged, forcing herself to eat a large bowl of oats sprinkled with a bit of brown sugar and pecans. "Rough night's sleep. I'm getting used to this house, to the creaks and groaning sounds. Everything makes me jump." She gave him a one-shouldered shrug.

"I'm in the same boat. The noise of this house is different than our mobile home noises."

She glanced at the clock up on the kitchen wall. It was six a.m. Bandit was eating his breakfast in the kitchen. At least their dog was acclimating to his new role as herd protector, and she smiled a little, loving the big fellow. "Bandit's settling in just fine," she noted.

"Isn't he, though?" Colin said, glancing in his direction, half his bowl of kibble gone already. "He's been good out at your ranch, too. I'm glad he follows you around, where ever you go."

"Me, too," she admitted. "He gives me a sense of safety. With you around, I do feel safe. I just don't like it when you have to drive to town. I feel vulnerable when you're away, Colin."

"I worried about that," he muttered, apologetic.

"But you have to make trips to Three Bars and into town all the time. I just have to get over my fear."

"Well," he said, stirring his oats, "you have good reason to feel that way, Dana. I wish this wasn't happening to you. Moving here was a chance to start over, a new life."

She wanted to reach out and touch his forearm but stopped herself. "I have a confession to make to you, Colin." She saw his brows move up, question coming to his eyes. "We haven't gotten to really sit down and honestly talk with one another. There's something happening between us and it's good. At least, I feel good about it." She finished off her bowl of oats and set it aside, picking up her cup of coffee, her gaze on him. "I've been less than honest or at least forthcoming, about how I feel regarding you in my life."

He frowned. "I hope it's positive?" His gut tightened.

"Very," she whispered, giving him a shy glance. "You make me happy, did you know that?"

"No," he began, hesitant. Panic started eating at him.

"I wake up every morning knowing you're in the house, in my life."

"I like that we're becoming friends, Dana." How many nights had he dreamed of this? Of Dana liking him as much as he liked her? And yet, the terror that followed right behind it was stark and real.

She brightened. Placing her hand on her chest, she added, "I'm so glad to hear that!" And then, "You're still so hard to read, Colin."

"I know . . . I don't mean to be that way, Dana, but I have a war going on inside me twenty-four-seven." He shook his head. "It's a major distraction to me . . . and to you."

Her brows dipped. "What do you mean? Your PTSD symptoms?"

It hurt to say it, but he said with bitterness in his low tone, "Yeah, that."

"I haven't seen it very much out at the ranch," she said, searching his expression.

"It's always there, Dana. Sometimes, I get lucky and it all goes away for maybe half a day, but that's rare. That's why I told Chase I couldn't be with a wrangler team on his ranch. When the symptoms hit, all I want to do is go away and be alone to wrestle them and keep control over myself. It's such a war of anger, irritation, and impatience going on inside me it takes all my energy and focus on it just to keep it from exploding outwardly and hurting people who don't deserve to be blasted like that at all." His heart shriveled with the hope it held because he saw sadness come to Dana's eyes. How badly he wanted to be exactly what she wanted: intimacy on all levels and in all ways. But he couldn't be. And he wasn't about to lead her astray and make her think otherwise. He would never lie to anyone, especially not to her because he *did* have feelings, powerful ones, for her.

"Look," he began, his voice roughened with emotion, "I wish to hell these symptoms would go away, but they don't, Dana. I never want to put you into the line of fire with me when I'm wrestling with them. And I'm sure to hurt you, whether I mean to or not." He dug into her widening eyes, feeling the disappointment washing from her to him. "I want what you want," he growled, "but you won't be safe around me, Dana. One of these days, I'm afraid I'd lash out and hurt you and that's the *last* thing I want to happen. You deserve nothing but goodness and happiness, not a washed-up warrior who has more scars inside him, than he wears outside of himself."

She sat there, digesting his low plea, holding his gaze. "Look, there's no one who is perfect, Colin. You think I don't have scars from what's happened to me? For the losses that remind me every day in small or large ways? You don't hear or see the tears I cry for being alone because I was so close to my parents. I could really talk to them, let down, and tell them what I was feeling. They were my beacons of light. They loved me as fiercely as I loved them. I miss them so much . . ." Her vision blurred. "See? Just talking about it makes me want to cry. Do you want to cry, too, Colin, for what you've had to go through?"

He reached out, gripping her hand. "That's why I need to be alone, Dana. Yeah, I cry. Men aren't supposed to, but if I don't, I'll implode. Crying is a release from what is churning inside me. It's a good thing, whether others think so or not."

She wrapped her fingers strongly around his work-worn hand. "Well, I'm not much better. When I get emotional, and I know I'm going to burst into tears, I go hide, too. Maybe I hurry to the house and to my bedroom, shutting the door so you won't hear me. Or"—her voice wobbled—"you might be outside and I'll hurry into the barn, go to the tack room and close the door and let it go, where you can't hear me." She wiped the tears from her eyes with her other hand. "So you see? We are more alike than you realize. We're both hiding and running."

He stared down at their hands entwined. "I didn't know that . . ."

"We need to talk, really talk with one another, Colin. I like you. I've never felt this way toward a man before. I wake up in the morning happy just knowing you're nearby. I look forward to meeting you in the kitchen, and we're working like the good team that we are, making coffee and breakfast. I love to hear what you're thinking, how you see things, and what makes you smile. Did you know that?"

Looking away, his mouth working, he rasped, "No . . . I didn't know that, Dana," and he forced himself to gaze into and hold her watery gaze. "I guess," he stumbled, "that I've handled my PTSD so long, I don't know how to reach out for help, or how to tell someone that I care deeply about them, and share what's going on inside me . . ."

"Do you feel better when you're around me, Colin?"

Nodding, he squeezed her hand. "My day always goes better when you're around. We may be in different parts of the ranch, but I know you're there, you're close . . . and it makes my PTSD a little less sharp and hard inside me."

"You affect me the same way," she whispered unsteadily. "Don't throw me away, Colin. Don't run. Why can't we run *toward* one another when we're feeling like this? If we make each other happy, why not do this, instead of slinking off to a dark corner to cry alone when all we really need is to be held by one another?"

The catch in her husky voice cut through his fear. "You're right," he rasped, reaching out and gently removing the tears from her pale cheeks. "What if . . . what if we keep talking honestly to one another? We're building a good friendship, Dana. For me, being friends is something I value and need. I trust you with myself. And since I got PTSD, I never trusted anyone before you walked into my life. I was feeling too damned alone and unable to do anything but crawl under a rock and hide when that stuff hits me internally."

She managed a weak smile, holding his gaze. "You're the first person since my parents were murdered that I trust. It just happened, Colin. It wasn't something I was searching for, it was just there . . ."

"Then, let's build on that, Dana. Let's keep growing into this relationship, and most importantly, let's really sit down and talk with one another when we feel the need to do it?"

"Y-yes, I'd like that. I just couldn't bear to have you walk out of my life, Colin. You're becoming that important to me . . ."

"I won't walk out on you, Dana. That's a promise." Shaken by her honesty, he felt her fingers tighten briefly around his. "I'm not that kind of man," he rasped. "I'd rather have a chance to see where this is going with you . . . us . . . and I'll never disappear from your life unless you want me to."

She managed a small sound in her throat. "I would *never* ask you to leave me, Colin. That's how important you're becoming to me. Just give us a chance? Please?"

He clasped her hand with both of his. "Listen to me, Dana. I will never leave unless you ask me to do so. I'm afraid of myself, of hurting you, but I'm more afraid of losing someone who is like sunlight to me in my darkest days. I like what we have. I like where it's going."

She gave a small sigh. "I feel the same way. You're an unexpected gift in my life, Colin. Every day I wake up and I feel happier than I have in a long, long time. And it's you. I know you're broken, but so am I. It feels to me as if we are somehow healing one another. Doesn't it?"

Giving a nod, he said thickly, "Yes, that's what I feel, too. We're good for one another, Dana. I don't want to throw that away and I know you don't, either. In some way, even with the jagged pieces of ourselves that have been destroyed, we fit together."

"Somehow," she choked, "and in some way, you're right. It's as if you are the salve for my losses, making me feel a little more of who I was before my parents were ripped away from me."

"And that's how you make me feel, Dana. I'm feeling more and more whole, the old Colin returning, than before. I think that's pretty magical, don't you?"

"Oh . . . yes . . . it is magic, a good kind . . ."

"Then, let's keep on walking together. We'll get through this thing with the bags of money under the floorboards of that poor old cabin of yours. I know there's a lot of darkness and anger swirling around you right now, but we've got a lot of help from Dan and the other law enforcement agencies. All we have to do is be alert, be smart, and only be out at your ranch during daylight hours."

"That sounds good . . . I'm so glad we had this talk, Colin."

He reluctantly released her hand. "Me, too. Now, I think we need to get out to your ranch. We've got a busy day ahead of us . . ." He reluctantly stood up, taking the bowls and spoons with him to the kitchen sink. It was the last thing he wanted to do, but they'd managed, somehow, to bridge and create an even more important connection with one another. His heart lifted. His hope grew in his chest. He held the greatest secret of all, that he was falling deeply in love with Dana. But she couldn't know that now. And probably? Never. But even he wasn't sure of that anymore, either. They just had to take it one day at a time. And with this criminal worry mounting, he had to remain quiet about how much he loved her.

May 31

Memorial Day had come and gone. There were throngs of tourists pouring into the Silver Creek Valley, a favorite destination of nearly one hundred thousand people, Sheriff Dan Seabert had told Dana. She tried to gird herself for whatever news he had for them. He'd called earlier, and tersely asked them to come in and see him.

Colin walked at her side, their hands sometimes brushing against one another. Every time it happened, Dana felt a moment's respite from her worry and mounting anxiety. What had the sheriff found out?

Colin opened the door to the lobby and the sergeant at the main desk waived them on by, saying, "He's in room two, to your left."

Thanking him, Colin placed his hand gently against the small of her back. He wanted that intimacy with her, to give her a sense of safety, that everything would be all right. As an Army Ranger, who worked black ops missions, he knew that was a fool's wish at best. Seeing some of the strain in her expression dissolve, told him everything. His world was one of nothing ever going right; that there were twists, turns, and corkscrews to it. He'd survived in that world, and done well until that night in the Afghan village. The years before, however, he had been requested by the Navy SEALs on many of their missions because he was a deadly force who knew his job and was a team player.

Dan met them at the open door to the conference room. "Come on in," he invited, stepping aside.

Dana saw a half-a-wall-sized projection screen whirring downward. There were six seats at the rectangular oak table. The blinds were closed and there was low light in the room as he invited them to sit down.

"There's a lot going on," Dan told them, sitting at his laptop and clicking on it.

A map of the area where the Wildflower Ranch sat, was thrown up on the screen.

"We still haven't gotten the flyover yet. There's a wait list, and satellite demands are taken on certain priorities."

"And we're not really one, right?" Colin asked.

"More or less," Dan agreed. "But what we have been doing is looking at the area across the highway from where you have your ranch, Dana. My ears perked up when I saw those ATV tracks to and from your main HQ at the ranch, and how they went up that hill slope. We've been able to work with the US Forest Service, and they've given us all kinds of maps. The one I'm most interested in is the massive trail system up in those mountains beyond the two small ranches that sit off the main highway. Their property lines go to the slope of the mountain, and then from there, it is forest service property. It's a state forest, and the HQ for it is here, in Silver Creek. You can see hundreds of small feeder trails. Some are marked for hikers, others for horseback riding, bike trails, and the others either ATV trails or a multiuse trail system."

"There are a *lot* of trails," Dana muttered, frowning. "Wow."

"In the summer months, this is a tourist mecca," Dan said. "We get a lot of city slickers pouring out of their digs and coming out West for some elbow room."

She grinned and nodded. "Understood."

"What about the edge of Dana's ranch property?" Colin asked, pointing to it on the screen.

"Well, that's what I was interested in, too. There is a trail there, and it is on USFS property, but it's not defined. I called up the supervisor for this area, Dave Roberts, and he said that was an illegal trail of some kind."

"Are there a lot of illegal trails in our area?" Dana wondered.

"According to Dave, there's some. But there's only two on this side of the highway, yours and another area about a mile down the road, heading out of town. All the rest are on the other side of the road and Dave said these were made by tourists back-country hiking, biking, or whatever."

"I see some other symbols," Colin noted.

"The house symbols are line cabins that are kept by the USFS," Dan said.

"There's a group of them strung out not far from that first ranch, going up to about seven thousand feet."

"Yes, it's a group of cabins that are out of the woods, but close enough for a fire entrance/exit area for firefighters and hotshots, should we get a wildfire in this area. There's a need to put the buggies there, and the groups of cabins are to house hotshots who need to eat, sleep, and recoup before they go out on the fire line again."

"Is there a garage area or something like that to house their buggies and other fire equipment?"

"I was up in that area about five years ago, just reconnoitering and familiarizing myself with it, Colin. There are two open garages for some fire equipment, but not a lot. During the winter, the USFS comes through and pulls down the garage doors to save them from snow blowing in. Usually, these are open from May through November every year."

"Have you asked Ranger Roberts if he's seen any illegal activity around my ranch?"

"No . . . nothing."

"So," Dana said, "this might mean that Hauptman isn't around here?" There was a hopeful note in her voice.

"Right now? Yes, I'd say that's a logical assumption."

Relief plunged through her. "That's good to know."

"I still want you to stay over at Three Bars until we can get more reliable and precise intel," Dan warned.

"Oh, I will," Dana promised. "But we're heading into the growing season big-time, and we have to be out in those fields."

"Understood." He changed to another picture. "Here's the drug lord, Gonzalez. Right now, intel has him in Guatemala and he's not illegally up here in our country. But he has been known to fly across the border and check out his drug drop-off points, too."

"But right now," Colin said, darkly studying the color photo of a man with dark brown eyes, black hair, and a thick mustache, "he's not up here and not in our area?"

"Correct. The FBI has an undercover agent in Gonzalez's group, and that has been confirmed by him."

"Good." Colin breathed, giving Dana a glance. She looked relieved, too.

"How long before we can get that satellite flyover?" Colin asked.

"They're saying another two or three weeks."

Grimacing, Colin growled, "Damn."

Dan shut off the laptop and the lights came up. "No one has seen any activity," Dan assured them. "I've sent out deputies to both ranches where that one trail leads to where that series of line shacks are located, and they have seen no activity, except for normal tourist-season movement in and out of that road. There's a hiking trail that parallels the two ranch boundaries and it's quite popular, but it's nowhere near those line shacks. The road gets really heavily rutted and almost impassible shortly after the parking area for that popular trail. No one goes up there."

"But you told the ranchers to stay alert?" Dana asked.

Nodding, Dan closed the laptop. "Absolutely. Right now, all I can say is it is quiet in Dodge."

"What about the money?" Dana asked.

"Well, that, at least, is coming along. The three bags are drug money that is confirmed to be from the Gonzalez drug cartel. Wc can tell that by different means, thanks to the FBI forensics lab."

"The bank robbery heist bag?" Colin asked.

"That is fully confirmed to be Hauptman's gang, as the FBI calls them. They've taken fingerprints off some of the money and identified not only him, but gang members who are known to run with him."

"How much did he steal?" Dana wondered.

"Half a million dollars."

Colin whistled. "That's a lot of money."

"Yes, and provided either DEA, ATF, or the FBI can find and arrest this gang, that money will be part of the evidence against all of them at their criminal trial. Hopefully, that will happen sooner, not later."

"And then the money will be given back to the banks and to the people who lost it?" Dana asked.

"Yes, but that may be years in the making. We have to catch this bad actor and his gang, first," Dan said.

"The sooner, the better," Dana muttered.

"Seriously," Dan agreed, getting up. "I'll keep you two apprised as more info comes in."

Rising, Dana shook the sheriff's large hand. "Thanks. You're helping me sleep at night. Really, you are."

He smiled a little and opened the door, stepping aside. "I've been in some squeakers and know what it's like to be hunted," he told them. "It's not something I'd ever want anyone to experience."

"Chase said one time you had been a Navy SEAL," Colin said, halting outside with them in the hall.

Dan shut the door. "Yes, nine years." He pointed to his knees beneath his tan slacks. "Wrecked me in some ways."

Nodding, Colin said, "I worked almost exclusively with SEALs and Delta Force when I was a Ranger."

"That's what Chase told me a while back," Dan said, walking them to the lobby. "You're one of us. How are your knees holding up?"

Giving him a sour grin, Colin said, "Probably about as good as yours are."

The men chuckled knowingly.

"Stay safe out there," Dan told them as he opened the door for them.

"You, too," Dana said to the sheriff. The fresh air lifted her spirits, or maybe it was knowing that Hauptman and his gang weren't nearby. She felt like celebrating. Joining Colin on the sidewalk, she slid her hand into his. She saw the surprised look on his face.

"You okay with this?" she asked.

"Well . . . sure . . ."

"I don't care if everyone knows that I like you, Colin." She saw him pluck up and grin. He was always so serious. Even her step was lighter as they walked to the truck out in the parking lot.

"The town will gossip," he warned her, meeting her smile. Opening the door for her, she climbed in.

"Ask me if I care?" she shot back, laughing.

Chuckling, he shut the door once she was settled.

Chapter 11

June 12

Colin was finishing saddling the horses in the corral. It was just after dawn, and less than half an hour ago they'd arrived at Wildflower. Dana went to clean out the box stalls in the barn, which was her normal chore to do. The day was threatening rain, and Colin wasn't sure they would be able to ride around the upper acres to check on the different plantings and how they were coming along or not, but they were going to give it a go.

They'd had a warm front come through five days earlier and the land was soaked. The soil was soggy at best and they couldn't use the truck on the dirt road, which was now far too muddy to get around on, so the horses would do the job this morning. At least they wouldn't get stuck in the mud, and he smiled a little, making sure the cinch was tight on Gypsy, Dana's mount.

The breeze was erratic, humidity higher as the cold front was pushing through the area. The sky was a lead color, cumulus clouds moving lower, blanketing the entire valley, indicating rain wasn't far away. He decided to get two rain ponchos that he'd stashed away in his truck, parked just outside the corral area. They might need them. Bandit had decided to be with him, and the Lab was casually waving his tail in anticipation of going out on the land with the horses and his humans. There was no question he was an athletic dog and loved these times when they would ride instead of drive out to check the fields.

As he opened the door to his truck to get the rain gear, he heard a sound, but couldn't make out what it was.

A bolt of lightning flashed above him, followed quickly by rolling, teeth-jarring thunder.

Bandit barked.

Pulling out of the cab, Colin looked up toward the barn on the other side of the road. A cold warning went down his spine. He knew that meant danger. What the hell! He shut the door, Bandit at his side, barking, but looking down the hill. With the barn, it was impossible to see beyond it, the old log cabin below it. Another noise. It sounded like an engine.

What the hell! He heard another engine fire up, the sound eaten away by another clap of thunder rolling through the valley.

What was going on?

Bandit barked furiously, looking up at him, and then looking at the barn. He moved to the corral, mounted up on Blackjack and pulled the reins to Gypsy, so she followed beside him. His heart was starting to pound. There was danger. But where? And who? Where was Dana? He knew she was deep in the first floor of the barn where the box stalls were located.

"Dana?" he yelled, guiding his black horse out the gate, Gypsy trotting beside them.

Bandit suddenly took off, barking furiously, heading straight for the barn.

Lightning flashed and he winced, digging his heels into Blackjack. The horse grunted and leaped into a full gallop. Gypsy followed, her nose near his left knee as they raced toward the barn. Mud splattered upward, and Colin knew the ground was slick. Blackjack was a solid, powerful horse and he could feel him beneath him, negotiating the clay that was now nothing more than slick mud.

Just as he approached the open doors of the barn, he heard several engines, unable to see them due to the size of the building.

"Dana!" he yelled, halting at the open door.

She wasn't there.

Suddenly, an ATV with three men in it roared by, down below the barn.

Where was Dana?

Urgency plunged through him as he pushed his horse into a gallop, getting around the side of the barn so he had a view of below. Who was in that ATV? As he rounded it, he saw a second ATV ahead of the one he'd seen. There was no mistaking Dana's red hair in the back seat. There were three other men in it, too!

Frantic, Bandit was barking wildly, running ahead, chasing the two ATVs that were heading toward the upper fifty acres and that slope that led up to the top of the ridge.

Bullets suddenly filled the air.

The men in the ATV, all wearing camo gear, had AR-15s and were shooting out the sides of the fleeing vehicle at him! Bullets sang wildly around him and the horses, but Colin didn't stop. There was no way he could return fire, for fear of hitting Dana by accident. Bandit was high-tailing it toward the ATVs, which were going at least twenty-five or thirty miles an hour, chewing up hunks of mud, sliding around, but heading straight for that slope.

Colin called out to Bandit.

The dog slowed, looking back at him, torn between running after the fleeing ATVs and going back to him.

"Bandit! Come!" he yelled, slowing the horses. His mind canted toward what to do next. The ATVs were making strong headway and were almost to the edge of the planted fields. In a few more minutes, they'd be clawing their way up that slope. Why hadn't he looked around? Since the incident in late May, everything had been quiet around the valley. Everyone was waiting for that satellite flyover, which was still on the wait list, and the sheriff couldn't do anything about it.

Who was taking Dana? Were they white nationalists? He didn't know. Pulling Blackjack to a halt, Bandit came back to him, his chest and neck covered in mud, tongue lolling out the side of his mouth. Colin could see how upset the dog was. Hell, so was he! What to do? He pulled the horses to a halt, told Bandit to stay, and hauled out that small, powerful radio, making a call to Dan.

"What's up?" Dan asked.

In as many words as he could, his voice hoarse with fear, Colin gave him the information.

"They kidnapped Dana?"

Colin heard the disbelief in Dan's voice.

"Yes . . . they did. I saw her in the back with a soldier

or some guy in camo with her. They're heading up that slope, Dan. The same one that's not a USFS trail."

"Can you follow them at a safe distance while I get my people together here?"

"Yes, I intend to. I'll keep you informed. They've got AR-15s and I can't get too close to them, but the ground is wet and muddy, so their trail is going to be easy to follow."

"Okay, if you can do that? It will help us. I'll be in touch. I have to call the FBI, DEA, and ATF and let them know what's happened."

"Who kidnapped her?" Colin rasped. "Was this Gonzalez's men? Were they down here to get the bags of money?"

"Maybe," Dan growled. "I'm putting one team on and around that log cabin. My other team will work with you. If we can just keep tabs on them, we may be able to capture them."

"Dana's in danger," he warned.

"We won't do anything to risk her life," Dan promised.

"Okay. I have to put a halter on the other horse. It's Dana's horse. We were going to go to the upper field this morning to check on the crops."

"Take that horse with you," the sheriff said.

"I've got Bandit, too."

"Use your Ranger skills, Colin."

"Roger that. Out."

He wanted so badly to chase the ATVs that were now climbing the slope. First things first. He took off Gypsy's bridle and tied it to the saddle horn. He snapped on a nylon lead to the halter she wore; it would be easier on her to travel without a bridle in her mouth. Remounting, he looped the lead around his saddle horn. By the time he was ready to go, it had started to rain. Hauling out the olive-green poncho, he threw it on and then clucked to his horse. He looked up and saw the ATVs both turn right at the top of the ridge. He had to get up there ASAP.

The rain pelted against his face and he lowered the black baseball cap he'd worn to protect his eyes so he could see ahead. Keeping Blackjack at a strong, steady trot, they hit that slope and it was a muddy hell. The horse automatically avoided the chewed up ditches where the ATVs' treaded tires had bit into the soil. Instead, as if his horse sensed that he wanted to follow the tracks, Colin gave him his head and they worked their way up the slope. Gypsy, being a wrangler's horse, knew to stay up, keep her nose just behind his leg. Bandit was running ahead, nose to the ground, following the scent of the ATVs.

His mind spun with questions. Where were they going? Were they at an encampment? But where? Colin had no idea, trying to stop the terror from eating into his steely focus as they topped the ridge. The rain was coming down heavily, the whole landscape in front of him gray and some of it hidden.

He saw the ATVs, still on that ridge. And in a moment, they disappeared down the other side of it. Urging his horse forward, they moved into a strong trot. He took his radio, checking in, giving Dan not only the information, but the GPS from his watch, so he knew exactly where he was. Signing off, he tucked the valuable radio away, his heart wringing in terror.

Why hadn't he fessed up to Dana that he loved her? He'd been a coward, afraid to tell her the depth of his feelings for her. And now? It could be too late. What would those men do to her? Why had they kidnapped her? The worst-case scenarios played out in him and he wanted to cry out of fear and frustration, but shoved it away. All his military training was coming to the foreground, and he found himself acting and thinking like the black ops soldier he'd been when working with the Navy SEALs. It was the only way to treat this situation. Yes, he carried a Glock in a nylon holster on his belt, but it was no match for an AR-15. It was time for him to go undercover . . . not seen, but seeing his enemy. The men who had captured the woman he loved more than life itself.

Dana felt the bite of a syringe needle enter the back of her thigh. One moment she was wheeling out a barrow of horse manure to the area where it was placed daily, and the next, a choked sound coming out of her as she turned. The man was white, baldheaded, wearing camo, his black eyes on her. *Who? What?* Mouth dry, she felt the world tilt, and then she saw a black curtain coming down over her vision. In moments, she lost consciousness, crumpling, the wheelbarrow tilting to one side as she lost her grip. It was the last thing she knew.

Voices . . . there were men's voices above the growl of an engine. Straps were biting into her shoulders and across her waist. Everything was black, but her hearing was coming around. The smell of a gasoline engine, the movement of whatever she was riding in, swaying, jerking, and jolting at high speed. More yelling by the men. She felt the vehicle she was in sway hard to the left. It hit something and there was a terrific jolt seconds later. Feeling like a rag doll, unable to control her muscles, she felt terror eating through her. She wasn't thinking straight or clearly.

More jolting and jostling. She heard the men swearing, but she didn't recognize the language.

Where am I? Where?

The smell of sour, unwashed bodies momentarily surrounded her. Sweaty male bodies. It made her gag. She felt so weak! She was blind! But she could hear and it had clarity now, whereas before the male voices yelling at one another were garbled and she couldn't understand them at all. Her fingers ached in her lap. Why? It was so hard to think straight! She moved her fingers very slowly and they were sluggish to respond. Something was biting deeply into her wrists. They ached. The pain drifted up through her forearms. Why? Why was she in pain?

Terror filled her as she became semiconscious, sitting between two males, and they were speaking in Spanish. Groggy, scared, her breathing shallow and fast. Whatever the vehicle, she was being knocked around, jerked constantly. And then . . . they were on pavement! Speed increased. Wind was whipping with rain against her face, soaking her clothing.

Suddenly, the vehicle lurched, and once more they were on a slippery dirt road, mud splattering on either side of where she sat. Where were they taking her? Her brain felt like it was in pieces, incoherent, and she was trying to think, trying to understand why she was a captive.

Dana had no idea how long they were climbing; sometimes it was a nasty uphill grade, and then down again, just as steep, the vehicle sliding, almost tipping over one time. With every passing minute, her mind became less chaotic. It dawned upon her that these men, Hispanic more than likely, were from the drug lord's gang. Why didn't she see them earlier? The log cabin was down below the barn, away from all the main buildings. She remembered looking at and around the log cabin, but didn't see anything remarkable or out of place. How did these men get there without being heard? Shame tunneled through her. She'd somehow missed the signs!

Her mouth was dry. She was dying for a drink of water. Rain continued to come into the vehicle, but now, she could smell wet Douglas firs. They had to be in the forest. Somewhere . . . What about Colin? Had they killed him? She remembered nothing. Nothing! Tears jammed into her eyes and she wanted to sob. Had they killed him? Was he a prisoner, too? Oh, no! No!

Everything had been so quiet around the ranch since they discovered that money! She had let her guard down. Wanting to cry, but fighting it, Dana wasn't sure she was going to live to see nightfall. The rain continued, heavy and unabated, thunder rolling around and making it sound as if they were all in some huge, invisible kettledrum being hit hard.

Dana lost track of time. She would fall back into that woozy world, weak, unable to lift her eyelids, unable to do much of anything. By the time the vehicles stopped, she was coming out of that state and she could see clearly, for the first time. There was a group of six men, all Hispanic. They wore camo gear. AR-15s were hanging in slings across their bodies. She realized she was sitting in an ATV, in the back seat. When her two captors climbed out, another man, lean, intense-looking and Hispanic, reached out and gripped her hands, which were tied.

"Can you walk?" he asked in stilted English.

"I-I don't know. Why are you doing this? Who are you?"

He managed a thin smile beneath his mustache. "In time, señorita, in time."

"My wrists hurt. I can't feel my hands."

He released her and reached back, produced a slender knife and expertly cut them away from her wrists.

She groaned as circulation flooded back into them, the pain intense and ongoing. Feeling faint, she fell back against the seat, eyes tightly shut.

"Here," he said, putting a canteen between her hands in her lap. "Drink this. It will make the dizziness go away."

It felt solid to her. She wrapped her fingers around it as she struggled weakly to sit up. The canteen was beat-up-looking and an olive-green color. "I'm so thirsty," she whispered.

"That will help. Drink up."

She watched as he turned and snapped out a number of orders in Spanish, which she didn't understand. Instantly, the men jumped and followed the orders. There were four ATVs she could see in front of a lean-to type of affair that they'd built. Nearby were cabins, log cabins, like the one on her property, only much more recently built and well cared for. She counted them: seven of them in a semicircle, hidden by thick woods all around them.

To her right she saw a muddy road. It must have been the one they'd been on. She found her arms weak, and it took a huge effort to bring the canteen to her lips. The water tasted delicious and she drank heavily. The activity around her increased. She allowed the canteen to rest in her lap, watching all the armed men, soldiers more than likely, that belonged to Gonzalez's drug cartel.

Her mind spun. How much to tell this man who looked in charge? What would they do with her? Kill her? The idea paralyzed her momentarily. She wanted to live! Not die! And yet, the looks these men gave her, made her skin crawl. Feeling as if she were naked, feeling horribly vulnerable, she tried to think, her brain slowly coming back online. The man in charge turned to her after giving a series of new orders to his men.

"I'm Lieutenant Alano Gallego. And you are?"

Anger stirred in her. "Captive. Against my will," she gritted out. She saw his very serious expression lighten.

"Ah, *le jaguar hembra*, the female jaguar."

"I don't speak or understand Spanish," she said. Desperately Dana wondered how much he knew about her ranch. Had they been watching them? Did they know of the money? Her life depended upon those answers. The officer was a very good-looking man, probably in his middle thirties, lean, fit, and hard-looking. But his eyes were a light brown and he didn't look like a killer, although she knew he must be.

The thunder clapped over the mountain, a rolling sound sending vibrations through her. She was damp and cold.

"Come," he said, gesturing for her to get out of the ATV. "We will get warm and dry inside my adobe."

Afraid not to obey, Dana stepped out of the vehicle, clinging to the frame, her legs weak, but she was standing. All the other men had scattered and gone into different cabins. The officer came forward, taking the canteen out of her hand.

"Can you walk or do you need help?"

"N-no, I'll make it on my own. Just give me time . . ." She saw him size her up, one corner of his mouth lifting and she sensed he respected her independence.

"This way." He kept in step with her toward the first log cabin in the crescent.

He opened the door for her and it creaked loudly. There were windows, allowing in some dreary, gray light. There was no electricity that she could see. But it was warm and dry in here, and for that, she was grateful.

"Sit in that chair," he instructed, coming around his desk and sitting down.

There was an old, dilapidated wooden chair, the green paint peeled off most of it over time. She sat down, tense, watching him. There was no way for her to run away. Her legs were shaking and trembling. "Why did you do this?" she demanded hoarsely. "You kidnapped me."

Holding up his long, lean hand, he said, "Señorita? If you will answer my questions I might let you go. But if you lie to me?" He shook his head, his eyes hardening. "You will not see dusk today. Do I make myself clear?"

Giving him a jerky nod, she clasped her cold, damp fingers together. "Why couldn't you have just driven into my ranch and asked? You didn't have to do it this way."

His smile was patient, like a father toward his petulant child.

"You are the owner of that ranch?"

"Yes," she said, tensing up. He didn't look like he'd kill someone, but her senses told her it was easy enough for him.

"And how long have you owned it?"

"Just this year . . . it was vacant. I-I wanted to farm the land."

Nodding, he leaned back in the chair, studying her. "And what about that log cabin?"

She froze, her gut clenching. "What about it?"

"When you bought the place did you go out and look at that cabin?"

"Yes. I was going to hire a construction company to come in and repair it."

"Did you?"

"No . . . not yet . . . I didn't have the money to do it."

"Hmmm. Well, my men went down there last night, to your cabin. And you know what? They did not find the bags that we had hidden beneath the floorboards." He stared at her. "What do you know about that?"

If she was going to survive this, Dana knew she couldn't lie. "About three weeks ago, I was inside it and my foot went through a floorboard, breaking it. I found a bag, but I didn't know what it was. The wrangler that I've hired came back to the ranch and he went to take a look at it. He found out the entire floorboard had four bags hidden beneath it."

"I'm glad you decided to tell me the truth," he said softly. "What happened to them?"

"I called the sheriff. He came out and they discovered there was money in those bags. They took all of them to their office. It was the last I saw of them."

Rubbing his chin, his eyes half closed, he said nothing, staring off into the distance.

Dana wanted to scream in fear. The energy in the room went from warm and pleasant to icy cold.

"What did he do with them?"

"I don't know. I'm just a civilian. I'm not part of law enforcement. He didn't tell me anything." That was partially the truth, and her stomach knotted.

"I see." He sat up. "You know nothing else?"

She squirmed, wanting to keep Dan and Colin's name out of this for fear this man, who reminded her of a lean wolf, would hunt them down. God only knew what kind of damage he could wreak on the town, too. "I only know he took them with him. I was questioned by him and he was convinced I wasn't the one who hid them in the cabin."

"What did he think?"

She tried to shrug. "He didn't say. He was very close-mouthed."

He tapped his fingers, studying her again. "We need those bags back. Three belong to my boss and the fourth belongs to a gringo bank robber and his men."

"Why tell me this? I don't want to know," she pleaded. "All I want to do is go home. I don't want to be here. I've done nothing wrong!"

"No," he said, "you have not. You are the unfortunate person caught in the middle. Now? If someone knows you are gone? They will be hunting for you. Especially law enforcement, because they now have the bags in their possession and they'll put two and two together, knowing you were kidnapped for information about them. You were the easiest target to capture and talk to."

"I've told you all I know. Please," she begged, "let me go."

"What is your name?"

Again, she froze. How much did he know about her already? Where was Hauptman, or was he even nearby? Terror ate at her. She gave her name.

"Very good. You told the truth."

Staring at him, she didn't want to ask what would have happened if she hadn't.

"Then, let me go."

"Can't do it, because you'll go to the sheriff and tell him what happened. And I have given you my name. They would like to have it, believe me."

Feeling as if she were on thin ice and never able to regain her balance or footing with this man, she swallowed hard. "Then . . . what are you going to do with me?"

He smiled a little. "For a few days, you will be our guest here. Someone, maybe that wrangler who works for you, will go to the sheriff and tell him what happened. I'm sure they will be out at your ranch very soon, searching for you."

"I have friends. And if I don't answer my cell phone, they'll wonder where I am. Or if something has happened to me."

"Correct," he agreed. "So, our bags of money must be in the sheriff's office?"

"I don't know where they are."

"The gringo. He's the one who watches your ranch. His money is there along with ours."

Shivering inwardly, Dana remained silent. "I don't know what you're talking about." She knew it had to be Hauptman. And she wasn't about to open that can of worms. Hauptman wanted her dead and had said so in court while she sat there. Rubbing her arms, she whispered, "I need to go to the bathroom . . ."

He pointed to his left. "Go right through there."

Slowly getting up, her legs feeling stronger, she made her way to the door and opened it. There was a full bath and it looked inviting. Mind whirling as she did her business, she wondered about Colin. Had they killed him? Injured him? She had no way of knowing. Her fingers trembled as she zipped up and buttoned her jeans. Dragging in a deep breath, she opened the door. The officer was on a satellite phone, speaking rapidly in his language to someone at the other end. When he saw her, he cut off the conversation and switched the phone off.

"I will have one of my men escort you to your cabin. You need to know it has no windows. When darkness comes, there is no light in it. There's a toilet, a shower, and a bedroom. The outside door will be locked and you will not be able to escape, so do not try."

Nodding, she saw another Hispanic soldier come in, this one very short and thin. He looked more like a teenager than an adult.

"Pablo, take Señorita Scott to that last cabin. You are to lock it from the outside so she cannot escape. I expect you to check on her hourly until night falls."

Nodding, Pablo looked at her and gestured for her to follow him. She glanced at the lieutenant, who appeared busy punching in numbers on his satellite phone as she left.

Outside, the rain was easing, but it was much cooler now, and she wrapped her arms around herself, hurrying toward the end cabin. It was the smallest of the group. There were two open garages and the ATVs had been put inside them.

Her cabin was on the other side of the garages, at the tail end of the line of shacks. Still, she was alive . . . he hadn't killed her. Yet. The dread of dying made her mouth go dry as Pablo opened the door and stepped aside. She walked inside.

The door slammed shut, making her jump. It was dark, save for a small lantern that sat on a roughened table. There were several canteens of water there for her, and something to eat. She wasn't hungry.

She was scared out of her mind.

Looking around, the floorboards creaking, she located the bathroom and the bedroom. A little bit of relief trickled through her. The officer considered her an accidental tourist to this whole debacle. He didn't seem to want to kill her. And maybe that was her idealism leaking through. Sitting down at the table, she pushed her palms against her face, still feeling the effects of the drug they'd given her. Her mind was working sporadically, and she hoped it would stay online. Somehow, she had to escape from this place. Somehow.

Where was she? She'd been unconscious for most of the trip. She might be a farm girl, but she was no hiker who could tell the four directions or even how to find them when in the middle of a huge forest. The only thing she knew for sure was that the ATV she was riding in, had crossed an asphalt highway. That meant she was on the opposite side of the road from where her ranch was. And how far did they drive up into the mountains? Being drugged, she had no idea because time didn't ebb and flow properly.

Holding her hands against her face, eyes closed, she thought of Colin. Was he dead? Injured? What had they done to him? She'd been afraid to ask for fear Gallego would ask her more questions. It bothered her greatly how much he knew of her. How did he get her real name? Did that mean he had a spy in Silver Creek? Someone under-cover, acting like a civilian when in reality he was a drug soldier under this man's command?

This was worse than she had realized at first. Her heart centered on Colin. She loved him! Oh, she loved him with her life! What had he seen? Where was he? How was he taking her kidnapping? The unknowns looked like the Grand Canyon to her. She glanced at her watch and blinked once, studying it. It was an Apple Watch. Could she, someway, text Colin? Let him know what happened? He didn't always wear his because of the hard, physical work required of him out at the ranch. He was always afraid that he'd break it, and therefore it stayed in the house.

Pressing once, it didn't work. They must be in a dead zone.

"Oh! If only," she whispered tremulously, keeping her voice low. How did she know they hadn't bugged this cabin? That they were already listening to her? Looking up, she stared around the dark corners of the cabin. Was there a camera or two hidden in here? Watching her? Sud-denly, she felt her spike of hope shatter. She knew nothing of drug teams like this one. And now, she wished she did.

Why didn't they take the watch off her? They should have. Nostrils flaring, Dana pressed the watch face. They probably knew there was no WiFi, and were out of range of cell service. That was why that officer was using a satellite phone, instead.

Nothing.

Her stomach churned and she felt suddenly more alone

than she had in her life. There was no WiFi or cell phone signal up here in the mountains and she was unable to text or get ahold of anyone, never mind Colin. It was a dead zone.

And she could be dead tonight, or tomorrow morning . . .

Chapter 12

June 12

Midway up the mountain, Colin and his mounts were drenched by a thunderstorm that had broken over the area. Luckily, the poncho kept him dry, the water dripping and running off the brim of his baseball hat. The temperature had dropped dramatically from sixty-five to forty. His elk-skin gloves werc wet. He was not immune to the falling, slicing rain and the wind whipping through the dense growth of Douglas firs that surrounded them.

His heart was squarely centered on Dana. Where was she? What was happening to her? Colin could barely go there, the scenes too horrific to imagine, and he grimly blocked it, concentrating instead on paralleling the muddy dirt road that was barely visible off to his left.

He couldn't afford to just ride up that road. He knew those two ATVs were carrying what he thought were either domestic terrorists or worse, the possibility that Gonzalez had sent drug soldiers to retrieve those bags of money. He didn't know which it was. On one hand, Hauptman could be running this terrorist group of white nationalists. Worse, Gonzalez's men had arrived to take their drug money.

His radio buzzed softly. He pulled to a halt, pulling it out of his pocket beneath the poncho.

"Dan?" he asked.

"Copy that. Are you out of WiFi range?"

"Yes, I checked with my cell phone and about a quarter of a mile earlier, I lost the signal. That last GPS I gave you is going to be it. Where are you?"

"We're out at Dana's ranch. We went to the log cabin. Whoever was there, pulled up that floorboard. It means either Hauptman and his crew did it or Gonzalez has sent a group of drug soldiers in to pick up the bags. My forensics team is at work to see if we can lift fingerprints or anything else that might help us ID the suspects."

"I hope you can find something," he said heavily, continually looking around, keeping his voice low, but not a whisper.

"Are you still paralleling that road?"

"Yes. I'm staying out of the line of sight of it, pretty much guessing where it's at. I can't risk being seen. If I am, there's going to be a firefight and I don't have an AR-15, so I will be pretty much a sitting duck."

"We're mobilizing at HQ right now. I'm going to wait at the ranch and then we'll pretty much follow how you are stalking them. We can't do much until you have eyes on wherever they are."

"What about a drone? Your department has one, don't you?"

"Yes, but it's out for repair. It's a special military type with an infrared camera on it. I called Cheyenne where it's getting fixed. They're waiting for a part that won't be

there until tomorrow. I'm sending a deputy to Cheyenne
to pick it up tomorrow morning. It's our only eyes in the
sky. We're going to have to go at this like it was a ground
mission."

"Got it. I don't like it, but it's all we have right now."
And that meant that it would take the deputy half a day
to drive the part back from Cheyenne, which was half a
state away, back to Silver Creek HQ.

"Keep shadowing the road. I'm hoping you'll run into
their camp."

"I worry for Dana. I'm sure they'll interrogate her
about the money."

"Yes," Dan said, "they will."

"Do you think they'll let her go?" His hand tightened
on the wet, slick reins for a moment because there was
hesitation in Dan's voice.

Finally, he said, "It's doubtful . . . she's seen them and
can ID them, Colin."

"Then it's a matter of time?" he choked out, terror siz-
zling through his chest, his heart contracting with a silent
scream.

"I'm afraid so. That's why you need to try and locate
that party as soon as possible. See if you can rescue her.
I'd like to be able to know where they're at and get adequate
help and backup from law enforcement to take them down.
But even then? They could have killed her already. I'm
sorry, this isn't what you want to hear, but I can't soften
this for you."

Mouth working, his eyes narrowing as he looked through
the gray drizzle that was now beginning to lighten little by
little, he rasped, "Okay . . . thanks. I'll check in about an
hour from now."

"Ten hundred hours," Dan said, breaking into military Zulu-time speak. The military used a twenty-four-hour clock.

"Roger that. Out." Colin carefully turned off the radio. It had a battery, and at some point it would die. Just like Dana might die. No! It couldn't happen. It just damn well could not happen! He leaned down, patting Blackjack's sleek, wet neck. Gypsy had hung her head, almost touching his right leg. The horses were feeling the urgency as well. And so did Bandit, who was always ahead of them, nose to the ground, following the scent.

Now he was back being a Ranger. Back on the stalk to find the bad guys, only this time, they weren't in Afghanistan; they were here, on US soil. Bitterness assailed him, along with a simmering rage. His PTSD had become his shield against a heavily armed enemy who was merciless. It didn't matter whether it was drug soldiers or Hauptman and his crew. Both were murderous and took no prisoners. They'd shoot him on sight and he knew it.

Pressing his heels into Blackjack, he asked the horse to move forward at a steady walk. There was no way he could trot through this forest; the trees too close together and he was constantly looking for ways to weave through it. The horses were much larger and needed more room, and he was constantly having to choose a new path through the area. Although the brown carpet of pine needles stopped the mud, they were slick, and more than once a horse had slid and had to catch itself.

The mountain ahead of him went up at a five-degree angle, and that was steep enough. They were approaching eight thousand feet, according to his last cell phone check-in before the WiFi was lost. The horses were laboring, sometimes snorting, and as much as he wanted to push them harder, it would be foolhardy.

To his right, less than a quarter of a mile away was the Buckthorn River, which snaked down through a mountain pass somewhere far above them, and he was now paralleling it, too. Once, he'd gone to the river so the horses and he could drink water. The animals had gulped it eagerly, drinking long and deeply. So had he and Bandit. Luckily, he had a canteen in one saddlebag and a lunch he and Dana had planned on eating once they arrived at the field to survey it. He would stop every half hour or so, dismount, allow the horses to eat grass and foliage from nearby bushes because they had no hay or grain to eat. Food was fuel. Luckily, Bandit had been fed earlier, so he was working off a full stomach.

Colin had to keep the horses watered and fed, or they would not be of any help to him. Silently, he railed against what was happening. What he wanted to do was use that muddy dirt road, follow it in his truck, which would probably sink to its axles with all this rain. And Dana? God, he couldn't go there. *No way.*

He led his horse forward, walking on the spongy brown needles, sometimes seeing the dirt road, sometimes not. Bandit came to his left side, looking up at him, a worried expression on his dog face.

Tears came unexpectedly into Colin's eyes, mingling with the rain striking his face. He loved Dana. Again, he lamented not telling her the whole truth when they'd spoken about their growing relationship a day earlier. Why hadn't he? Why? She was alone now. No one to protect her. She was vulnerable and there was no safe place for her. Nothing . . .

Shaking his head, he pulled up the hood of the poncho, keeping part of his head dry.

Bandit halted, frozen, ears up, looking toward the unseen muddy road they were paralleling. Suddenly, Colin also heard the growling sound of an ATV somewhere to his left, a long way away, but coming in his direction. Halting, he turned the horses so they faced the road because there was a small rise in front of them that would hide them. Positioning himself next to a large fir, Colin's whole focus was on that sound that was drawing closer and closer. Bandit remained steadfastly at his left side and sat down, ears forward, eyes on the sound that was growing louder and louder. Colin took out his cell phone, turning it on, positioning it against the bark because where the slope ended, he might be lucky and be able to get a photo. He couldn't send it, but if he could ID these bastards, that was better than nothing. Was Dana with them? Would they, by some miracle, let her go? His heart began a slow pound and he waited.

The horses heard the approaching ATV, lifting their heads, ears pricked forward.

Pushing his shoulder against the tree trunk, Colin aimed his cell a little past where the slope was lessening. In less than a minute, the ATV growled and was sliding back and forth down the slope. The road was on a wide curve and as the ATV roared into sight, Colin snapped a number of photos until it disappeared down below them.

He hadn't been seen. There were two men, heavily armed, wearing camo, in that ATV. They carried AR-15s.

They were Hispanic. His gut clenched. Drug soldiers. Mercenaries who never took prisoners. They shot first and asked questions later. He did not see Dana in the ATV. Moving the cell toward his body, protecting it from the rain, he quickly assessed the three photos and then pulled the radio out, contacting Dan.

"I've got something for you," Colin began without preamble. "Two drug soldiers, both Hispanic, in camo gear and carrying AR-15s, came down the mountain on that muddy road, heading toward the highway, maybe."

"That's good news," Dan said.

"No cell coverage. I can't send the photos to you for ID."

"That's okay. At least now we know whom we're dealing with. That's a step in the right direction. Was Dana with them?"

His voice fell to a gravelly growl. "No . . . no sign of her."

"Could you estimate the distance from when you heard the ATV up above where you're at?" he demanded.

"I would guesstimate a mile," Colin replied, listening as the ATV sounds disappeared and the quiet patter of rain in the forest returned. "Bandit heard them first, which tipped me off."

"If you are right, the ATV sounds you heard started a mile away; it could mean their camp is a mile away."

"Yes, but that's when the engine noise came into earshot," Colin parried. "They could have been much farther up on that mountain, maybe miles farther away, and just because its hearing distance? It doesn't mean their camp is a mile away from me."

"Yeah," Dan muttered, "I thought about that, too. What's your plan now?"

"I'd like to know where that ATV is going, but I'm going to continue to follow the road up this mountain at a safe distance and keep going until I find where they're at. Dana is my priority. Bandit has a scent on them, as well, so that's helping me."

"Good to hear. Keep trying to find out where they are. And if that ATV returns?"

"Once I hear it, I'll dismount and hopefully get more photos of them returning. I'll call you if that happens. They may just be doing recon, is all."

"With them heading down that road, they could also be setting up an early warning system," Dan pointed out. "Maybe the leader, whoever he is, has ordered two of his men to stand watch at the entrance to that road off our main highway. We don't know where Hauptman is, or even if he is a part of this group. Right now, we're in touch with both nearby ranches that are possibly in danger, too. We've had them vacate their property. We don't know where this drug group is, or what they're planning. We have unmarked cars with deputies going to each of the ranches to be lookouts."

"That means you need to approach that road, whenever you decide to come up it, with a helluva lot of caution, Dan."

"Don't worry, we will."

"I'm going to keep heading up the mountain," he told the sheriff. "I'll check in maybe an hour or so from now, unless something happens before that."

"Whatever you do, Colin? Do *not* put yourself in the

line of fire. You're far more valuable to everyone concerned by remaining in recon status and giving us reports."

The military lingo was correct for this situation, Colin knew. "Roger that. Out."

He listened for a few minutes, but no other sounds came. The rain was easing even more, the thunder over the mountain, heading away from them now.

Colin took time to check the horses' legs and hooves. So far, no scratches, cuts, or injuries. He needed his game horses to be sound. He also checked out Bandit, making sure there were no cuts or injuries to his paws and legs. Everyone was healthy so far.

Mounting up, he moved out and started weaving in and out. They were somewhere between eight and nine thousand feet. In his experience, woods began to thin at this altitude, and that meant fewer trees, more of a straight line that he could shadow that dirt road. It would be easier on his horses as well. Bandit remained on the left side of Blackjack, panting heavily, easily keeping up with the horses. Colin swore that they all understood the urgency of their journey.

June 13

"That bastard," Hauptman snarled. "Gonzalez has sent his men and stole our money before our meeting date!" He stood with his six men, staring at the floorboard that had been lifted in the old log cabin on the Wildflower Ranch. Their flashlight beams showed the floorboard had been removed, and nothing below it except dirt and gravel stared back at them. Richfield Jones, his second in command, cursed softly.

"We were supposed to meet this Lieutenant Gallego at three a.m." Richfield looked at his watch. "It's five a.m., almost dawn, and they never showed up or called us, and they have your cell number. Now, we know why. They got here earlier, maybe yesterday . . . We just don't know . . ." He looked around. "No one's here at the ranch. Or the mobile home. Everyone is gone. Gonzalez agreed to meet us on June thirteenth, and together we'd lift the floorboard and they'd take their three bags and we'd take our one bag."

Snorting violently, Brock glared around the darkened log cabin. The door had been unlocked when they'd arrived at two a.m. and they'd parked their ATVs at the rear of the structure where they could not be seen. "I was leery when none of Gonzalez's men were here to meet us," he said, shaking his head. "I shouldn't have trusted him. When I tried to call him, the phone number no longer exists. That's how I know he's taken our money."

"He was using a burner phone. Now what?" Richfield asked.

"Turn off our flashlights," Hauptman ordered. "It's almost dawn. We need to disappear back into the forest. And I think I know where Gonzalez's men might be holding up right now."

"They could be long gone," Richfield said.

"Remember when they were meeting us two years ago when we first came to Wyoming?" Brock said, thinking out loud. "There was one of his lieutenants, Gallego, the same man who was supposed to meet us here, tonight. I remember talking to this dude about the US Forest Service line shacks on that dirt road located on the other side of the highway, and that it would be a good place to hide for a day or two before they headed back south. Hell, I talked to him two days ago, confirming the time and place to be here. It was all a ruse."

"You think they still might be around here?" Richfield asked.

"They've got four bags of money. They're illegally in the US. They probably have a plan on how to return to Mexico, to cross the border, but they have to have some kind of help involved, from the other side, to do it. I want to go up that other road where the line shacks are located and check it out."

Richfield grimaced. "It's muddier than hell right now. So is the road we have to take back to our tent city."

"We need to try and nail them now," Hauptman growled, turning, walking out the open door. "My gut tells me they're up at those line shacks. They can't have that many men. I want our damned money back."

Richfield hurried out to catch up with the long-striding Hauptman. "We only have six men, Brock."

"I'm betting Gallego has fewer than that. They can't be traveling heavy on a mission like this. Let's go . . ."

Near dawn, drugged with tiredness, Colin pulled the horses to a halt behind a large hill that paralleled that dirt road. The top of it was decorated with a lot of thick bushes, not pine needles. It reminded him of an egg in a frying pan, the top like the yoke.

The forest had thinned a lot and he guesstimated they were near seven thousand feet. It was certainly more of an effort to breathe. He had gone earlier to the river to let the horses drink and eat grass, and shared half his sandwich with Bandit, and drank his fill from the icy-cold river. It was a large river, nearly one-quarter of a mile wide at some points. It was the main water source for Silver Creek Valley and all the ranchers and farmers who irrigated, used it.

As exhausted as he was, his heart hovered over Dana. He still hadn't run into those line shacks. Maybe he'd un-derestimated how far up the mountain they really were. Dawn was a gray line along the horizon as he stood in the partial clearing, the hill in front of them so they couldn't be spotted by anyone on an ATV going up or down that muddy road. The rain had quit at midnight and he was glad about that. As he walked, his feet did not sink as deeply into the wet bed of brown pine needles beneath his boots. The air was clean, the resinous scent of the forest, surrounding them. As always, he kept his hearing keyed, as well as watched Bandit for a first warning, the dog's hearing and smell a helluva lot keener than his own. The last time he'd checked in with Dan, who also sounded just as exhausted, was at four a.m. It was time for another check-in.

A sound like gunfire, far below him, faintly drifted up to where he stood. Scowling, he heard more shots, fired in rapid succession. Bandit froze, ears up, looking at where the sound came from. Colin knew it couldn't be Dan and his law enforcement team because they weren't planning on coming into the area until he'd located the drug soldiers, possibly at the line shack. They had no eyes in the sky in the way of a drone to find them faster. Blind, he understood Dan's hesitancy to go on a wild-goose chase without absolute proof that the drug soldiers were located at or near those line shacks. Bandit whined, standing near Blackjack, his ears perked, looking down the road.

Both horses lifted their heads, ears forward, listening to a gun battle below them. Rubbing his jaw, Colin knew something or someone had found those two drug soldiers in that ATV that had come from somewhere above his position. A sense of urgency thrummed through him and he mounted Blackjack, clucking to Gypsy, who was on a halter lead, to follow closely. Bandit moved about ten feet ahead, always picking the easiest ways through the mighty firs for the group.

Something was wrong, but Colin didn't know what or who it was. Otherwise, why would those drug soldiers be in a skirmish below him? The woods had thinned a great deal and he continued to be unseen as he paralleled the road. Urging his horse into a trot, he headed, his heart pounding, and it wasn't from the altitude.

Something woke Dana up. Instantly, still fully clothed, the thin blanket on the bed drawn around her shoulders because it was cold, she sat up, snapping wide-awake. All afternoon, and into the darkness, she had feared someone coming through that only door to kill her. She'd been so emotionally pulverized by the event, that she fell into the bunk bed near dark, on a seedy, thin mattress, and pulled the wool blanket around her body. She fell asleep, picturing Colin's serious face hovering above hers. Was he trying to find her? How would he know where to look? Was the sheriff on this and looking for her, also? How could they find her? It all felt so hopeless.

The food on the table, all snacks, had filled her belly

just before she went to bed. She'd drunk all the water. Once, she tried the door, but it wouldn't open. There was a lock and key for it on the outside, not the inside where she needed it to be.

She heard something and got up, dropping the blanket on the bed and walking out to the main area where the table and chair sat. The sounds were muted . . . and she couldn't make them out.

And then, the noises stopped. Her watch read 5:15 a.m. It would be grayish light outside at this time of year. Could she escape? She'd searched the cabin for any kind of instrument she could use to jimmy the door lock.

Making a frustrated sound, she realized she had a Buck knife on her belt! Quickly, she pulled open the case and pulled the longest blade out. Moving to the door, the crack between the door and the jamb was about one-quarter of an inch. Leaning over, she gently pushed the long blade forward. It struck something. Twisting the blade, she tried to get below the obstruction and did. Lifting the blade above it, she held the blade in place, wriggling it gently. Could she get the thin steel blade into the mechanism and put enough pressure on it to pull it back, thereby freeing her? Dana didn't know, but she was going to try. Escaping Gallego and his men meant she had a chance to live! To be with Colin!

Mouth thinning, she knelt down and took another try at the lock. To her surprise, the blade slid into the lock itself. That was progress! Now, Dana wished she had some knowledge of such mechanical devices. She'd have a template in her head and she'd know what to do and where to do it in order to open the door.

She kept her ears keyed to any more sounds, but there

weren't any. The logs on this building were thick and stout. What was that sound she'd heard? Gently, she maneuvered the blade a little this way, and a little that way in another direction. Something moved. Breath hitching, her heart started to pound with anticipation. She kept repeating, *Move, just move, let me out of here . . . I want to live . . . I want to tell Colin how much I love him . . .*

Suddenly, the latch released! Gasping, she leaped to her feet, hand closing around the doorknob. Holding her breath, she twisted it slowly, afraid there might be a guard outside. The door moved. She cracked it open. Everything was quiet. Fear roared through her. Heart pounding so loud, she could barely hear anything! She had to escape!

Opening the door cautiously, she looked to see if there was a soldier or guard around. There was not. Mouth dry, she slipped out, quietly shut the door, and eased around the corner so she couldn't be seen. Ahead of her was the slope of the mountain, small knobby hills popping up out of the land, and thousands of fir trees.

She had to be quiet! The needles were slippery. Up ahead in the grayness, she saw a hill about a quarter of a mile away from her. If she could get there? Maybe she could stop, think, and figure out where to go and where she might be. Fear made her knees tremble so badly that she thought she might fall, striding ahead, keeping that cabin between herself and the rest of them. What would Gallego do when he found out she'd escaped? Oh, God. He'd kill her!

Adrenaline shot through Dana and she hurried faster. The need to put more space between her and them, pushed her into a slow jog. Her breath was raspy sounding; she had no idea what the elevation was, and she felt like her chest was going to explode either from sheer fright of dying or the thinning air.

Another sound reached her ears. Growling engines, far, far below where she was. Who was it? Was it the sheriff? Colin? Unsure, she broke into a run to hide behind that hill covered with pine needles, which looked like the hump of a camel.

Hurry! Hurry!

Slipping and sliding, breath tearing out of her contorted mouth, she lunged upward, her thighs beginning to ache and burn from her sudden effort.

Just a few more yards!

As she whipped around the hill, there was a tremendous explosion below her. Gasping, she jerked to a halt and then peeked around the edge of the hill.

NO! Oh, my God! There were four ATVs, camo-covered men pouring out of them, throwing grenades or some other kind of weapon, at the six cabins. There were screams, curses, and the air filled with sounds of violence, the popping of rounds being shot, and fire arcing up and out of six of the seven cabins. To her horror, she saw the first cabin, Gallego's office, explode upward like a thousand matchsticks had been lit under it, wood shrapnel flying in every direction. The whole roof blew off, the shakes like rectangular squares falling like a different kind of rain. The sounds hurt her ears. She felt a powerful pressure wave pass by her, and she cried out, falling to her hands and knees, hiding her head with her arms. Sobbing for breath, she got on her belly and crawled to where she could see below. There was no way she could be discovered! Men were on their knees, AR-15s blazing, spitting out death toward those cabins that were all on fire. The drug soldiers inside were screaming, trying to get out of the burning cabins, shot dead as they ran out the doors. It was carnage, and Dana squeezed her eyes shut, her hands over her ears, her face pressed to the damp pine needles.

Who were those guys? Who? She was too far away to be able to identify them; only that they, too, had AR-15s, wore camo clothing, and were snapping off shots with deadly accuracy. There were six of them. Gallego had about the same number of men. The air turned smoky and she coughed, slapping her hand across her mouth, not wanting to be heard. There wasn't much chance of that happening, though, because now all the line shacks were on fire, including the one she'd been kept a prisoner in. Luckily, they had been built in an area where the trees were at least three hundred feet away from the structures. She worried about the forest being set on fire.

She saw two of the men who had started the fight, fall over. They didn't move. Fear ate at her. She rolled over and hid behind the hill. Looking around, she saw another hill about the same distance from the first one. Could she use this series of hills to remain unseen, and escape? She had no idea where she was because they'd given her a shot that made her unconscious. The woods seemed the same to her, except that there was a summit far above her, the sunlight hitting the tip of the craggy mountain that still had a lot of snow on it.

Shaking violently with fear, she pushed herself up, her knees feeling like mush, as if they wouldn't support her run to that next hill. She had to get away from this! It wasn't Dan and his sheriff deputies, that was for sure. This had to be some kind of turf war between drug gangs, she thought. Pushing forward, bent over, she walked swiftly, always turning, and always making sure that the hill was between her and the activity below so she couldn't be spotted.

The crackle of fire took over as the major sound by the time she reached the second knoll. Sneaking around the edge of it, she realized it was smaller than the first one. But it would hide her. Sinking to her knees, mouth dry and parched, she wished for water, but there was none around.

The shooting had stopped.

Wanting to look, but too afraid, she huddled there, listening, trying to hear what was going on. There were a couple of single shots, but that was it. The smoke was drifting over her now, like a thin, gossamer, brownish-yellow blanket. It was being pushed upward by the mountain's air currents. Gaze darting here and there, Dana tried to figure out which way to go.

Who was left down there? Did she dare look? *No*, her mind screamed at her. *Keep climbing, keep going. Get as far away from this area as fast as possible! If they find you they will murder you! Just like your parents were murdered!*

The reality sunk starkly into Dana. She saw several other little knolls here and there. This second knoll had gone off to her right from where she'd first knelt. Squinting, the light getting better, she tried to find the road, but couldn't. Maybe the road stopped at the line shacks? Yes, that was possible. How she wished she knew the area better than she did. She had no compass, just her jacket and what she wore, and her Buck knife, that had saved her life.

Trembling, pushing her hands across her sweaty face, she realized if she hadn't gotten out of the cabin she'd either have been burned to death or shot. The horror of her situation deluged Dana as never before.

Forcing herself to look around, to strategize how to get out of this area, the only thing she could do was keep going up at an angle, and make it across that mountain that rose far above her. Now, with the sun rising a little more, she could see snow about half a mile farther up the slope. If she could use these knolls, she could angle off to the right and perhaps find a path or hiking trail. If nothing else? She saw snow and that meant water for her. She'd give anything to taste water melting into her mouth. Her parents had taught her survival skills because she grew up on a farm out away from everything except raw nature and the landscape surrounding it.

Slowly standing, Dana turned and looked back, that hill her shield. The smoke was thickening, but the trees weren't on fire. She heard nothing else except the popping and crackling of the burning cabins far below her,

Grimacing, she felt suddenly weak and tired. It didn't matter. She had to get going. A person could live for weeks or months on water, but only about four days without water. And that snow was her savior at this point. She could eat the snow and get liquid into herself.

As she moved upward, keeping that knoll as her safe-guard once more, she hurried as fast as she could toward the third one. Her breath was coming harder and harder. Was she around nine thousand feet? Dana knew trees and brush quit growing at ten thousand feet. And she could see the bare area and the snow above her. Looking back every few minutes to make sure no one was sneaking up on her, she kept putting one foot in front of the other.

She was alive! That's all that counted. Somehow, someway, she would find her way back home, or to Silver Creek. Maybe by climbing this mountain she could see the land below it and figure out exactly where she was.

Heartened, her breath rasping, lungs burning, she forced herself to step over branches and not crack one, which would make a sound. She had to be quiet. Silent, if possible. Never had she felt more alone in all her life. She wished Colin were with her. She loved him. This event had torn away any questions or trying to hide from the truth. Would she be able to get home? Throw her arms around him? Kiss him? Love him? Dana wanted nothing more than that. He was part of her heart, part of her life. And she ached to be with him once more.

Colin's heart bounded once when he spotted the first in a line of cabins. There was a rise farther up, and it would hide him and allow him to dismount and tie the horses to the trees while he took out his binoculars from his saddlebag, take Bandit, and go lie on his belly, assessing the situation.

In no time, he was in place, Bandit lying to the left of him. The road was in front of him and the seven line shacks, plus two large open garages where he spotted the ATVs parked, within them. There was no movement, the gray light of dawn telling him the drug soldiers were asleep. How many of them? He didn't know. But those ATVs could hold four men apiece, so there could be sixteen. And he was but one man against all of them. It almost felt like the Afghan village that got overrun that night when he and his men could not save or protect them, the numbers in the hundreds when they attacked.

Where was Dana? Or was she already dead? He shook his head, denying it. No! Not Dana! Not now! For a moment, he felt cursed, but shook it off. She couldn't be dead! And yet, the possibility was very real. Mouth going dry, he focused on each cabin. Most of them had windows. The one on the end did not, next to where the ATVs were parked in those two garages.

Another sound rolled his way. What the hell? He turned on his side, looking down the slope. Bandit looked, too. It sounded like a group of growling, clawing ATVs coming up the mountain on the road. Coming toward him. Was it part of the drug soldier group coming to join them? Colin didn't know.

Chapter 13

Colin grabbed his radio and called in to the sheriff's office, not knowing if Dan was awake at this time of morning or not. Almost instantly, he answered.

"Where are you?" he asked Colin.

"I'm about seven hundred yards east of the seven line shacks, hiding behind a knoll. I have a clear view of them. There's four ATVs near the cabins. No movement outside. I'm assuming there's men inside those cabins, but haven't been able to ID them or know how many, yet. I just heard noises—first, like military rifle gunfire for about fifteen seconds, and then two minutes later, like ATV engines fired up, far below me, at the area where the main highway and this road connect with one another. The engine noises are growing closer to us. Someone is coming up the mountain."

"Stay put," Dan ordered. "I've got men ready to roll. Our SWAT team leader, Hunter Grant, is loading his crew into the van right now. I'll need your input and we were just waiting to see if you could spot the perps. Good work."

"I've discovered something. Not sure who or what." The noise coming up the road grew louder. "I'm not sure who is coming up this road, Dan. Stand by, those ATVs will crest this hill any moment now . . ."

"Standing by," Dan said.

Keeping low, with Bandit lying down next to him once more, the unmistakable sound of ATVs approaching broke the peaceful morning stillness. In the first ATV, he recognized Hauptman in the passenger seat. Colin's eyes widened. He held a grenade launcher, at the ready, in his arms. Of all things!

Confused, Colin watched as the two ATVs, which held six men in camos, pulled out on the other side of the road opposite the cabins. He watched Hauptman get out, aim the grenade launcher and start firing at the line shacks, one after another, in rapid, sustained succession.

A massive series of explosions rocked the first cabin, wood and roof exploding outward. Automatically, Colin opened his mouth, equalizing the pressure in his lungs with the outside air so they wouldn't turn to jelly. A pressure wave from each explosion hit the knoll and shook it. He held on to Bandit, his arm like a vise around the frightened dog's shoulders, keeping him against his body. The horses jumped around, but their halter leads were well tied around trunks of trees.

Hauptman fired off round after round, in quick succession. Six of the seven cabins were on fire! He saw men running out of them, rifles in hand. But they were no match for Hauptman's men, who were ready and fired their AR-15s into the stunned, confused group. No one ran out of the seventh cabin that had not been set on fire. These men were in T-shirts and boxer shorts, firing back at Hauptman. A few bullets sang by the knoll.

Screams, shouts, and gunfire filled the air; the crackle

of fire, and smoke billowing upward, thick and black, combined into a battle. Worrying about his horses, who were still jumping and leaping around, Colin slid down the knoll, taking Bandit with him, got to his feet and walked over to Blackjack and Gypsy, trying to calm them with his low voice and hands. He stood with them, keeping a tree between himself and the gunfire. Bandit huddled at his feet.

Instantly, the horses settled down as he talked to them in a low, soothing voice, his hand on each muzzle, quieting them. Bandit sat up, leaning against his left leg, whining. Wanting to put a hand on the scared, trembling dog, he couldn't because he didn't have three hands. Right now, it was important that the horses calm down despite the noise and ongoing carnage. He couldn't see anything because the knoll was in his line of sight. It would protect all of them from getting hit by flying shrapnel or bullets that sang around the area like bees buzzing above all their heads.

In a matter of two minutes, the gunfire abruptly stopped. The horses calmed. Bandit stopped whining. He patted Bandit soothingly on the head and gestured for him to follow him back up to the top of the knoll. Lying on his belly, Colin moved cautiously to the top.

Six cabins were on fire. Luckily, there was a huge circular fire break around them, so the trees had not caught on fire. He saw six men near the cabins, lying unmoving. He could see bloodstains across their bodies. On the other side, he saw Hauptman and two of his men. They were tending the other two, who had been wounded in the melee. Hauptman strode down the line of carnage, toward the seventh cabin. He had his AR-15 up, ready to fire, as he used his boot to kick in the door. He ran in but came out less than a minute later, scowling. Apparently the seventh cabin was not being used, with no enemy soldier within it to shoot.

Pulling the radio out of his pocket, Colin gave Dan the intel, describing it in detail. When he was done, he waited.

"Hauptman fired on the men in those cabins with a grenade launcher?" There was shock in Dan's voice.

"Yes, it's a black ops China Lake grenade launcher, the type Navy SEALs use. Hauptman's men brought over seven rounds for him to utilize. Where he got that weapon, I don't know. He's adept at using and reloading it in a helluva hurry, too. I don't know how much more ammunition he's got for that weapon. Two of his men put the ammo he did use, nearby, so he could easily reload and fire. That's why he could take out six of those seven cabins in a matter of ten seconds."

Colin heard the sheriff swearing softly and then he put his hand over the radio; Colin could hear him giving orders to someone else and couldn't make out what was said. Bandit remained next to him, lying down, ears up, remaining on guard.

Returning, Dan asked, "Can you tell *who* they are?"

"My guess is they're Gonzalez's drug soldiers who came looking for their drug money under the floorboards of Dana's cabin."

"They must have gone to the log cabin on Dana's ranch earlier?"

"Yes, that's when they kidnapped her and took off in their ATVs," he said, his voice turning raw.

"And they came to these line shacks," he murmured,

thinking aloud. "Maybe to regroup? Figure out what to do next? I wonder if Dana told them we had the bags?"

"I haven't a clue. All I know is Hauptman just blew them away with a grenade launcher."

"We're mounting up in the SWAT van right now. We'll be there in twenty minutes. Stay where you are, Colin. You can give us updates. We don't know what Hauptman will do next."

"Right now, he and the other two men who aren't injured are going to the garages where those other ATVs are parked. They're looking for something . . ."

"Maybe these unidentified men were Gonzalez's soldiers," Dan said. "And they might have arrived first to go look for the bags under the floorboards of Dana's log cabin. And maybe Hauptman was supposed to meet them at a specific time and place, but he got there after these other dudes had realized the money wasn't there and then kidnapped Dana? They probably hoped she would know where the money was located."

"Sounds plausible," Colin agreed, watching the men thoroughly search each ATV. "Right now, Hauptman and his two soldiers have ransacked the ATVs, which lends credence to your idea."

"Looking for bags of money?"

"Yeah, it could be. They don't look happy at all. Now, they're going back to the cabins they destroyed. They're still on fire. My guess is they might think the money was in one of the cabins?"

"Well," Dan chuckled darkly, "if that's so, Hauptman thinks he just destroyed his stolen bank money. He doesn't know we have the money, and in fact, the FBI came by and picked up all four bags in person about an hour ago, so it's no longer on our possession, either. It's headed to the forensics lab at the main FBI HQ in Washington, D.C."

Colin muttered, "Karma." Lifting the binoculars, he added, "Yeah, looks like they're now focusing on the cabins. They've gotten some long branches and are poking through the fire and ashes, definitely looking for something."

"Maybe it will keep them busy until we can get there. I'll need you to stay right where you are. This SWAT van won't make that grade or muddy road. We'll have to park below at the turn-off and hoof it on foot up to those line shacks. It will be longer than twenty minutes to get up there."

"Roger that," Colin agreed. "Yeah, you'll need ambulances, too. I don't see any of those guys they shot, moving. Probably already dead."

"Any sign of Dana?"

His heart fell. "No . . ." he managed, his voice roughened with emotions, "no sign of her. I hope . . . I hope she wasn't in one of those cabins . . . but I don't know where she could be. She was kidnapped by those drug soldiers. I'm going crazy trying to figure out where they might have taken her."

There was a long pause. Dan choked out, "Let's take this a step at a time, okay? Hang in there. Keep the faith . . ."

"Yeah," he rasped. Colin knew without him in place, the SWAT team would be blind and could walk right into Hauptman's crew. He stared at where the leader had laid that grenade launcher down on the lead ATV they rode in on. He clicked the radio. "You need to know besides their AR-15s and the sidearms that look like Glocks, Hauptman has a grenade launcher and he sure as hell knows how to use it. I don't see any more ammo for it, though."

"Remember, he was a regional drug dealer on the West Coast before he ever started robbing banks," Dan said.

"I forgot about that . . . Yeah, it makes sense. All drug soldiers and drug lords go high tech for black ops weapons when they can lay their hands on them. That explains everything."

"I want to know if he's got any more ammo for that grenade launcher."

Colin surveyed the ATVs Hauptman's gang came in on, looking at both of them carefully. "I can't pick up anything in them that looks like weapons or ammo, but I only have one angle."

"I'm going to put my SWAT team in a semicircle so that as we move up, they're also moving to the other side of the cabins and probably in front of where you are located."

"A bowl strategy. That's a good one. I'll keep you apprised as you come up this road."

"Copy that. Out."

Now, the waiting began. Colin was sure that everyone on the SWAT team was in superb physical condition and they could take this high altitude with little problem. Checking on his horses, they were no longer jumpy, but they remained hyperalert. Animals almost always were frightened by gunfire, never mind that whooshing sound that the grenade launcher made. Right now, he was in the most protected place of all, and he was glad because he didn't want the horses or Bandit injured or shot in the coming melee. He was too far away to use a pistol, which was only accurate to seventy-five yards, and he was far beyond that range. Besides, it would be a one-sided battle bringing a pistol to an AR-15 fight or that lethal grenade launcher. He figured that Dan's team was armed with AR-15s, as well. And, they wore body armor, to help them remain protected against bullets. No one could survive a grenade launcher, however.

Hauptman gestured to his two men who were not wounded. The others were sitting on the ground, waiting stoically. They were not badly wounded from what Colin could ascertain, just flesh wounds.

Hauptman then strode back to one of the two ATVs, climbed in and headed to the cabin at the end of the line. Maybe he was too lazy to walk the distance? But it seemed out of place. Colin wondered if the man, who lived on his animal instincts, felt the coming showdown.

Getting out, Hauptman surveyed the seventh cabin closely. He had slung his AR-15 across his body and leaned down, picking up a long, fallen fir branch to poke through the debris. The cabin, too, had burned down and was nothing but hot, glowing coals, ash, and very little smoke at this point.

Swallowing hard, Colin couldn't wipe out the fact that Dana had been in one of those cabins. Or worse, that the drug soldiers had gotten what they wanted out of her and shot her in the head, leaving her body somewhere out in the forest. Squeezing his eyes shut, he wrestled with his violent emotional reaction, wanting to deny all of it. There was just no way he'd believe any of it, although logic told him it was entirely possible. Grief spilled through him and he had to focus even more to push it away and stay on top of other men stirring through the ashes of cabin one and two.

His mind whirled with the many things that could happen. He was sure the SWAT leader, Hunter Grant, who had been a US Navy SEAL for nine years, would be leading his team of ten specialists. He had earned notoriety in Wyoming; the Silver Creek team had been called in too many times to count, to assist with other law enforcement situations around Wyoming, always successful when called upon. There was no question that Hunter's name was apropos—the man was a hunter. He lived up to his name. Hunter wasn't a swashbuckling dude, but a quiet, intense, focused leader that the women and men on the team had full confidence in. That line of work required just such a man.

Colin felt his muscles tightening, his breath growing shallow, as he waited. In ten minutes, the team was in place. He could see two SWAT officers, dressed in black, Kevlar vests in place, carrying AR-15s, to the left of the hill where Colin hid, taking their positions. The one closest to him was a man, but he didn't recognize him. He made eye contact with Colin, threw him a thumbs-up and then knelt, his rifle aimed at the smoldering ruins of the line shacks.

His heart started a slow pound. Colin felt time slowing down, like it always did during battle. There was no past or present; just *now*. Right now. He slowly slid down the hill, Bandit with him. He wanted to be with the horses should Hauptman and his group decide to stand and fight it out instead of surrender to the sheriff.

"This is the sheriff," Dan Seabert called through a megaphone. "You are surrounded. Put down your weapons and put your hands above your head."

Instantly, Hauptman ran to the ATV, leaped in and

gunned it, pine needles and dirt spurting as the tires spun madly to get purchase.

The horses jerked, wild-eyed, as gunfire erupted. Colin couldn't see who fired first, his whole focus on the horses, calming them. This time, they remained calm because he was there, soothing them with his voice, even though it was drowned out by the popping and cracking of the rounds. A few bullets sailed over the heads of the horses, rattling them. He saw Hauptman make his escape, gunning the ATV up the slope trying to keep bullets from taking him down.

Looking to his left, he saw the nearest SWAT person lying on his belly, slowly, methodically, firing his weapon. Looking to his right, he saw Hauptman disappear behind the first knoll. The noise of the ATV suddenly became loud as the area became silent. All the gunfire had stopped. He saw the SWAT member leap to his feet, running forward, disappearing from his view.

"Colin!" Dan yelled into the radio.

The horses settled, snorted, but were not moving around restlessly.

Grabbing the radio he had buttoned in his shirt pocket, he said, "What is it?" Had they seen Dana? His heart leaped hard in his chest.

"Go after Hauptman! We have no way to follow him because we can't find the keys to these ATVs. Take your horses and dog. We have to get him! I'm going to try to find the keys to get one of these other ATVs going."

"I'm on it," he said, quickly untying the halter lead and hitching it around the horn of the saddle. "I'll try to follow him."

"Be careful! He's got an AR-15 and you only have a pistol."

Colin grinned as he swung into the saddle. Bandit instantly got on his feet, tail wagging. "Got it. I'll give you updates."

"I can get another deputy to stay on the highway if he goes that direction. If he does? Let me know immediately?"

"Roger. Out." He pushed the radio down into the pocket, snapping it shut. As he galloped from out behind the knoll, he saw that the entire SWAT team was at the cabins. Two men from Hauptman's team lay dead. The other two had their hands up, surrendering. He saw Dan running hard toward the parked ATVs that belonged to the drug soldiers. Would he find a key or not? It didn't matter. Sometimes, a horse was a better choice in a situation like this.

Gypsy galloped at his leg, staying up with Blackjack's long, ground-eating stride. The wind whistled past him as they hit that slope and his horses began to push hard, their hind legs like mighty pistons, tearing up clods of dirt in their wake as they lunged repeatedly forward. Colin looked back to see Bandit trailing them. That was a safe place for him to be under the circumstances.

Slowing at the first knoll Hauptman had disappeared behind, Colin pulled his pistol, slowing his horses down. He could hear the ATV, and it sounded loud in the forest.

Not wanting to get blindsided by Hauptman, he pulled Blackjack to a trot. Glancing around to locate Bandit, the dog was still behind them. As he cautiously rounded the knoll, pistol poised to shoot, Colin saw the ATV heading toward a second knoll that one couldn't see until they were where Colin was presently. Holstering the gun, he called Dan. "He's heading for a second knoll, Dan. Do you have a map of this area available? I need to know where he's going."

"Hold on . . ." he muttered. "There's no keys. Those drug soldiers must have had them and they're in the ashes somewhere. We'll never find them. Keep after him."

In a minute, he was back on the radio.

"There's four knolls between you and where they're heading—in the direction of the Buckthorn River. Do you see the river from where you are?"

"No. But I watered the horses there, earlier. I know, generally, the direction of it. Does that river lead down to the main highway?"

"Yes, there's a bridge there, too. Does it look like Hauptman is working his way in that direction?"

"Maybe. He's over half a mile ahead of me." Squeezing Blackjack's flanks, the horse took off in a gallop in that direction, Gypsy following. "I don't want to be within half a mile of the perp," he told Dan, threading the horse between some of the trees that were now much sparser and easier to ride around. "The AR-15 has a half mile range. If I get inside that? He could take out me, the horses, or the dog."

"Roger that, hang outside that perimeter. Call me when he gets to that second knoll. He'll have a choice of either going straight up this mountain to a pass, or to turn east toward the river."

"Roger that, out."

Grimly, Colin rode hard, heading toward the river. He

didn't mind trailing Hauptman, but that AR-15 was powerful and lethal. Getting killed wasn't on today's menu as far as he was concerned. The wind tore past his ears and his narrowed gaze swiveled from left to right, not trusting who or what else might be out here. Fighting himself emotionally, wanting desperately to find Dana, it became tougher and tougher to block her out, because she was in his heart. She *owned* his heart. How could this have happened? They were two broken, lost people trying to mend and knit their lives back together again. Why them? Why *now*?

Suddenly, he saw a flash of dark blue. Hauling Blackjack and Gypsy to a skidding halt, his eyes squinted, he saw someone . . . someone . . . running up the steep slope from a knoll less than half a mile from him.

Who?

His heart started to pound. He looked down at Bandit, who was panting hard.

"Bandit?" He gestured toward the human on the slope. "Dana?"

Instantly, the dog's ears perked up and he focused on where the person was scrambling, falling, and trying to make it up toward a thick grove of fir trees.

Barking, Bandit took off as if his tail were on fire!

Could it be? He swung the horse around, asking the animal to catch up to the speeding dog.

Bandit was lunging ahead, digging into the now almost dry pine needles. His booming bark continued, relentless, as he threw himself up that steep slope, barreling toward the person, swiftly closing the distance.

Not far behind, leaning forward in the saddle, Colin

asked everything of his tired mount and Gypsy as they hit that steep interface that led to the trees. He couldn't see the person because of the hood on their head. He'd *swear* that it was Dana, by her build. He knew how she ran. He knew every little minute thing about her, had studied her and absorbed her into his heart.

Don't let me be wrong!

In less than five minutes, Bandit caught up to the person.

Colin's eyes widened as the person turned toward the dog.

DANA!

It was *Dana*! He wanted to shout. To cry. He saw her staring at him, as if disbelieving that it was him. Bandit was leaping all over her, licking her hands, her face. As he drew up and halted, he heard her laughing. But it sounded hysterical. Anxiously he looked at her face. She was white. Scary white. Her eyes were huge, her lips contorted, as if she were in pain.

"Dana!" he called, dropping the reins, running toward her.

"It's really you!" she cried, sobbing, her hands against her mouth, staring at him as he came up to her. "Colin?"

"Yes . . ." He halted, rapidly assessing her. "A-are you okay?" he managed, reaching out, touching her slumping shoulder.

She pushed the hoodie off her head, her shoulder-length red hair disheveled. "I-I am now," she sobbed, throwing herself into his arms, her head buried against his chest.

Nothing . . . nothing had ever felt as good as Dana

hurling herself into his arms, holding him so tightly he could barely breathe, but he didn't care. He slid his gloved hand around her head, holding her tightly, as she sobbed like a frightened child.

"You're alive . . . you're alive," he managed, his voice shaking. Tears jammed into his eyes, sliding down his cheeks and he didn't give a damn. Dana was in his arms! Warm. Alive! *Oh, God, she was alive!* And he couldn't stop crying, their faces wet, their hungry, needy mouths seeking, finding one another. The saltiness and warmth of the tears were shared between them. They came up for air once, and then kissed one another wildly a second time, making small, pleasurable sounds between them.

Colin couldn't get enough of touching her, running his hand along her waist, holding her tightly, wanting to let her know how much she meant to him. "I love you, Dana . . . I love you," he rasped against her ear. "Never forget that. I'm sorry I didn't tell you before this happened . . ."

She moaned, closing her eyes, kissing him as hard as she could, her arms wrapped around his broad, capable shoulders. Bandit was dancing at their feet, yipping and whining, as if celebrating right along with them, his thick yellow tail beating and thumping against their legs from time to time. "I love you . . . Oh! Colin, I love you," she whispered raggedly against his lips.

Closing his eyes, he held her tightly, her heart against his. *Never* had anything felt so good! Her breath was warm against his chest and he gloried in the strength of her body firmly against his, her arms around him. "I—I thought I'd lost you, Dana . . ."

"I thought I was going to die!" she cried softly, pulling

her hand up, pressing it against her cheek, more tears coming. "I was so scared . . . so scared . . ."

Easing her away from him, he gave her a watery smile, drowning in her darkly shadowed green eyes that were filled with anxiety. "I was scared for you. No one knew where you were. Can you tell me what happened?"

"They punched a needle in my thigh and they pushed me into one of those ATVs," she began, her voice low and wobbling. "I lost consciousness. The next thing I knew, I was coming around when we stopped at those line shacks. They pushed me into the end cabin and locked the door." Wiping her eyes, she pulled out of his arms, standing close, gripping his hand. "There was no way to escape. Later, the leader, a guy named Gallego, wanted to know where the money was."

Grimly, he touched her mussed hair. "What did you tell him?"

"The truth. He said if I lied, he'd kill me on the spot. I believed him, Colin."

Nodding, he said, "You did the right thing."

Gulping, looking around warily, she studied the grove of trees partly surrounding them. She quickly told him the rest. "When I got back to that cabin, they had locked the door. I was their prisoner. I didn't know what they'd do with me. I went to sleep. Maybe four hours later, I woke up, realizing they hadn't taken my Buck knife off me. I managed to pry the door open, Colin. I ran."

"That was fantastic," he praised, touching her wan cheek. "And then you ran up the slope?"

"Yes. I was using the knolls, going from one to another, because they hid my escape. But then I saw two

ATVs coming up that road, and all of a sudden, hell broke loose!"

Colin told her of Hauptman's arrival and the grenade launcher. He saw her eyes widen enormously. "I was so scared at that point. I felt like sooner or later, they'd come hunting me. I-I didn't know Hauptman was there . . ."

"Well, when it was all over, none of the drug soldiers survived, that I could tell. I don't think Hauptman knew you were there?"

Shaking her head, she whispered, "I don't know . . . I don't know . . ."

He pulled the canteen from the saddle, opening it for her. "How long has it been since you were hydrated?"

She gripped it and slugged down the water, head tipped back.

Bandit came and sat near her left leg, panting happily, looking at both of them. Colin leaned over and said, "You found her, big boy," and he patted the dog fondly, watching his golden eyes sparkle with unfettered joy.

Just as she handed him back the half-emptied canteen, Colin picked up the sound of an ATV. Scowling, he capped it and put it in the saddlebag. It couldn't be Hunter. What?

Shifting, he moved behind his horse, looking toward the area where he last saw Hauptman. His heart slammed into his ribs. Turning on his heel, he grabbed Gypsy's bridle, putting it on.

"Dana, can you ride?" he demanded in a low voice.

"Well . . . yes . . . where are we going? Can we go home now?"

He winced at the look of longing, and almost the pleading in her husky voice. "No. Hauptman saw us. He's coming at us on an ATV. We've got to get out of here now! He's got an AR-15 and all I have is a pistol. If he gets within half a mile of us and starts firing? He can kill us. Come on, I'll help you into the saddle!"

Chapter 14

Dana climbed into the saddle, her legs shaky, hands trembling as she picked up the reins on Gypsy, who was dancing around nervously, sensing the danger coming at them. She looked toward the ATV. It was heading straight at them. Her heart felt as if it were going to break in two. Hauptman. Murderer of her parents. Tears burned in her eyes as she tore her attention from the ATV that was a good mile away, from what she could judge. She watched Colin leap lithely into the saddle. Bandit was waiting, his attention on the ATV in the distance.

"Ride ahead of me," he told her, pointing toward the east. "We've got to get lower, into the thick of the woods where his ATV can't go!"

"You want me to take the lead?"

"Yes," he shouted, wheeling his horse around. "Just head east. Look for thick timber. We've got to stop him from following us!"

Nodding jerkily, she turned Gypsy through the nearby grove. The mare sensed the threat, hindquarters lowering, digging into the soft pine needles and soil, ears laid back, neck stretching out as she raced through the woods. Dana wasn't the most practiced of riders recently, but thank goodness she knew how to ride. The woods were fairly open and an ATV could dodge and move among the trees, but it would slow the vehicle down. Her heart raced in time with the beat of Gypsy's hooves as she pounded down the slope.

All of her attention was on what was ahead. Once, she jerked a look over her shoulder and saw that Colin was far behind her. Why? And then it struck her hard that he was protecting their rear from Hauptman, who could trail them through these woods. Choking on her love for him, for his trying to protect her, she leaned low, the mane stinging her face as she urged Gypsy down, down, down the slope, looking for dense woods where the ATV would not be able to follow them.

Her whole life was a cascade of emotions rushing through her. She loved Colin! And yet, as she had felt the power of his mouth against hers, still, there were no promises that either of them would survive this.

Looking over her shoulder, the wind making her eyes water as Gypsy valiantly continued down the slope, she saw that Colin was closer now. The black horse was tall, long-legged and mostly thoroughbred, so he had the bloodlines and stamina to catch up with her smaller mount, who was no less valiant. She checked on Bandit, who was running ahead of Gypsy! The dog was incredible! It was as if he was leading all of them to a safer place where trees grew closer together.

Up ahead, she saw the forest beginning to grow denser, vaguely aware that they had probably dropped to seven thousand feet. In her mind, she wondered how the sheriff was doing. The SWAT team were at the line shacks. Couldn't they turn back and race to Colin and her for assistance? She didn't know all the facts. But she trusted Colin's instincts regarding this situation. Some of the ground began to get rocky—black, lava-like rocks, peeking up out of the pine needles, which hid them and it made it dangerous ground to be galloping across.

Gypsy slowed considerably as they hit the field of rocks that were laid out for as far as she could see. If her horse tripped, Dana knew her brave mare could break a leg. Dana could be thrown off and break her neck. She slowed Gypsy to a trot. Bandit raced ahead, the slope even more steep. She had to be careful and sat up, shifting her weight and balance to Gypsy's rear haunches, sliding and almost sitting on her rump at times, as her horse dodged larger and larger black rocks. Off to her left, she saw the land falling away, as if there was a cliff or something there. Moving Gypsy in that direction, she wanted to see what was causing the land to drop like that. The trees were now closer together and she knew the ATV could not follow them here. *Success!*

But it was short-lived as she drew Gypsy to a halt, standing up in the stirrups, straining to look over where the land fell away. She could see there was a rocky cliff, the black rock everywhere. It was a good hundred-foot drop down to the floor below where the trees grew thickly.

Colin rode up. "What did you find?"

"I don't know. It's really rocky around here . . ."

Sizing up the vertical cliff, he grunted. "Volcanic rock."

She warily looked around. "Where's Bandit? He was with me just a few moments ago . . ." She stood in the stirrups once more, searching the steep incline. "He went that way . . ."

"Let's follow him. We're going in a southeasterly direction. That's still working toward the river somewhere out there." Colin gestured toward the area.

Worriedly, she whispered, "Where's Hauptman? I don't hear his ATV . . ."

"Hopefully, by being on pine needles, the imprints left by the horses have disappeared and he's going to have trouble following us." Colin grimaced. "At least, that's what I hope."

"The trees are close together down there," she said, a little relief in her tone. "He can't get us."

"Don't count on that," Colin warned. "Hauptman can't be trusted to do anything that's logical."

"Why was he coming back toward us?" she asked, her voice thin with terror.

"I don't know, and I wish I did."

"Did he see *me*?" Her voice cracked.

Colin rode up closer to her, lifting his glove, moving it across her tight, tense shoulders. "There's no way he could have, Dana. I don't know why he circled back on me . . . us . . ."

"I'm so scared," she said, continually looking around, her hearing keyed to any sounds and watching Gypsy's ears, because her horse would hear it first.

"We all are," he assured her. "Let's walk the horses down this incline, and be careful. Give Gypsy her head and let her pick her way through all the rocks at her pace."

"Yes," she said, nodding. "Where's Bandit? I'm worried about him, Colin."

"I don't know. It's not like him to take off like that."

Her hand went to her throat as she gazed into the

woods before them. "Did he hear or smell Hauptman, I wonder? Is he going after him? Oh, God, I hope not . . ."

"He's a trained service dog, Dana. There must have been something he smelled or heard that we can't pick up on. Come on, we have to keep moving. I'm sure he'll show up. He knows where we are."

Dana wanted to believe him. Gypsy was breathing hard. Both horses were covered with sweat from that long, downhill run. Her breath was coming in shallow gasps, too. Settling back into the saddle, she gave Gypsy her head. allowing the horse to pick the safest route through this black minefield of lava rock. She looked back. Colin was about a hundred feet behind her. He was looking over his shoulder from where they'd just come. Once more, he was the Army Ranger and they had a real enemy out there with a lot more firepower than they had. Because her father hunted, she knew a rifle had a longer range than a Glock. And that was all Colin had on him.

She had so many questions to ask him! And talking right now wasn't a wise thing to do. What if Hauptman left his ATV behind and was following them on foot? Why *would* he be following them? Shaking her head, Dana swiveled, looking for Bandit and anything else that looked out of place. Where was their dog? She worried about him. Why had he taken off?

It took nearly thirty minutes at a careful walk to get through the steep lava field strewn with branches and debris that hid many of the rocks. At the bottom of the incline, she felt as if she could breathe a little easier. What was their elevation? The woods were very close together now, and Gypsy was doing a strong walk, weaving in and around them. That gave Dana some solace. Every time she looked back up the incline, Colin was looking around, looking for Hauptman. That sent an icy chill down her spine.

The trees, because they had grown so thickly , cut off the light. It was dark and dreary to Dana. The breeze picked up, and she could smell the soil and fir trees from the rain the day before. Beginning to relax, she wondered obliquely where Buckthorn River was. She knew the one Colin was talking about. It fed a stream that crossed her ranch.

Suddenly, she heard Bandit barking. It sounded far off and a little to her left, near the edge of this cliff they were finally leaving behind them.

Colin rode up beside her. "Hear Bandit?"

"Yes," she said, excitement in her tone. "Over there? That direction?"

Colin nodded. "That's what I'm hearing."

"I'm so glad he's barking! Does it sound like he's coming toward us?"

"No," he said. "Bandit's found something, but I don't know what it is."

"Hauptman?" she barely whispered, giving him a worried look.

"I doubt it. Let's ride in that general direction and see if we can find him."

Relieved, glad that Colin was riding closely behind her, she angled Gypsy off toward Bandit. She hoped he was all right. The mare picked up her pace as the rocks seemed to have diminished in this crowded grove of firs. The flat area dipped downward once more, curving to the left. Her heart thumped in joy. There was Bandit far ahead of them!

"I see him!" Dana called back to Colin. "He's over there." She pointed.

"Good. Let's go see what he's barking about."

To her delight, she saw Bandit standing beside a small stream of water. It wasn't the river, but she was thirsty and she knew the horses had to be, also. Near the stream there was a huge pile of black rocks rising about fifteen feet high. Bandit was wagging his tail, pink tongue hanging out the side of his mouth. He was dripping wet. Dana laughed and pointed to the dog. She saw Colin's taut face break into a smile.

"He's a Lab and a water dog." She laughed.

"He was thirsty, so he headed to the nearest water source," Colin said, smiling broadly.

The horses picked up the scent of water, hurrying even more, weaving among the trees.

As Dana broke out of the trees, no more than fifty feet from the burbling spring, she turned, looking at the massive black rock formation. Gasping, she said, "Colin! This is a cave! Look!" and she pointed at it, dismounting and leading Gypsy to the water.

Bandit came over, wagging his thick tail, licking her hands and whining his hello to her.

Colin dismounted and gave Blackjack his head, the horse plunging his muzzle into the icy cold water, gulping like a camel.

He stared at the cave, which was facing east. It was protected by spindly pines as well as thick bushes a good ten feet or more in height. With the water and opening in the forest, even grass was growing on both banks of the stream. This was what the horses needed: water and grass. It was the perfect place to stay, at least for the moment.

Dana looked over at him. "Can we rest here? Put a nylon lead on their halters, take off their bridles and let them eat?"

"Yeah," he said, "for sure." He pulled the nylon lead out of the saddlebags. "Good idea."

Dana went to her saddlebags, getting the red nylon lead and hooking it on Gypsy's halter when the horse finally lifted her head, having gotten her fill of water. Taking off the bridle, she hung it over the saddle horn, holding the lead as Gypsy quickly began to hungrily eat the grass.

"Do you have the time?" Dana asked.

"Noon. Did you have any food in your saddlebags?"

Shaking her head, she said, "You were packing us a lunch. Is there any in yours?"

He gave her a sheepish look. "There wasn't much and I ate it over the past day as I was reconnoitering for Dan and his SWAT team."

"There's a lot I don't know," she said, patting Gypsy's sleek, wet neck.

"Well," he said unhappily, "that radio I was given by Dan has dead batteries. I tried to call him on it when the ATV turned and came back toward us." He patted the pocket where it sat. "Deader than a doornail."

"Then . . . we're alone, and Dan doesn't know where we are? He probably doesn't even know I'm here with you. Right?"

"Right," he answered, allowing his horse to quickly

gorge on the rich, succulent grass after he'd removed the bridle. "It was the only way I could keep contact with him."

"What will he think when he tries to get ahold of you and you don't answer?"

"I don't know, Dana. He's got his hands full with a lot of dead bodies right now down at that line shack site."

"Couldn't we backtrack?"

"We don't know where Hauptman's at," he answered, pushing his hat up on his head. "We have to keep moving east because that river will eventually lead us to the main highway and then we can cross it and get home."

She sighed. "Home sounds so good right now . . ."

"Doesn't it?" He gave her a warm look. "We've just got to hang together on this, avoid Hauptman, and run into the river. Once we reach the ranch, we can call Dan on the phone and let him know I found you and that we're alive."

Looking up the slope, she said, "I have a horrible feeling, Colin," and she moved her shoulders as if to get rid of the psychic weight of it.

"About what?"

"Hauptman. I feel like he's tracking us. I know it sounds crazy. Why would he abandon his ATV to follow the horses' hoofprints? What are we to him? Or did he really recognize me and he's coming to kill me?"

Walking over to her, he put his arm around her shoulders, drawing her gently against him. "It's impossible that he would have recognized you at that distance, Dana." He kissed her wrinkled brow, felt the tension radiating around her. "Impossible," he repeated.

"Then, why?" she croaked, looking up into his shadowed eyes.

"I simply don't know. It doesn't make sense if he's trying to track us. He knows we're on horseback and we can get away from him."

"Maybe his ATV ran out of gas?" she ventured.

"That could happen, for sure. But if that's so, why come after us? Why not continue his escape up and over the pass on this mountain and try to avoid getting caught by the SWAT team? I'm sure they're going to send a group up that mountain to find him. There were other ATVs at the line shacks. All they need to do is find the keys to start them."

"But what if those keys were on the men who drove them?"

With a grimace, he muttered, "Hauptman sent a grenade launcher into every cabin. That pretty much killed them. They didn't stand a chance. And those keys might be on some of the drug soldiers who made it out of those burning cabins, or they are on someone who's nothing more than a burned-out hulk in the cabin ashes." He saw her wince. "Sorry, didn't need to be that graphic."

She placed her hand on his chest, kissing his cheek. "You're in Ranger mode, as I call it. You're on guard and you're protecting us."

He marveled at her wisdom, and kissed her brow. "You're right, I am. It's all come back, Dana. I tried to get rid of it, push it away, ignore it, but when this blew up in our faces, I reverted right back to all those years when I was a hunter behind the lines, going after Taliban leaders."

"Well," she whispered, resting her head against his shoulder, brow on his unshaven jaw, "it could save our lives right now . . ." She closed her eyes, absorbing him, as a man, as someone who loved her. She knew Colin would give his life to protect her and she opened her eyes, sadness flowing through her. "I don't want to lose you," she whispered tremulously. She felt his arm tighten briefly around her shoulders.

"We'll get out of this, Dana." He kissed her brow. "A lot of things have gone wrong, but an equal amount of them have gone right."

"I just couldn't believe it was you riding up that hill. I was in such shock . . ."

"You are in shock," he said gently. "The past has come back to confront you. That's hell."

"But that's PTSD for you, isn't it? Something you go through every day in some small or large way?"

Colin valued her understanding of the emotional scars that would never leave him alone. "Yeah," he began, his voice roughened with emotion, "that's exactly how it is, Dana. I'm sorry you had to realize what someone with PTSD has to go through daily. It can be a particular smell, the way another person behaves, a scream, a cry, and it sets off the entire chain of events of what happened to me before. It's . . . hard to keep going when your pain and emotions are right on top of your life, the first to react, and the first for me to feel, and it's always emotional . . ."

She turned, pressing her body against his, drowning in his saddened gaze. "Then? If for no other reason than I honestly realize what you're going through daily, this is a blessing in disguise for me, Colin. From now on, if we get out of this alive, I'll be far more sensitive toward you and when you suddenly withdraw from me, go away . . . hide."

"It's the only thing I can do when it hits," he managed, searching her eyes, absorbing her brutal honesty and understanding. His love for her surged through him as never before. Reality had ripped away the life he'd tried to hide from her. Why would he *ever* want to share it with anyone because it was so damned eviscerating, pulling his attention to the past again and again, unable to focus fully on the present, never mind a future. Searching her warm gaze, the soft corners of her mouth lifting a little, he felt her pride in him, her understanding of him on a whole new level.

"Are you still going to want me around now that you know?" he asked her haltingly, unable to believe anyone would want this kind of person in their life for a minute, much less a day, week, month, or year.

"Yes. A thousand times, yes, Colin. You don't see yourself and I do. I always have." She stretched upward, seeking, finding the compressed line of his mouth, her lips moving against him, feeling him beginning to melt beneath the fierce love she had for him. He was a hero and a patriot serving his country. He was a good man caught in the hell and nightmare world of war.

She closed her eyes, hearing him groan, holding her tightly against him, his mouth softening beneath her gentle onslaught, his breathing matching her own, shallow and warm.

The world dissolved until there was just Dana, her arms coming around his shoulders, her lips firm, sweet and wet against his. For just this one moment out of time, only the two of them existed as they honestly, with their hearts, reached out and clung to each other, as one. And slowly, sweetly, their lips parted, eyes barely opening, drowning in the other's gaze.

Colin felt his heart swelling in his chest with such

utter, raw joy, that he couldn't speak for a moment, a knot of emotion forming in his throat. When Dana's lids lifted, her forest-green eyes shining with such life and happiness, he felt something old and hard break within him. And then, he felt it dissolving, forever. Having no idea what it was or why it was happening, he lifted his hand, moving a few errant red strands away from her temple. "If nothing else," he began in a guttural tone, "we've found one another and we're standing on the same ground. Together."

"I like what we have," she admitted, her voice nearly overwhelmed with emotion. "I remember after waking up from that injection, that I'd never told you that I love you, Colin. I cried in that line shack then, because I was so afraid they were going to kill me, and I'd never get a chance to let you know how much you really mean to me . . ."

He managed a deep sigh, looked up at the sky that was cloudy, with breaks of sunlight through them. Dipping his chin, he met and held her green gaze, feeling all her love being transferred to him. "I think I began to become aware that I love you maybe three weeks into us working together at the ranch. At first, Dana, I tried to deny it. And then, when I couldn't, I tried to ignore it and you." He managed a shake of his head, his smile wry as he held her laughter-filled gaze.

"And how'd that work out for you?" she teased, grinning widely.

"As you suspect, it didn't," he admitted, a one-cornered grin tugging at the corner of his mouth.

"So what did you do then?"

"I began to have this silent love affair with you," he

admitted. "I allowed myself to be filled with happiness every time you gave me that look."

Tilting her head, stymied, she asked, "What look?"

"I noticed almost right away after I came to your ranch, that sometimes that secret little smile"—he touched one corner of her mouth—"would lift, and then I would look up into your eyes . . ." Shaking his head ruefully, he rasped, "Your eyes . . . do you know that I see your every emotion in them? Your soul? Because you'd give me this flirty look and I felt like whether we admitted it or not, we were so damned drawn to one another, and it was useless to fight it because in the end, we were going to come together as man and woman. You have beautiful eyes, Dana, large, wide, and so readable." He leaned over, kissing her brow. Straightening, he added, "Your green eyes change color. I noticed that right away. If you are stressed, tired, or upset, they are more olive colored. But when you are around me, they are like spring leaves that first come out, green and gold highlights. I could *feel* the emotion you were feeling. And at first, it scared me because I had stomped my emotions into a dark hole within myself, and I didn't want to feel. I was afraid that your joy of being around me, would open Pandora's box, and I was scared."

"So?" she whispered, touching his cheek with her fingertips. "What happened?"

"At first, I could control it so my emotions wouldn't escape. But then, you'd laugh so freely and happily that I found them escaping, anyway. In the end, Dana, it didn't matter. If I could drown in your eyes and your laughter, it actually helped me, and my emotions didn't harm me like I thought they would. Over the time we've spent together, that box where I tried to cram away all my feelings, has opened. I haven't been drowned in them. And I feel that was because I was falling in love with you . . ."

"You trusted me, Colin, with yourself. And you finally trusted yourself."

Her words haunted him as her love seeped into the wounds within himself. And then, those quiet, gentle words of truth began to melt away some of his scars. He could actually feel it. "I guess," he began haltingly, "that I began, over time, to trust you. I couldn't believe it, Dana, that you actually liked someone like me."

"Someone who was wounded, right?"

"Yeah . . . for sure." He looked away, feeling close to tears. "I knew you didn't know how damned broken I am. And yet, you honestly liked my company; even if I slunk off to be alone and hide, it didn't seem to matter. That was when I realized that something good and solid was being built silently between us."

"I felt that," she admitted. "I was scared for other reasons, Colin. I didn't really understand your PTSD until just now. But I wasn't afraid of you or it. I could feel your strength, your ability to control whatever war was going on inside you. Never once did you take it out on me. I knew when you would leave after dinner, after helping me wash the dishes and put them away, that you needed what I called 'alone time,' and I was fine with that."

"Because you needed it, too, right?" he asked, holding her somber gaze.

"Yes, I did. So often, when we have been living together

in that mobile home, and we share laughter, a joke, or something that makes me happy, it immediately brings back those times I had as a child growing up with my parents."

"So? These were good times?" he wondered, trying to understand.

"Very much so. But what it triggered in me, after feeling that moment with you, and then reconnecting with their memory, I instantly felt grief afterward, because I would never have another shared laugh or love with my mom and dad . . ."

He saw tears welling up in her glorious emerald eyes. "I'm so damned sorry that happened to you, Dana. No one deserves that. No one."

"You didn't deserve what war did to you, either. You trusted the military and they put you in godawful situations and wounded you to your soul. And now, every day, you pay a price for the trust you put in them."

"It's a little different than that," he said. "When you're in the military, it is the people who work with you every day who become your family. You are faithful and trust them, Dana. I never blamed the military for putting us . . . my family . . . into dangerous situations, because I volunteered to be a Ranger working with other black ops groups behind the lines. That was *my* choice. I could have gotten a cushy job in another, far safer base in that country, but I wanted to take out the Taliban leaders who were making their own people suffer horrifically, for their own greed, money, and power. But yes, I became deeply wounded by what I'd managed to survive."

"We're a fine pair, aren't we?"

"I just can't believe," he whispered, kissing the corners of her eyes where the tears watered, "that you love me. I can see clearly why I could love you."

She managed a little laugh and opened her eyes, seeing his blue eyes filled with teasing. "Well, I feel the same way about you. Your PTSD didn't scare me off, Colin. I *wanted*, *needed* to get close to you, I guess, to help you heal those wounds over time. I didn't care how long it took. I was looking forward to a lifetime with you. I thought the Wildflower Ranch was the most important thing in my life, but it wasn't." Her voice lowered. "It was you. Only you . . ."

Groaning, he brought her into his arms, holding her tightly, her heart against his, the beat synchronous, warm, and so full of life and promise. "You," he rasped against her ear, "are all I'll ever need or want, woman of mine. I want to get out of this situation we're in right now and go home and live a life of possibilities with you. I trust you with my life. I always have and maybe that's why I began to allow myself to trust you little by little."

She kissed his neck and then rested her cheek against his shoulder. "Trust is earned, Colin. It can't be bought. It can't be stolen. It's something that happens over time, place, and space. I knew you didn't trust me at first, but then, you didn't trust anyone that I could see, except maybe for Chase."

"Chase was in the military like me," he admitted thickly. "He understood my PTSD and hired me as a wrangler, but gave me a lot of jobs where I could be alone. If I worked in a team or group, it was too stressful on me and he understood that."

"Probably because he wrestled with his own PTSD?" Dana guessed, moving her hand gently across his broad chest. The blue plaid cotton cowboy shirt was damp with sweat from the ride they had to make, to escape a nightmare that had returned to stalk her. She pushed that aside and focused instead on the joy bubbling up through her at being in Colin's embrace, his ability to show his emotions to her, to be honest even if it hurt to say those words to her, that he trusted her with his broken soul.

"Yeah, he has a pretty bad case of it, too, but over time, it has faded and he's in a lot better space than I am . . . or was." He pulled her away from him, holding her gold-green gaze. "You are healing me whether you know it or not. At first, I didn't know what was going on, but after two months, I realized just being around you, working with you, having dinner with you every night, things were changing inside me, good changes, Dana. I never realized that one human could do that for another." He shook his head ruefully, giving her a look of apology and awe.

"Had you ever fallen in love before you met me?" she wondered.

"No. Sure, I had girlfriends, but it was nothing like what we share. You move me emotionally, Dana. When I wake up in my bed in the morning? Instead of dreading the day ahead, I'm looking forward to it because shortly I'll see you. In some ways, I guess I live vicariously through your ability to be emotional, to be like a happy child, or to trust whatever it is you're doing and the gusto and life you feel with each task. I've had nothing but good moments with you, and I'm so damned glad I've got this time to share with you."

"I saw my parents affect one another just like that, Colin. And when I realized about a month into our working together, that we were beginning to behave the same toward one another, I was overjoyed. I couldn't share my joy with you because I saw you wrestling with your PTSD every day. I didn't want to intrude. I didn't want to make it worse for you, so I remained at a distance with what was going on inside me. I was hoping that if you were drawn to me as much as I was drawn to you, that one day I could share how I felt."

"How much time was wasted," he muttered, shaking his head.

"No, I don't feel it was wasted at all. I had time to be around you in many different situations, and so that knowledge and education was like a solid foundation that occurred magically between us."

He looked around, always checking the area. Bandit was sitting in the stream again, cooling off, his panting much less now. Devoting his focus to her, Colin said, "I feel like I'm in some kind of good dream and I'm afraid to trust it, for fear that's all it is. I'll wake up and it will be gone . . . you'll be gone . . . I know that sounds crazy . . ."

"No, it doesn't. With your PTSD, there are no happy moments to remember. Only sad ones, bad ones or grief-stricken ones, I'd bet."

Making an unhappy sound, Colin nodded. "Nothing good. Not ever."

"Then," she whispered, "let's agree to make so many happy moments to come, that it will balance out what you're working on inside you?"

He felt his heart expand, loving her more than life.

"Yes . . . I'd like that. But first, let's get out of this mission we're on, in one piece, alive and safe, okay?"

"That sounds good," she managed, suddenly emotional.

He cupped her cheek, holding her fraught gaze. "Hold on to this, then: I want to wake up every morning with you in my arms. I want to love you until we melt together and are one. I want to hear your laughter, see your smile, welcome your kisses, to continue to heal me, but I also want what I can give you to help ease and heal your wounds, too."

Chapter 15

Colin was bridling the horses near the creek. Blackjack and Gypsy had gotten their water and eaten their fill of grass, having rested for nearly an hour. Nearby, Dana was on her knees, filling the only canteen they had between them.

Looking around, he didn't feel good, the energy—or whatever it was—having shifted after their incredibly deep, honest discussion with one another. His heart, however, was ballooning with such a wealth of joy, he was having a tough time remaining focused on the fact they weren't out of the woods—yet. Bandit sat nearby, stretched out in the luxury of the green grass, absorbing, he was sure, Mother Earth's energy. For the moment, things were quiet.

As he cinched and tightened the saddles on each horse, he frowned. His trainer in the Rangers always told him, "Look for what is out of place."

Resting his gloved hands on the horn and cantle of Gypsy's saddle, he looked toward the hill above them, thick with woods. Something *was* out of place, but he couldn't define the threat. Looking darkly into the woods above them, he sensed danger. His instincts while hunting Taliban kicked in big-time.

He glanced over at Bandit, who was lying down, eyes closed, soaking up the sun, just as exhausted as they were by their earlier run. The dog was doing what Colin wished he could do right now, feeling that same bone-deep tiredness pulling him to go lie down and rest.

But they couldn't. Looking at the horses, they seem completely relaxed, eyes half closed, a back leg cocked, showing they, too, were resting and trying to sleep standing up, which they could easily do. Everything seemed fine. The gurgle of the stream was inviting.

Something was missing. What the hell was it? Looking up at the sky, he didn't see any birds, just midafternoon blue sky polka-dotted with white, fluffy clouds. The scene around him looked idyllic, beautiful, and how badly he wanted to let down his guard and talk further with Dana. Both of them knew they were alone, without a way to communicate with the sheriff, and were sure Dan was worried about them and where they might be.

And then it hit Colin. The birds were *not* singing. Scowling, he studied the forest above them. When birds quieted, it meant a predator was nearby. He'd always seen it happen when hunting Taliban. It was as if the world had stopped spinning, that everything was holding its breath, that deadly silence blanketing him.

"Dana?" he called, catching her gaze as she stood, capping the canteen.

"Yes?"

"The horses are ready to go."

She frowned, looked up at the hill and then back at him. "What's wrong, Colin?"

He rubbed his unshaven jaw. "Something doesn't feel right, and until I can spot or pinpoint it? I want all of you in a safe place. " He saw her grow tense, the pink color in her cheeks dissolving. "Do you feel anything?" he asked, pulling the reins over Gypsy's head and handing them to her after she'd placed the canteen in the saddlebags.

Nodding, she moved toward him. "Maybe fifteen minutes earlier, I began to feel uneasy, but it's a vague thing . . ."

He met her halfway. "Look, I'm sensing something," he told her in a low tone, giving her the reins to the horses, which she took. "I'm getting a piece of rope out of my saddlebags. I want to put it on Bandit so he'll go with you." He saw alarm come to her eyes, a slight tensing of her body. "I need you to relax. Act as if nothing is wrong, Dana." He took the rope and looped it around Bandit's collar, handing it to her. "I think Hauptman is up on that hill above us. I can't see him, but I feel him coming . . . I'm sorry," he said, giving her an apologetic look. "We're going to walk toward the cave and stream, as if nothing is wrong. I don't want to alert him I'm on to him."

"Are you *sure*?" she squeaked, her voice low and cracking as she began to walk toward the cave.

He came to her left side, to protect her in case Hauptman was up there drawing a bead on them. "I'm sure," he rasped, his hand resting on her shoulder, giving it a squeeze. "I think I finally figured out why he's trailing us. It has nothing to do with identifying you. He must have looked at the gas gauge on his ATV, knew we had horses and were pursuing him, and turned around, figuring he could catch up to us, take our horses, and leave the empty ATV and us, dead."

"Oh . . ." she choked. "Oh, no . . ."

"But it didn't work, Dana. We outrode him and out-smarted him. He knows generally where we're at. And I think he just spotted us." His hand tightened on her shoulder momentarily. "Here's what I need you to do as soon as we get to the mouth of that cave. I want you to mount Gypsy. I'll tie Blackjack's lead to your saddle horn and he'll follow. You're going to have to keep Bandit on your left side and keep that rope on his collar. I can't afford him to get loose and decide to follow me."

They reached the mouth of the cave. She halted, turning, staring up into his darkened eyes. "You're staying behind?"

He nodded, lifting his baseball cap and then settling it back on his head. "I'm going to stalk and find him, Dana. It's the only way. I don't want you, the horses, or Bandit here in the area. It's not safe. In case I get shot before I can shoot him, he'll come down here after you and kill you—and most likely, our dog. He'll take the horses and hightail it off into the mountains where he'll not be found." Touching her cheek, seeing her blanch, he rasped, "You're too precious to me, Dana. I need you to go. Now. I'll be okay. My plan is to have you ride due east, and I think the river's only about two miles away. Once you reach it? Find some shade, and wait for me. If you hear gunshots, do *not* turn around and come back to look for me." His voice grew lower. "It will be easy enough for me to jog two miles. I can do a mile in twelve minutes and this is all a slight, downward slope to the lower elevation to the river. It will be easy for me to do it. I'll meet up with you there and then we'll follow the river to the main highway, ride across it and get to the ranch. From there I can call Dan and let him know we're okay."

"And if you don't show up?" she rattled, her eyes huge with terror.

He pursed his mouth for a moment, unable to meet her gaze. Looking up, he said thickly, "I'm either dead or too badly injured to meet you." He cupped her cheek. "Listen to me, Dana. This is a war. Hauptman will kill all of us, pure and simple. If I don't stalk and find him first? We'll be dead. It's only a matter of time, is all." Leaning down, he kissed her lips gently, longingly. Wanting to continue kissing her, he knew it was time for them to part. "Come on, I'll help you mount Gypsy . . ."

Huge tears rolled down from her eyes as she settled into the saddle. Colin was utterly calm. She'd never seen him like this before. He made sure the lead was snug around Gypsy's saddle horn and led Bandit over to her right side, handing her the leash. "Isn't there some other way, Colin?" she asked, her voice quavering.

Shaking his head, he gave her a sad smile. "My past has come back full circle, sweetheart. This is something I'm doing for all of us. Something good. Evil isn't moral, has no integrity or values. Hauptman is the Taliban, in my eyes. Nothing more or less."

"B-but he's got a rifle! It can hit you at half a mile!"

"If he's in the woods, which I think he is, and nearby amid all those trees that grow so close together, he can't hit me at half a mile. And all things being equal, that rifle is pretty much useless in this kind of warfare. He needs a wide-open clearing with no objects in the way to get a clean shot at me." He gripped her hand. "I'll be all right. I'll meet you at the river. I love you . . . never forget that . . ."

Dana gave a jerky nod. "I love you with my life, Colin . . ."

"I know you do. And I feel the same way about you." He patted Gypsy's rump. "Now, get going. Keep riding due east until you get to the river . . ."

Hesitating, she finally clucked to her mare and they took off at a slow trot. Colin watched them go, making sure that Bandit would be okay on that leash. Well, of course he would. He'd been on a leash all his life, and Colin shook his head, turning and pulling his Glock out of the holster at his side. Making sure the cartridge had bullets, he slid one in the chamber, left the safety off, and placed it back into the black nylon holster.

It was time to hunt.

He moved to the other side of the cave where the thickly wooded forest began. Thankfully, he was wearing dark clothes and as he slipped into the almost sunless woods, he would become the shadow he'd been for so many years before. Now, with Dana safely away, he could fully focus on hunting the hunter. Not knowing Hauptman's background, Colin didn't think he had the upper hand. Colin had five years of stalking Taliban leaders. The late afternoon sunlight disappeared. He knew how to walk to avoid being heard, all that practice coming back as easy as breathing. Narrowing his eyes, he allowed his senses to become full-blown. It was as if he were back in that foreign country, using the darkness and melting into it, becoming one with it. Smells became stronger and more intense. His hearing picked up sounds few humans would ever be aware of. All of his PTSD, the high cortisol levels that set his six senses at maximum strength, were now fully online. He wasn't doing flight. He was going to make a stand and fight.

Taking swift, long strides, moving up the treacherous terrain of black lava rocks peppering the brown pine needles, his mouth parted, breathing through it instead of his nose, he turned into the animal that man always has been capable of becoming. The veneer of civilization no longer covered him. It dissolved completely, leaving him to become one with his surroundings, a shadow jogging steadily upward, avoiding fallen limbs or branches so he wouldn't snap them and alert his foe to his whereabouts.

Sweat trickled down the sides of his face, but he was oblivious to it. Every shadow, every movement in the trees, registered instantly on his eyes, and it was easy to separate tree trunks from something that should not be there.

Look for what is out of place.

Halfway up the hill, Colin spotted his quarry. Sure enough, Hauptman was walking along like he was not being hunted. He was cocksure of himself. A big man, at least two hundred and fifty pounds, all muscle from years of weight lifting during his prison time, the AR-15 resting on one meaty shoulder as he was looking around, he was exactly where Colin wanted him. He was oblivious. But he was heading down toward the cave, so Colin was sure that Hauptman had spotted them riding to it. His shaved head gleamed like a cue ball as shadows and light danced around him.

Kneeling down on one knee, allowing a large tree to hide all of him, Colin watched him. Hauptman was constantly tripping and sliding, cursing because the jagged rocks were slippery with those needles. He was over a hundred and fifty yards away. Colin's pistol had accuracy to seventy-five yards. *Wait. Just wait.* Hauptman was coming Colin's way on an angle, aiming toward the cave. Even if Colin wanted to take a shot, there were too many trees in the way. No, Colin knew a clean shot when he had it.

And it wasn't now.

His heart began a slow, heavy beat in his chest, even though he was breathing hard from the altitude and climb. It always became this way at the critical moment. His whole world suddenly magnified and enveloped him and his quarry. Every muscle in his body ran with energy and tension, ready for an instant leap or run.

Taking the pistol out of his holster, he slowly began to push up on his knee, taking over a minute to stand fully, the trunk hiding him. Convinced that Hauptman had never stalked another human being in this kind of environment, his sloppiness—looking around, slipping, almost falling, not looking where he was going to put his feet next—fed Colin more information.

That didn't make his quarry any less dangerous. He had a rifle; if one of those bullets tore anywhere through his body, it would leave a path of widening carnage so that when it came out of his body, he had less than a five percent chance of surviving. It would take only one bullet. *Just one.*

His heart whispered of his love for Dana. The sharp relief that she was out of harm's way was the most important thing in his life in this living instant. Every breath he took, he felt at cell level, the oxygen coming into his mouth, moving down his throat, expanding his lungs, and then just as quietly, being released back into the world around him. His whole body felt as if it were more than just a physical shell at this crisis moment. He felt every part of himself vibrating like a frequency all of its own. The path between him and Hauptman was narrowing. Step by sliding step. It brought Hauptman closer and closer to where Colin stood, waiting for him. Colin knew he was impossible to see. The shifting light and shadows danced above and around them, like a tiger's black, vertical stripes appearing and disappearing as it moved soundlessly through the jungle.

As Colin slowly lifted his pistol, taking his time, Hauptman was within that seventy-five-yard radius. And only two trees stood between him and his quarry. He had a clean shot.

"HALT!" Colin yelled. "DROP YOUR WEAPON OR I'LL FIRE!"

Hauptman's face turned to shock, and he jerked around, taking the AR-15 off his shoulder, fumbling with it, trying to get his finger around the trigger. Frantic, he was looking everywhere for where that booming male voice had originated.

Just as he lifted the AR-15, Colin fired one shot.

Hauptman screamed, flying backward, the rifle leaving his hands. He hit the ground, swearing and screaming, grabbing at his bloodied right shoulder. His gun shoulder.

Colin stepped out to the left, away where his quarry was screaming and cursing, heading silently for the rifle that had fallen a good ten feet away from Hauptman. In moments, he scooped up the rifle before Hauptman realized he was there. Quickly, he settled it over his head, the strap across his chest, the rifle against his back.

"Stay down," Colin snarled, "or I'll blow your head off."

"You bastard!" Hauptman screamed. "Who are you? Why'd you shoot me!"

"If I didn't, you were coming to kill us." Moving around the criminal, a good ten feet away from him, Colin finally faced him and gave him a chilling smile. He had hit him in the upper right shoulder, probably shattering the rotator cuff area so he couldn't lift a rifle, much less anything now. Hauptman was disabled. There was some blood, but not a lot of it. His shot was designed to avoid hitting a major artery. He wanted to cripple him so he couldn't use it at all. "Now get up! We're taking a walk."

Glaring at him, breathing like an angry bull, Hauptman's little eyes grew squinty as he sized the man up. "Are you a cop?"

"No. Get up or I'll put a bullet in your head right where you sit." He lifted the Glock slowly in his direction. "*Now*." His voice was low, lethal. Hauptman hesitated and then gingerly scrambled to his feet, holding his left hand against his wounded shoulder, breathing harshly.

"I'm hurt. I'm bleeding. You can't do this! I know my rights!"

"You're lucky I'm giving you the chance to get up and live," he rasped, hard anger in his voice. "You never gave the people you murdered a chance to live. Did you?" Inwardly, he shook and trembled with such rage over the deaths of Dana's mother and father, that he was afraid he'd lose control and put a bullet into this monster's head.

Giving him a wary look, Hauptman growled, "Who the hell are you?"

"Your worst nightmare, Hauptman." Colin pointed down the hill. "Now get your ass in gear and start down that slope. I'll be behind you. Make one move I don't like? And it will be the last one you make."

Cursing, Hauptman limped down the slope, glaring at him.

Once on the level, in front of the cave, he made Hauptman sit down. "You have a cell phone on you?" Colin demanded.

"Yeah," he muttered. "So what?"

"Get it and toss it toward me."

Grudgingly, Hauptman took it out of his shirt pocket and threw it to Colin.

"Now roll over on your belly, facedown, and don't move."

Hauptman cursed, but did as he was told.

Quickly, Colin turned the cell phone on and saw that, miraculously at this elevation, he actually had bars on it, indicating it was usable. Punching in numbers to Dan's personal cell phone, he waited, keeping all his attention on Hauptman.

"Who is this?" Dan growled

"It's me, Colin," he said, quickly explaining what happened. When he finished, he heard Dan's voice lighten considerably.

"Damn, we lost you in the melee! You and Dana are okay? Unhurt?"

"We're fine, fine. Let me give you the GPS of where I have Hauptman."

"Got it," he said, relief in his tone. "I'm looking on my phone and it shows you're about one-and-a-half miles from the river and roughly a half a mile from the highway. We can meet Dana with our ATVs and then come hot-footing to where you have Hauptman."

"Sounds good to me. I'll just wait here at the cave next to the stream until you arrive. Be sure and tell Dana I'm fine. She'll worry."

Dan laughed. "Yeah, that little filly has her eye on you."

Grinning lopsidedly, he replied, "I have my eye on her, too."

"My hunch was right. First time I saw you two, it felt like something good was happening between you."

"Sure was," Colin agreed. "Now come and get this piece of shit. I want him out of our lives once and for all."

All he wanted right now was Dana, in his arms, where she belonged.

Dana jumped when the cell phone in her blouse pocket rang to life. She was standing beneath a grove of cotton-wood trees with the horses and Bandit. Fumbling, she got to it and hit the button. Who was calling *her*? And she didn't even realize that she was in cell phone tower range!

"Dana? This is Dan."

"Dan!" She nearly shouted his name. "Colin—"

"He's safe and alive," he reassured her. "We're coming your way right now. Stay where you're at, I've got a GPS fix on you. We're coming by ATV. There's an ambulance waiting half a mile from where you presently are. You're very near the bridge."

She sobbed and then choked out, "How?"

"Colin winged Hauptman, got his cell phone and called

me and filled me in on everything. I told him I'd call you. I have your cell on speed dial." He laughed.

Relief shattered through her, tears running down her face. "I—it's over?"

"Will be shortly, so just take it easy there. Stay where you are. Are you okay?"

"Y-yes . . . I am now . . . I was so afraid I'd lose him, Dan . . ." She burst into tears, covering her eyes with her hand.

Bandit whined, coming closer, sidling up against her leg, as if to give her comfort as he looked up at her with concern.

"Hey, it's okay," Dan said gently. "As soon as we can reach you, I'll leave one of my women deputies with you, and then the SWAT team and I are heading up to that cave where he's got Hauptman hog-tied."

"Swear to me Colin isn't wounded? Isn't hurt?"

Snorting, Dan said, "Dana, he's a *Ranger*. He worked black ops, hunting down Taliban leaders in Afghanistan. He's *not* a dude you want to meet on a dark night, believe me. He's *fine*. No wounds. Now, we'll be there shortly. Hang on . . ."

Colin saw the column of ATVs coming his way. He kept Hauptman on his belly where he could do no harm.

"Son of a bitch!" Hauptman yelled. "The ants are eating me alive!"

The corner of Colin's mouth twitched. "Good. Think of how the people you murdered felt under your gun?"

Swearing, Hauptman didn't move. He believed the shooter would take him out.

In another ten minutes, Dan Seabert led in the SWAT team. He was grinning ear to ear, throwing Colin a thumbs-up and then dismounting from his ATV.

"Hey, you sure you don't want to join SWAT?" he laughed, coming up, slapping Colin on the back, grinning.

Hunter Grant took over where Hauptman was concerned. They'd brought two paramedics with them and the other ATVs could carry six people apiece.

"In a pig's eye," Colin growled at Dan, taking the bullet out of the chamber of his Glock and putting the safety on, sliding it back into the holster. "I thought I left my old life behind."

Dan gave him a wolfish grin. "Oh, believe me, it's a part of us for the rest of our lives. Why do you think I got into law enforcement? Closest thing to the military that would use my skills, PTSD, knowledge, and experience."

"Yeah, well it's not my gig, brother." Colin rested his hands on his hips, watching the paramedics work on Hauptman's shoulder wound. He'd winged him enough so he couldn't lift a weapon and fire at anyone, that was all. If he'd aimed lower, he'd have put a hole through the top of his lung, and then he'd have been in real fucking trouble.

"Winged him just right," Dan said, a pleased tone to his voice. "You knew right where to disable without killing this piece of scum."

"Hopefully, he'll get thrown into a prison where he won't ever break out again and cause more deaths."

Nodding, Dan said, "Got that right." He shook his head. "I don't know if I'd been in your boots, if I'd just winged him. One hit to the head and this evil piece of work would be gone forever from this earth."

Sighing, Colin rasped, "I thought about it, Dan. I really did. I've seen the awful agony and ongoing grief Dana carries around with her every day because of what that vermin did to her parents." He held up two fingers. "I came this close . . ."

"I don't know that much about your black ops background, but I'd wager to say you killed a goodly number of Taliban enemy, and you were tired of killing?"

"Yeah, it came to that . . ."

Dan shook his head. "Me, too. I had too much first-hand experience, just like you did. I was tired of it."

"I see every man's face I took out. All I have to do is close my eyes, and their faces are there." Shaking his head, he muttered, "I've had enough, Dan."

"Listen," the sheriff murmured, clapping him on the shoulder, "you come in tomorrow and we'll take an official report on all of this. There's an ATV waiting for you." He pointed to the smaller one that held only one person. "Dana's about one-and-a-half miles away, under a cottonwood grove with the horses and Bandit. She's pretty shattered by everything, so I'm sure she'll be glad to see you, pardner."

"Roger that," Colin said. "Thanks for the ATV. I'll leave it at the grove and you can pick it up on the way out. We'll ride the rest of the way home."

"Copy that, brother. My deputy sheriff will take it. Go be with the woman who loves you."

Colin felt heat moving into his face, but he gave Dan a boyish grin. "I'm going to do just that . . ."

* * *

Dana's breath caught when she realized the ATV speeding in her direction held Colin at the wheel. The ATV was kicking up dirt clods and grass, it was going so fast. Bandit sat up, beginning to bark. She still had him on a leash, but the yellow Lab could tell it was Colin, too. Her heart beat hard in her breast. She'd managed to stop crying after Dan arrived. The deputy sheriff with her, a woman named Brenda Hanover, was smiling, too.

"He's got his tail on fire, Dana!"

Managing a choked laugh, Dana nodded. "He's going to kill himself before he gets here. He's going too fast."

"I think he wants to be with you," Brenda said slyly, giving her a knowing glance. "Give me the reins to the horses. Go meet your guy . . ."

Thanking her, Dana ran out from the grove, toward the ATV. As it came closer she could see Colin's face, with the biggest smile in the world on it. He braked it and climbed out.

She ran into his open arms, taking him back a couple of steps, the fierceness of her love overwhelming her as she kissed him repeatedly.

His arms went around her, hard and possessive, crushing the breath out of her as their lips met and hungrily captured one another. The scent of his sweat, the pine fragrance, all swirled around her, her eyes closed, simply melting into his hard, masculine arms, her body pressed fully against his, and he lifting her off her feet.

The world stopped in the best of ways as his mouth voraciously took hers and she eagerly returned the raw joy exploding through her in every possible way. Colin was alive! He loved her! She had never loved a man as

294   *Lindsay McKenna*

she loved him! And he was alive! Alive! And here, with her. She couldn't think, overwhelmed with exploding feelings, sexual hunger, and a joy so profound that she floated in it like being on a glistening, white cloud, floating. Just . . . floating.

Making happy sounds in her throat, she felt his gloved fingers moving through her red hair, down her neck, across her shoulder and caressing her spine. He was memorizing her! It was such a delicious sensation to be adored like this. She felt like a loved goddess from mythology reacquainting herself with her long-lost warrior lover. She had grown up on myths, always loving them, daydreaming that she was the goddess Venus, or perhaps Helen of Troy, whose lover worshipped the very ground she walked upon. And that was the feeling that rolled like tidal waves through her right now.

His lips tore from hers, kissing her lids, brow, temple and hair. His hands were loving movement enwrapping her within his embrace.

Finally, Colin gently set her feet back on the earth, releasing her, looking down into her dreamy, she was sure, looking eyes. Her lips parted, feeling wet, absorbing the hungry power of him and at the same time, surrounded by his quiet, fierce masculinity. Dizzied by his effusive show of loving her, she felt his hand wrap around her upper right arm, because she was a little off-kilter.

"Okay?" he asked, laughing.

"Really okay," she assured him, grinning like a fool who had found real gold, not fool's gold.

"Are you ready to go home with me?" he asked, walking

her slowly toward the horses that the deputy was holding for them. He drowned in her smile and shining eyes as she looked up at him.

"Oh, am I ever, Colin! Home has never sounded so good as right now!" she whispered.

He slid his arm around her shoulders, bringing her close to him and she rested her head against him. Colin did not want to let this woman out of his sight, much less release her.

He knew Brenda, and thanked her for staying with Dana. Colin helped the woman he loved into Gypsy's saddle, released the rope from Bandit's collar, and he ran free. The first thing the Lab did was leap upon him, barking and whining, his thick tail going like an out-of-control metronome, gone wild.

Taking a minute, Colin loved up Bandit. The dog was deliriously happy to see him once more. He knew that Bandit hated the leash, and would rather run free. Well, now he could!

Mounting Blackjack, he waved good-bye to Brenda and they started off at a slow canter, following the grassy bank of the wide, quiet but deep-running river. He brought the black horse alongside the blood bay mare and traded a smile with Dana. Her face was flushed and the joy sparkling in her leaf-green eyes made her look more like a dream he might have had, but she was real. And she loved him. Their boots would sometimes touch as they cantered that half mile up to the main highway. Traffic was coming and going. When there was an opening, the three of them moved across the highway, down the berm and onto a path made by wild animals over time, paralleling the Wildflower Ranch fence.

Up ahead, Colin could see the new wooden sign above the massive timbers that made up the gate and entrance to Dana's property. This really was her home. A start-over home. A new chapter in her life, he realized with gratefulness, because it included him, too. Him . . . the loner. The man who couldn't be around crowds, or even a team of wranglers, had finally found so much of what he'd lost out in the sands of Afghanistan.

Watching the wind curl and pull at the red strands of Dana's hair, the sunlight glinting upon them, colors of copper, gold, and crimson danced across her head. She was more a figment of his imagination than real. For so long, he'd been so afraid to dream of anything coming into his life that was happy. That emotion simply didn't exist for him any longer, snuffed out in his black ops life. How could someone kill and still be happy? The two never equated or met inside Colin. Ever.

Until . . . until Dana walked quietly into his life, so full of vitality, promise, and hope despite her own tragic background. She exuded hope for him. That was another emotion that got bled out of him over there in the Sandbox. Whether she knew it or not? She fed and infused him with *life*. Wanting to live once more, not just exist or barely survive.

His eyes watered as they cantered single file along the fence with Bandit barking and leading the way, and Gypsy right behind him. The animals knew they were coming home, too, all of them eager to do just that.

He was the luckiest man on the face of this sorry-assed

earth. He really was. And he was going to spend the rest of his sorry-assed life showing Dana just how much he loved her and how much gratitude he held in his deeply wounded heart. He could hardly wait to get home—with her.

Chapter 16

June 13

The sun was low in the western sky as they rode the horses to the barn. Dismounting, they cared for Blackjack and Gypsy as if they were their children, bathing them, scrubbing the sweat and salt off their skin from the long runs they had made in order to save their lives. It was the least they could do, Dana thought, leading Gypsy to the grassy paddock that had ample food for her, plus a tank of clear, cold water. Blackjack followed her.

Bandit had trotted to the stream outside the pipe corral, leaping in to cool off and happily lapping the water, always keeping an eye on his two humans.

Colin pulled Dana beneath his arm after shutting the gate and they watched their yellow Lab lie down in the shallow stream that gurgled happily, surrounding him, cooling him down. He smiled down at her. "Our dog knows how to do it right."

"I'm hot and sweaty, but I'm heading for a shower,"

she said, chuckling, her arm around his waist. "How about you?"

"Let's get cleaned up," he agreed. "Are you hungry?" he asked as he walked with her back to the wide-open barn doors.

She gave him a one-eyebrow-raised look. "I'm hungry for many things. First, I need to know about you and Hauptman. How did it go down? Is he dead?"

Shaking his head as they went down the breezy center concrete aisleway, he said, "No, he's not dead. But he's sure as hell out of commission for good."

She frowned. "Don't be so sure. He escaped prison once."

"I don't think it will happen again," Colin reassured her, seeing the worry come to her eyes. He squeezed her gently as they reached the gravel, heading for their home, together.

"I hope you're right."

"Listen, we're alive, Dana. Everything worked out in the end."

She sighed and searched his serious-looking gaze. "All I want, Colin, is you. I want to get cleaned up. I want to love you in every way." Her heart lifted from her worry as his blue eyes danced with a joy she'd never seen before.

"We want the same thing, sweetheart."

"I want the cell phones turned off," she warned. "If Dan needs something? He can leave us a voicemail. Right now, I'm exhausted, relieved, and so happy all at the same time."

He halted and unlocked the door to the house. "Then

it's time to celebrate for so many good reasons. Go on in . . ."

She looked back toward the barn. "Bandit will stay in the stream and then he'll go lie in the paddock with the horses."

"He's not coming inside for a while," Colin agreed, grinning.

"No . . . not for a while . . ." She climbed the steps, moving into the house that had become a true home for her—and for Colin. In no time, she was in her bathroom, taking a hot, soapy, fragrant shower with handmade calendula soap that smelled of vanilla.

Colin took his shower in his bathroom. Scrubbing his hair, washing not only the sweat off his body, but the smell of stalking off it, too. His whole world centered on Dana, her softly spoken words, the look of love shining in her eyes for only him. Climbing out, drying off, he wrapped a white towel around his waist, tucked it in, and walked out barefoot to the living room and kitchen.

As if they were invisibly strung to one another, he saw Dana open the door, in her thin cotton purple robe that hung to her knees. He smiled to himself, seeing she was barefoot, too. Walking toward her, he said, "Let's go to bed. I want to love you . . ."

Nodding, she turned, going to the open door of her bedroom.

He followed, watching the gentle sway of her hips, knowing that he would cherish Dana until his dying breath. She walked in, pulling the robe off her shoulders, allowing it to hang over the end of the brass headboard.

As he quietly turned and closed the door, he absorbed

her naked form standing before him. Pulling the towel off, there was no mistaking how much he wanted her. But it was so much more than about sex as he walked up to her, holding her luminous gaze, silently applauding that woman's strength and fierceness that burned so brightly within her.

"Come here," he rasped, leaning over, picking her up and into his arms. Just the shocking and wonderful quality of their flesh meeting, sliding together, took his breath away as he carried her to the bed and then gently settled her in the middle of it, releasing her.

She lay down on her back, opening her arms to him as he came to her side. Lying down lengthwise next to her, inches between them, he slid his arm beneath her long, slender neck, his other hand moving from her shoulder, tracing her ribcage and rounded hip to her long, firm thigh. There were no words now, just holding her gaze, watching her lips part as he adored her with his caresses. He could feel the dampness of her red hair beneath his arm, inhaled the scent of vanilla around her, and leaned over, placing his mouth against her parting lips that awaited him. There was such profound beauty, a swelling of love in his chest that almost made him think he was going to have a heart attack, but he wasn't. It was the emotional wave of love thundering through his entire chest as her lips met his, molded and moved with such tenderness that they shared that coupling between them.

Closing his eyes, all of his senses were screamingly online, but this time, he was focused only on pleasing the woman he loved with his life. Curving his hand across the side of her small breast, he heard her moan and she pressed her belly and hips wantonly against the hardness of him. Her fingertips dug into his neck and shoulder as he deepened the exploratory kiss between them. And as he lifted his hand and trailed his fingers in a massaging motion across her damp scalp, he felt her trembling, but it wasn't from fear. It was desire. Every time she sensually rubbed her hips against him, he groaned, the sound reverberating through him.

Taking his time as he slowly left her wet lips, he kissed each of her closed eyelids, her smooth brow, promising her mentally that he would keep her safe. She would no longer have to worry about her past. He would focus her fully on *them*, on the present. And a future that was so rich with possibilities.

Her hands were busy, too. She wasn't a limp doll in his arms. Anything but, and he smiled as he placed a trail of light kisses from her earlobe, down across her neck, her shoulder, hearing her sighs and sounds of pleasure whispering from her lips as he stroked her, provoked her in the best of ways, wanting her wet and welcoming when she let him know she wanted him to enter her.

He wasn't surprised at all when she pushed him onto his back, urging him to lie down, and then swung her leg across his narrow hips, the wetness of her hot core meeting his own heat. Groaning, he gripped her hips, pushing upward, asking her to move against him. The scent of her womanly fragrance filled his nostrils as she placed her weight upon him, sliding slickly up and down him.

Gritting his teeth, he had to stop from coming from that one, simple loving act on her part. Her hands settled on his shoulders, and he opened his eyes, staring up into her gloriously gold-green ones. The smile on her lips tore his heart open with such a profound, deep, ongoing love for this brave, courageous woman who loved him. And when she invited him to enter her, his hands gripped her upper arms, thrusting his hips upward, surrounded by that hot, tight glove that made him nearly lose his control.

It was her softened groan of utter pleasure as he moved within her, his hips like a slow-moving rocking horse, back and forth, and within a moment, she tensed, she cried out, frozen in place as her orgasm exploded between them. He felt the hot, lush rush of juices surround him and he joined her groan, both of them, in those seconds, paralyzed with the ultimate pleasure they could give to one another.

Colin forced himself out of that golden cloud of Nirvana and kept thrusting, engaging that beautiful flower within her, and again, she had a second . . . and then a third orgasm. Dana moaned, eyelids fluttering, and sank exhausted on top of him, her brow nestled against his temple, breathing shallowly, her fingers moving in adoration along his left shoulder, torso, and hip, simply appreciating him as her partner.

It wasn't until she was fully satisfied that Colin allowed himself to release deep within her loving, sweet body. His cry of raw pleasure vibrated through both of them as he gripped her hard with his hands upon her upper arms as the white-hot surge of liquid fired through him and spilled hotly into her receptive body. Nearly passing out from the long, pulsating release she coaxed even more out of him. When he nearly passed out, she eased away from him, fell beside him, snuggling, her arm beneath his neck, her other on his hip as she nudged him to roll on his side and meet and meld the front of their sweaty bodies with one another. Colin's arm went around her shoulders, drawing her against him, taking her offered lips, crushing them with his own, his hand then sliding down her ribs, opening and flattening against her hip, keeping them pinned to one another.

And that was the way they fell into an exhausted, joyous sleep with one another shortly after they parted from their celebratory kiss. Her head was nestled against his shoulder and jaw, her leg across his waist growing languid as sleep claimed her. And minutes later, sleep came to him as well. The last thought Colin had was that he felt reborn, a sensation, a knowing, he could never have anticipated. Love, her love, was healing him as never before. And then, he slept.

July 13

Colin found Dana riding Gypsy back from the fifty acres of vegetables and herbs that had been planted earlier in the spring. The hot summer sun felt good on his shoulders as he walked toward the barn to greet her. She was wearing her baseball cap, as usual, her red hair in a ponytail, as usual. Today, she was wearing a pale pink tee with cap sleeves, her jeans and work boots.

He could tell she'd been walking some of the many rows of growing plants, checking on them, checking the leaves, making sure they were getting enough water and not being eaten by insect predators. Her boots were good and dusty. She had planted a lot of marigolds throughout the acreage; a natural insect deterrent, and now it was paying off. By early August, there would be a huge amount of vegetables that would have to be picked, processed in the new aluminum building nearby, and then packaged for Mary's store. Everyone was looking forward with great anticipation and eagerness to Dana's first crop.

There was a wonderful teamwork with Silver Creek Valley people. When a ranch or farm needed people for harvesting of food, fruit, vegetables, nuts, or hay, they would bring their wranglers to that farm or ranch, and together they would bring the crop in. Box it. Bring in the eighteen-wheel trucks and wheel the boxed produce into them, until the produce was loaded and ready to be shipped.

And then there was always a barbecue celebration afterward, and the community congratulated itself, because they'd learned a long time ago if they helped one another, everyone won and it was a success. Dana had already lined up the amount of people needed to pick the veggie crop that would be ripe to harvest. Colin was working with Chase on the barbecues that would be taking place all during late July and all of August. The squash were special; they would be ready in September and October. More barbecues to look forward to! Summer was a time of harvest celebrations for everyone. And everyone contributed in small or large ways.

The women who lived in the women's shelter in town, came out and did a lot of the administrative work, filled the work orders, did the billing and other paperwork so that Dana did not have to do it all by herself. On some days, there were babies and young children all over the living room, their mothers at work not only in Dana's office, but Colin's own. Bandit loved the babies and young ones, always a faithful babysitter to them, tolerating all the pets he got, allowing the young infants learning to walk to crawl all over him, treating him like a big, warm blankie of a sort. Or maybe a yellow teddy bear.

Yes, their home rang with nonstop joy. Someone was always taking cell phone photos of Bandit with their baby or youngster. They were sent to parents and family, raising everyone's spirits.

And to Colin's surprise, having all these children and babies underfoot did not cause him rancor or make him want to run and hide like he used to do. Instead, he often was the other babysitter for all of them, learning how to take off and put on a clean diaper, holding a baby and giving it milk from a bottle, or taking a mother's pumped breast milk and putting it into the fridge when needed. He found himself smiling a lot with the babies. And it gradually sunk into his heart and mind that maybe . . . just maybe . . . if his PTSD seemed to evaporate little by little, that he and Dana could one day have their own babies.

The month since the capture of Hauptman had been healing for Dana, too. He waved as she galloped up to the barn door and dismounted. She no longer had nightmares. But then, neither did he. And sometimes, maybe once a week, one of his PTSD episodes would flare, but he wouldn't run off and leave her alone in her bedroom where they slept and made love. She insisted on him staying. She'd make them some lemon balm tea and they would sit in the living room and he would talk out the experience. He'd never given voice to them before, but with her love, her care of him, he was able to finally give these events words. And the miracle of doing that was the nightmares were receding . . . slowly going away and seemingly, not to return.

There was also a new woman psychiatrist who had moved to Silver Creek, Molly Rutledge. She had been a Marine officer, a psychiatrist, but her experience of working with PTSD started with herself. She'd been in combat, in many Afghan villages over her six years of duty. And with her experience and knowledge of the human psyche, she was helping him in ways no one had ever been able to do before. As Molly told him: It took a wounded healer to help another who had experienced similar events to mend their soul. Colin respected the forty-five-year-old woman, a widow who had lost the love of her life, a Marine recon officer, who had been killed in a firefight in the Sandbox. Molly knew a lot of grief and had been severely wounded psychically and emotionally—just like him. She, too, was helping him to heal internally as he put her suggestions to work, daily.

Two women in his life, sort of like proverbial bookends, were helping him to lift himself out of the nightmarish world he'd struggled in for so long, alone, before they entered his life. One he loved with an undying fierceness; the other because she was a combat sister who knew the ground he'd survived on and he trusted her, quite literally, with his vulnerable and raw emotional wounds. Both women were salve for his soul in different but very important ways. And he was never more grateful than right now.

As Dana led Gypsy into the barn and into the ties, Colin came to her side and unsaddled and unbridled the mare. She leaned up, kissing him spontaneously, her arms wrapping around his shoulders. As they parted, the gold-green of her shining gaze filled him, as it always did. Taking the equipment to the tack room, he returned with a box of brushes. Together, they washed the sweat off Gypsy and then began to brush her down.

Bandit, who always accompanied Dana out in the fields, lay nearby after soaking himself in the creek. She gave him a bucket of water, which he slurped happily.

"How goes the veggies this morning?" he asked, taking a comb to Gypsy's black mane, forelock, and tail.

"Great!" she said, using the coarse brush across the thick, muscular parts of the mare's body. "The broccoli is going to be ready in a week."

"Do you have that scheduled?" he asked.

"Absolutely. All the women from the Women's House are volunteering to come out."

"Uh-oh," he teased with a grin, "looks like me and Bandit are gonna be babysitters while you ladies go out and get the crops in?"

"That's it." She traded in her short brush for a dandy brush, which had long, soft bristles. Using it for Gypsy's legs and face, she stooped down, held her one hand against the mare's right leg and began to gently brush the entire area. There was little muscling in those legs and they were sensitive, so a dandy brush was a great way to clean, but keep her comfortable during the process. Dana looked up where he stood, combing Gypsy's mane. "Where did you go this morning?"

"Oh . . . had some things to do," he hedged.

"Usually you tell me where you're going, Colin."

"True . . ." he murmured, finishing Gypsy's mane and giving her a friendly pat on the neck. "Maybe, once we get Gypsy done and let out to the paddock, we can go inside and have a cup of coffee?" It was 10:30 a.m., and normally they would do that. He liked their rhythm that had established itself, and so did she. Sometimes? They skipped coffee and went to their bedroom, instead.

"Coffee sounds good," she said. Rising, she finished up and led Gypsy by a nylon lead to the rear paddock where Blackjack, Domino, and Trigger were. The four horses were the best of friends and it made Dana happy to know how well they got along. Blackjack was standing at the gate to the paddock, watching them come toward him. He whickered a loud greeting to Gypsy, who returned it. Two old friends greeting one another, and it made her heart sing.

As she washed her hands in the kitchen sink, her baseball cap on a peg near the door, Colin joined her and she handed him soap to wash up with, moving aside and grabbing a towel. "You're looking black ops," she teased, handing him the towel.

"Am I?" he asked coyly, giving her a grin.

She poured two cups of coffee and handed him one. "Let's go sit at the table?"

Nodding, he took the cup, their fingers briefly touching. He liked touching Dana. Always.

Dana took the chair at the end of the table and he sat to her right. "So? Did you see Dan at the sheriff's office?

Checking up on what's happening since our battle out there in the woods?" she asked, sipping the coffee.

"Yes, as a matter of fact, I did," he said. "Hauptman is now in jail in Cheyenne. The attorney general for the state is pressing charges against him, with the investigation completed."

"And?"

He heard the worry in her tone.

"And he's had so many federal and state charges thrown against him, plus the California attorney general has joined in on the charges because Hauptman and his crew robbed three banks in San Diego. He's screwed. Dan said given the charges, Hauptman will either go up for the death penalty or be in prison the rest of his life without the possibility of parole."

She grimaced. "They do know he's already broken out of a maximum-security federal prison in California. What's to stop him, Colin?"

He reached out, taking her hand and squeezing it, hearing the terror in her tone. "Dan thinks that once Hauptman is indicted and goes to trial, he'll be sentenced and sent to Rikers, in New York State. It's one place that the odds of him ever breaking out are at a bare minimum."

"I've heard about Rikers."

"Yeah, not a place you ever want to go."

"So, what else did Dan share with you?"

"The money under the boards of that log cabin of yours? The FBI has gone through every bill. The three bags were drug money, and it's all focused on the Gonzalez drug cartel out of Guatemala. There was four million dollars in those three bags."

Dana's eyes widened. "Wow!"

"In Hauptman's bag, it came out to about six hundred thousand. It's all in federal hands and the bank money will be sent back to the banks that were robbed. Happy ending there."

"And what about that drug lord coming into Wyoming?"

"They're sending FBI, ATF, and DEA agents out here to work with state law enforcement and try to stop the incursion."

"It's something we just have to be watchful about. No one knew Hauptman and his men were here. Or how Gonzalez was able to get his men up here, either," she muttered, shaking her head.

"Dan is on it. And the other county sheriffs are banding together to trade intel and info, too. They're tightening the net on all drug traffickers."

"At least something is going right for us," she said, brightening, squeezing his hand.

"Like what we have?"

Her grin widened. "Well, I can't say we're not getting sleep deprived, Colin."

"Not from nightmares."

She laughed. "No . . . but I'm not complaining and I'm not going to stop loving you whenever it feels right."

"Good to hear," he said, pulling a paper sack he'd set on the table earlier, toward her. "Open it." He released her hand.

Stymied, she looked at the sack and then at him. "What is it?"

"Oh . . . something."

"You're going black ops on me."

It was his turn to laugh. "Yeah, a little. But open it up. You'll see soon enough what it is . . ."

Dana took the sack. It was a small one. "You been over to Mary's? Did you get me my favorite chocolate?"

"I wouldn't say chocolate. And, no, it's not from Mary's grocery."

"Hmmmm," she teased wickedly, opening it up, "this is getting interesting, Colin."

"I hope you think so," he said, watching her expression closely as the bag opened. Dana looked down into it. "Don't worry, it's not going to bite you."

Giggling, she nodded. "I'm just cautious by nature, you know that."

"No bear trap in there, either." He met her widening smile.

"What is this?" She pulled a box out of the sack. It was a black velvet box. She gave him a wary look. "Colin . . ."

"It is what you think it is." His grin slipped, his emotions surging. Would she like it? He lived in fear that she wouldn't.

Prying the clasp open, she gasped, eyes huge as she stared down at a gold wedding band. Jerking a look to him, her lips parting, she whispered, "Are you serious?"

"As serious as it gets, sweetheart." He pointed to the gold band that had flowers engraved around it. "What do you think? Would you marry this beat-up wrangler? Spend your life with him whether he's crippled or not?"

Instantly, tears burned in her eyes as she wriggled the band out of the box, looking at it closely, appreciating the design and work that had gone into it. "You know I would,

Colin. And I don't see you as beat-up or crippled. Only you do. And that's slowly being shed because of the work Molly is doing with you weekly."

"Hey," he said, brushing the tear from her flushed cheek, "Molly helps. But you know what has really started the healing process in me? It's you, Dana. Only you." He choked up. "I want to spend every last hour I have left on this earth with you. Will you marry me when it feels right?"

Sniffing, she reached out, catching his hand, holding it tightly as it rested on the table. "Of course I will. Like I told you out there, I started falling in love with you shortly after you came here to help me out. That hasn't changed, Colin. We're both broken people. Somehow, our pieces fit together with one another and they are supporting our path to healing."

"Love heals," he told her gruffly, watching her expression closely. "Your love is doing that for me and I hope that mine is doing the same for you . . ."

"Oh, it is," she murmured, giving him a watery smile. "I love the ring, Colin. I like that I can wear it when I'm working, and it won't fall off or rip out a gemstone."

"Molly was counseling me on that," he admitted drily. "Said anything with a stand-up gem in facets will get ripped off sooner or later. She knows, because her husband had given her a diamond engagement ring and a gold wedding band to go with it. She told me one week she had lost the diamond in the ring during combat. Never did find it and she said it broke her heart. So, I went to the town jeweler and told her what I needed. They engraved the flowers on it because, to me? You are the flower in my life. You're beautiful to look at, wonderful to smell, and you always make me feel better, like a vase full of flowers."

She wiped her eyes and kissed the back of his hand. "I love how you see me."

"You're the bouquet in my life, sweetheart. You always will be," he rasped, tears coming to his eyes. "I want nothing more than you, Dana. Just you."

"Well . . . what about after we get married? Is there room for one more besides you and Bandit?"

Chuckling, he gave her a warm, loving look. "You know there is."

"I'm surprised you liked babysitting all those babies and youngsters, Colin."

"They make me smile. To me, they're all heart and love, a blank slate that parents will write on to make them into little carbon copies of themselves."

"Well," she said, placing the gold ring back in the box, "we need to talk about that. I don't believe children should be carbon copies of us. I see them telling us what *they* want to become."

"I like that idea. I really do."

"Good, then we can think about starting a family maybe in a year or two?"

Nodding, he said, "I'd really like that. We can always let Bandit babysit."

They both laughed heartily.

"Come here," he said, standing and pulling her up from her chair. Taking Dana into his arms, he kissed her long and hard and she returned it in kind, her arms wrapping around his shoulders, drawing him close to her. For the next minute, they languished in one another's embrace, the world no longer existing around them. When they finally broke their kiss, Colin whispered, "I love you, Dana. You are my life. My reason for hope. For finding happiness again when I never thought any of this was possible."

She became somber and slid her hand against his recently shaven face. "And yet? It was your past as a Ranger and black ops soldier that saved our lives . . ."

He grew serious. "I realize that. Now . . . I can't unmake what I became. Your love is like a healing layer over that chapter in my life. It won't ever go away, but it won't take overriding importance in my life going forward with you."

"That's because we have our own chapters to write that are before us, darling." She kissed him on the mouth, wanting to fill him with all her sweetness and womanly strength that had helped her get to this point in her own life. Leaving his lips, she whispered, "Love is the greatest emotion all of us possess. It is the one emotion that can heal us . . . and we are healing one another . . ."

Caressing her hair, cupping her cheeks, he rasped unsteadily, "As you are healing me . . . and I'm going to love you forever, Dana. Forever . . ."

We hope you enjoyed

STRENGTH UNDER FIRE
by
Lindsay McKenna

Don't miss the next book in the Silver Creek series:

SILVER CREEK BODYGUARD

coming to your favorite bookstores
and e-retailers in April 2022!

Chapter 1

Alone. What had changed? *Nothing*.

Wes Paxton had always been alone from the day his unknown mother had placed him on the doorstep of a fire station in Ft. Worth, Texas, and abandoned him to a heartless world.

No one wanted him, passing him from one foster family to another. In his teens, he was always in trouble, rebelling, angry because he got the message every day that he was seen as worthless. No one wanted a black-haired, gray-eyed, lanky kid. His only claim to fame was that he was damned good on the football field, a high school quarterback, his team taking the state championship, with him at the helm in his senior year. Not even that win could fill the hole in his heart that had been there for as long as he could remember.

The stars twinkled and danced above Wes. Standing momentarily outside his Ft. Worth, Texas, apartment where he'd stayed during a year-long rehab from a wound, he looked up at the night sky that had always been a comfort to him. Maybe because there were so many stars, all crowded and packed together like one big, happy family that got along with one another, was the reason. Remembering many times when it became intolerable in the next foster family he'd been passed on to, he would go outside at night and lie down on the grass, hands behind his head, and get lost in his star family, as he silently referred to the Milky Way. There, he felt a kinship. Stars did not kick you out of their family. Nor did they care if he was an orphan no one wanted. Outdoors, it was quiet compared to inside the foster home. He needed the quiet. Craved it, because it settled his roiling inner life and shut up that yapping voice inside his head that reminded him that no one had ever really wanted him. He was nothing but a check from the state every month for the family he lived with. He'd been nine years old when he realized he was a body that was worth so much money per month, and that was all.

Lifting his tan Stetson, moving his fingers through his short, dark brown hair, he settled the hat back on his head. Despite being a perennial problem child growing up, he'd managed to graduate with a high school diploma. He'd made friends with a police officer, Tom Harvey, who had spent ten years in the US Navy SEALs, got out and then went into law enforcement. Wes had been a rebelling fourteen-year-old, and Tom had given him something he'd secretly craved: care and attention. Tom was like a father to him, although Wes never said those words to him. He had always daydreamed of what a real, loving father would be like.

Tom, who was in his forties and with a family of his own, took him under his wing when Wes was a freshman in high school. For the first time in his life, Wes felt wanted and he lost his angry, rebelling disposition. Wes became part of a citywide project called Tom's Boys, in Ft. Worth. For once in his life, he knew that someone cared about him. At times, it felt like he was a drug addict; high on the praise and sincere attention, a smile, or a pat on the shoulder from Tom, made his heart burst with joy. And how he looked forward to when Tom would wrap his arm around his shoulders and give him a bear hug. It had been Tom's introducing him to football that had allowed Wes to not only bloom, but fiercely excel beneath Tom's tutelage, attention, and genuine care. Tom was responsible for teaching him to be a quarterback. The police officer had been one himself as a kid in high school, and he told Wes that he had the smarts to do the job and do it well. How much he looked forward to the twice weekly workout times with him! It fed his starving, thirsty soul, and salved his shattered heart, and for the first time in his life, he felt like he wasn't worthless, after all. He likened himself to a potted plant that was slowly dying due to no water being given to him; and two times a week, Tom watered him emotionally, giving him hope, his care and attention feeding his deeply scarred soul. For the first time, Wes had hope, his life steadying out beneath Tom's quiet, gentle nature, and he began to grow into a strong, thriving young man, his confidence and self-esteem soaring.

How lucky he'd been those last four years of his young life. Turning, Wes looked at the darkened building one last time. His mind moved back to after graduation when Tom suggested he go into the navy and become a SEAL; that he was a good fit for it.

He'd managed to survive BUD/S, the first step in becoming a SEAL. Tom and his wife proudly looked on in the audience, clapping for him as he graduated. The SEALs became his new family, one that embraced him, fed his hungry soul, and he excelled again.

At twenty-nine, he was shot in a battle. The upper part of his right lung was damaged and had to be removed; and he was forced to leave the SEALs.

Mouth tightening, Wes turned, walking toward his black Ford pickup in the parking area. In the truck was the next chapter in his life, and all his possessions in the back. He was moving to Wyoming, taking on an undercover bodyguard assignment that his old friend from his SEAL days, Jack Driscoll, had offered him after completing a year of therapy and transition. He was still adjusting to the loss of one-third of his right lung, but improving every day to the point that he could work once more and earn his own paycheck.

As he slid into his truck, the black and silver cab on the back of it holding his life, he slowly drove through Ft. Worth, where he'd been born thirty years earlier, looking for an exit that would take him west and later on, north, to Wyoming. His mind wandered back to that fateful day when he lay in the hospital, recuperating from the lung surgery he'd undergone.

While in the San Diego naval hospital, his cell phone

had rung one day, and it was Jack Driscoll, owner of the Night Hawks Security Company, whose headquarters was in Silver Creek, Wyoming. The phone call was like a lifeline to him. Driscoll had spent twenty years in the navy, and been a master chief to his SEAL team. He had left the military and created the world-renowned security company. Night Hawks seemed like a crazy name, he had thought at the time. But Jack was born and bred in Wyoming cattle country, grew up on a ranch, was a wrangler, and he wanted to hire women and men with that kind of background. The term night hawk, Jack told him, referred to the cowboy who rode around a cattle herd at night, keeping them safe from predators. And his business was hiring contractors who kept their clients safe from the same. Now, the name fit for Wes.

As a teen, Tom used to take him and a group of "at risk" boys out to a nearby cattle ranch outside of Ft. Worth every summer and on many other weekends. They worked as a team, and learned the rudiments of becoming a wrangler. Riding horses, branding, vaccinating, and herding cattle was something Wes grew to love. Being out in nature, out of the suffocating city, gave him a new appreciation of ranching, which was big in Texas.

And since he had that background, Driscoll had met him shortly after he had got out of the naval hospital and separated permanently from the navy. Jack had filled him in on his new security company. Wes liked the fact that they shared not only a wrangling background, but were part of the brotherhood of SEALs. SEALs took care of their own, which is why Jack flew into San Diego to talk to him about a future job with his company. Wes decided to throw his lot in with Jack and the other military vet men and women who he employed at Night Hawks. Wes had a year of rehab to do in order to get back to full strength. Jack was willing to wait to hire him after he'd successfully completed the rehab in Texas.

Jack had called him as soon as Wes had finished the strenuous rehab. He'd said he had an *interesting first assignment and I think you're a perfect fit for it. Let's talk.*

The light from the dash reflected into his thought-filled gray eyes as he continued to drive west. It was April and where he was going, it was going to be damned cold. And icy. Or both. Wes had gotten used to warmer climates; most of his SEAL assignments had been in Central and South America, because Spanish was a second language to him.

Rubbing his jaw, he knew that when Jack used a word like interesting, it was going to probably be an offbeat-as-hell assignment. The master chief only used that word sparingly when his team was under his command. Wes found out quickly when he used that word, it was going to be a mission that was really outside the normal boundaries their black ops unit operated within.

Jack reminded him that a wrangler was someone who could do anything with nothing. They were hardwired MacGyvers who could figure out what was broken and how to fix it or if trapped, how to get out of the situation alive. Baling wire and chewing gum, Driscoll drilled into them. Two really good items to have in one's arsenal, that was for sure. One corner of his mouth crooked upward.

Jack had a sick, twisted sense of humor. What SEAL didn't? Black humor was part of their stock and trade. Well, pretty soon, he'd find out about this "*interesting*" first assignment that Jack thought he was the "right fit" to take on. . . .

Connect with U(s)

Visit us online at
KensingtonBooks.com
to read more from your favorite authors, see books
by series, view reading group guides, and more.

Join us on social media

for sneak peeks, chances to win books and prize packs,
and to share your thoughts with other readers.

**facebook.com/kensingtonpublishing
twitter.com/kensingtonbooks**

Tell us what you think!

To share your thoughts, submit a review,
or sign up for our eNewsletters, please visit:
KensingtonBooks.com/TellUs.

More from Bestselling Author
JANET DAILEY

Calder Storm	0-8217-7543-X	$7.99US/$10.99CAN
Close to You	1-4201-1714-9	$5.99US/$6.99CAN
Crazy in Love	1-4201-0303-2	$4.99US/$5.99CAN
Dance With Me	1-4201-2213-4	$5.99US/$6.99CAN
Everything	1-4201-2214-2	$5.99US/$6.99CAN
Forever	1-4201-2215-0	$5.99US/$6.99CAN
Green Calder Grass	0-8217-7222-8	$7.99US/$10.99CAN
Heiress	1-4201-0002-5	$6.99US/$7.99CAN
Lone Calder Star	0-8217-7542-1	$7.99US/$10.99CAN
Lover Man	1-4201-0666-X	$4.99US/$5.99CAN
Masquerade	1-4201-0005-X	$6.99US/$8.99CAN
Mistletoe and Molly	1-4201-0041-6	$6.99US/$9.99CAN
Rivals	1-4201-0003-3	$6.99US/$7.99CAN
Santa in a Stetson	1-4201-0664-3	$6.99US/$9.99CAN
Santa in Montana	1-4201-1474-3	$7.99US/$9.99CAN
Searching for Santa	1-4201-0306-7	$6.99US/$9.99CAN
Something More	0-8217-7544-8	$7.99US/$9.99CAN
Stealing Kisses	1-4201-0304-0	$4.99US/$5.99CAN
Tangled Vines	1-4201-0004-1	$6.99US/$8.99CAN
Texas Kiss	1-4201-0665-1	$4.99US/$5.99CAN
That Loving Feeling	1-4201-1713-0	$5.99US/$6.99CAN
To Santa With Love	1-4201-2073-5	$6.99US/$7.99CAN
When You Kiss Me	1-4201-0667-8	$4.99US/$5.99CAN
Yes, I Do	1-4201-0305-9	$4.99US/$5.99CAN

Available Wherever Books Are Sold!

Check out our website at **www.kensingtonbooks.com.**

Books by Bestselling Author
Fern Michaels